She must be on the right track if someone wanted to kidnap her...

Harley made one last trip to the nightclub's bathroom. One glance in the bathroom mirror was enough to convince her that four beers were past her limit. She looked like something out of Fright Night.

Suddenly, the bathroom light went out. "Hey! I'm still in here!"

She fumbled with the latch on the stall door, then eased out and felt her way along the tiled wall. She bumped into the sink and ricocheted off the opposite wall. Swearing loudly, she wrenched open the bathroom door and ran right into a solid wall of muscle. A smelly bag was yanked over her head and her arms were pinned in a viselike grip as she was dragged down the hallway and out into the alley.

Whoever had her was trying to force her into a car, and she was just as determined not to go. Somehow, she got her legs up with one foot braced on each side of the open door. She blindly grabbed for a handful of his clothes to pull him off balance. He made a high-pitched sound like a loose fan belt and dropped her. His family jewels were probably missing a few stones by now. She crawled away and stumbled to her feet, ripping the bag from her head to yell for help.

That was when someone smacked her on the side of the head and she saw stars explode in front of her eyes. She hit the ground in the alley hard. Unable to move, she just lay there staring up at the stars.

Then someone bent over her, squeezing her cheeks together and peering into her eyes. "Hey, are you all right? Talk to me, honey. Focus . . . that's right, both eyes looking in the same direction at once, now."

A face slowly came into focus. She blinked. Diana Ross? "Why'd you break up the Supremes?"

Diana laughed and said to someone else nearby, "She's coming around. She's just not making much sense yet."

"Trust me, she doesn't make much sense when she *hasn't* been hit in the head," a familiar voice said. "I've never met anyone who can't even go to the bathroom without getting into some kind of trouble."

That would be Morgan, Harley thought hazily. *He sounds upset.*

The Novels Of Virginia Brown

The Blue Suede Memphis Series

Hound Dog Blues

Harley Rushes In

Suspicious Mimes

The Dixie Divas Series

Dixie Divas

Drop Dead Divas

Dixie Diva Blues

Divas and Dead Rebels (2012)

General Fiction

Dark River Road

Harley Rushes In

The Blue Suede Memphis Mysteries
Book Two

*

Virginia Brown

Bell Bridge Books

This is a work of fiction. Names, characters, places and incidents are either the products of the author's imagination or are used fictitiously. Any resemblance to actual persons (living or dead,) events or locations is entirely coincidental.

Bell Bridge Books
PO BOX 300921
Memphis, TN 38130
ISBN: 978-1-61194-098-5

Bell Bridge Books is an Imprint of BelleBooks, Inc.

Printed and bound in the United States of America.

Originally published as *Deadly Designs* by ImaJinn Books, a division of ImaJinn, Canon City, CO

We at BelleBooks enjoy hearing from readers.
Visit our websites – www.BelleBooks.com and www.BellBridgeBooks.com.

10 9 8 7 6 5 4 3 2 1

Interior design: Hank Smith
Front cover art and design by Don Thurakichprempri

:Lrhi:01:

In Memory

of Baby and Ranger, two wonderful dogs who left me behind as they went on a great adventure to the next life, where I hope there are plenty of squirrels to chase, biscuits to eat, and sunshine to keep them warm. No longer in my life, but forever in my heart.

Dedication

To my mother, Dorothy Leathers Lipsey, from whom I inherited my love of reading, and to my father, Wayne Nelson Moose, from whom I inherited my love for writing. Thank you both for enriching my life with these gifts. You always gave me the best.

And to a temperamental cat that will race from the back of the house to attack me when I sing. Of course, if you heard me sing, you'd probably do the same.

One

"You da *One*, baby." Tootsie grinned, then tossed back a strand of his long auburn hair and inspected his newly painted nails with a critical eye. The smell of Raspberry Soufflé nail polish thickened the air of Memphis Tour Tyme offices. "Now you da famous *One*," he added.

"You mean infamous." Harley tried and failed to be modest. She rustled the front page of the Sunday edition of the Commercial Appeal, Memphis's only major newspaper. There it was, in black and white and blurred color:

Local Tour Guide Breaks Jewelry Theft Ring and Helps Crack Murder Case, read the large headline. The leading sentence in the article said so much less than had really happened:

Harley Jean Davidson, 27, tour guide for Memphis Tour Tyme, had a narrow escape from jewelry thieves Friday night that ended with an arrest on charges of grand larceny, attempted murder, and two counts of murder. Ms. Davidson was instrumental in capturing the suspect . . .

She looked up with a satisfied smile. "I just love it when justice works."

"Don't get too excited yet," Tootsie said as he applied a top coat of clear polish over the bright raspberry color on his nails. "A jury could always set him free."

Harley frowned. That was daunting.

When Tootsie added, "But at least it's a good photo of you," she studied the blurred color of the picture apparently taken as she was leaving the warehouse. Her short blonde hair stuck straight up, her green eyes looked red, the man's tee shirt she wore hung almost to her knees, and she had an expression on her face like she'd just been hit with a stun gun. She'd been so focused on skipping out, she hadn't even noticed the reporters or photographers at the crime scene. Just her luck. She sighed.

"I bear a startling resemblance to Billy Idol. My hair looks like porcupine quills. And my mouth is open. I think I'm drooling."

"A natural look for you, baby."

"That's unkind," Harley said, but all in all, wasn't totally displeased. The article gave her credit for hunting down dangerous felons, which in a way she had, although after running for her life, it'd certainly seemed more like she was the one being hunted. An unpleasant memory, but not without some residual benefits.

"So," she said as she handed Tootsie yesterday's paper, "with all this free publicity for Memphis Tour Tyme, I'll bet Mister Penney is happy."

Mr. Penney owned and operated Memphis Tour Tyme, and while rarely seen on a daily basis, frequently made his presence felt. Never in a pleasant way.

Tootsie lifted a perfectly arched brow. "The ogre isn't often happy."

"How true. He always looks like a basset hound. Sad brown eyes. Floppy ears—did I say that last out loud?"

Tootsie grinned. "You did. I'm trying to picture a bald basset hound."

"Spare yourself. It's not pretty."

"He wants to see you first thing this morning, you know."

She grimaced. "I was afraid of that. And his mood is . . . ?"

"Inscrutable. Like the Sphinx."

"Or the basset."

"Right." The phone rang, and he punched a button and gave his usual "Good morning, Memphis Tour Tyme, how may I help you?" spiel. After he transferred the call he handed her a stack of pink message slips and said, "The phone's rung all morning, people wanting you to find their dog or cat, and one even wants you to find her iguana. No lie. A Mrs. Beasley wants you to find a necklace she lost when she was in high school way back in the sixties. Oh yeah, and your aunt Darcy said she has to speak to you as soon as possible."

"Aunt Darcy?" Harley blinked. Her mother's younger sister never called her at work or anywhere else. "I can't believe she called. She never calls."

"Not everyone is unappreciative of your talents. Your aunt seemed very impressed."

Harley took the pink slips of paper he held out, amazed and gratified. If even her family was impressed, then all was not lost. It usually took events of gigantic proportions to impress them. After all, her family knew all her flaws with annoying attention to detail, and they could be counted upon to regale complete strangers with youthful foibles that still had the power to make her cringe. Aunt Darcy was not only *not* an exception to that fact, she was the poster celebrity for it.

Tootsie lowered his voice to a dramatic baritone. "And Mike Morgan called. I assume that you'll be returning *his* call first."

A flutter in the pit of her stomach reminded her of the lazy Sunday spent lying in bed with the gorgeous man who'd ended her months of celibacy. Who could have foreseen that she'd enjoy it so much? What a delicious way to celebrate still being alive. And with a souvenir which still leaned against her bedroom mirror, a reminder of her narrow escape and life's possibilities. It had been pretty harrowing, running for her life in a warehouse crowded with cheap wooden statues and china dogs, especially when the man chasing her had no scruples about shooting her. Fortunately, she'd been able to hide behind a wooden statue with an astounding erection that did not prove to be impervious to bullets. It did, however, make an interesting souvenir. Somewhere there was a fertility god without his goods.

"Why would you think I'd call Morgan first?" she asked out loud, and Tootsie gave her a knowing look and pursed his lips.

"You have that just laid look, baby."

"Bitch," she said fondly, and went down the hallway to use the phone in privacy. She'd have to remember to bring him the dress she'd promised last week when he'd used his computer hacker talents on her behalf. Tootsie really should utilize his mind and talents in a better job, but he said this one suited him very well. Harley had often wondered just how the conservative Lester Penney had been induced to hire a man who spent his spare time dressed as Cher or Julia Roberts, but that wasn't really any of her business. If someday Tootsie wished to share his secrets with her, fine, but she cherished him as a friend too much to intrude on his privacy and ask.

Besides, since he was only a little taller than her five-six, and his extra thirty pounds were distributed quite differently on him than her one-hundred and twenty—one-fifteen on good days—were on her, sometimes they swapped clothes. She had leftover dresses from her days of wining and dining as a corporate banking employee, and Tootsie had some cute tee shirts that he rarely wore. He liked silk, she liked cotton. It made for a symbiotic friendship.

The tiny office down the hall, which was used by all the drivers, had been a storage closet in another life. It could be a tight fit, but she managed to wedge herself behind the oak teacher's desk that had come from a Memphis School District surplus sale. Reminders of its former use were in the form of insults and obscenities carved into the sides and top. City school teachers had to be tough to survive. The old wood chair squeaked a loud reminder to feed it WD-40 as she sat down and reached for the phone.

Like Tootsie had predicted, she called Morgan first.

"You aren't answering your cell phone," he said, his low, raspy voice making her tingle all the way to her toes.

"I know. It's broken."

"Oh yeah. I'd forgotten. How many does that make in less than a week?"

"Three. I have insurance. Not that it helps much. Apparently there's a limit on how many times they'll pay for new phones."

He laughed, and Harley's toes curled inside her Nikes. Honestly, he made her tingle in places she didn't know could tingle. And it'd be emotional suicide to let him know that.

"Maybe I should buy stock in Nokia," he said. "At the rate you go through cell phones, it should make a nice profit."

"Right. So what's up?"

"Baroni's through with the stun gun if you want it back. It's not needed as evidence."

"Mr. Penney will be delighted. Not that it did me any good. I didn't even get to use it."

"Better luck next time."

"Oh no," she said. "There won't be a next time. I'm leaving police work to the police. I'm not cut out for it."

"Yeah, I didn't want to point that out to you. Glad you got there on your own."

"Hey, at least I proved Yogi didn't kill Mrs. Trumble."

"We'd have gotten there eventually. What are you doing for dinner tonight?"

"Any suggestions?"

"Oh yeah. And one of them even involves food."

There went that tingle again. "Taco Bell," she said. "Burrito. Extra sour cream on everything. And no beef."

"You're a vegetarian?"

"That's Diva. I just happen to prefer the bean burritos today. And yesterday. Probably tomorrow."

"You frighten me. See you around seven."

When she hung up, she caught a glimpse of her reflection in the large mirror on the small wall. Where had that big smile come from? It stretched from ear to ear and made her look like an idiot. Not that another bad hair day didn't have the same effect. Her short hair usually stuck up in gelled spikes that she considered attractive, but today she had more of an early Meg Ryan look. The "just laid" look Tootsie had mentioned.

Jotting down a note to replace her broken cell phone, she dialed her aunt.

Darcy Fontaine answered on the first ring. "I'm so glad you called," she said in a rush, or what passed as a rush for her normally slow Southern drawl, which had sped up to an almost normal tempo. "I need to talk to you privately. Not now. It's too—dangerous."

Dangerous? How melodramatic. "Well, I'll be at Grandmother's for lunch Saturday. We can talk then."

"No. I can't wait. Harley, it's vital I speak with you soon. And this has to be kept between us, all right?"

Harley sighed. "Okay. So, what is it?"

"Well for heaven's sake, we can't discuss it over the *phone*. Meet me for lunch today. At The Peabody. I'll be wearing red."

She made it sound like international espionage. Harley swallowed another sigh. "I'm at work, Aunt Darcy. And I can't afford The Peabody anyway."

"I'll buy, and it doesn't matter what you look like, either. Just meet me in the lobby at twelve-thirty, okay?"

Without waiting to hear if it was okay, she hung up, leaving Harley listening to a dial tone and scowling. That was so . . . Darcy. No one else's plans ever mattered. And of course, she just assumed Harley was dressed inappropriately. She was, but it probably didn't matter anyway because they'd never leave the lobby bar. Aunt Darcy liked to drink her lunch. Gin and tonic. Or just plain gin.

With that in mind, Harley decided she might as well get the interview with Lester Penney behind her. Monday mornings were quite often fraught with peril anyway. If she saw Mr. Penny now, the rest of the day had to be better.

It was a short walk down the corridor to Mr. Penney's corner office. She tapped on his closed door, then went in when he responded with what sounded like an invitation, but he could have been just clearing his throat.

Lester Penney was on the phone, and he looked up with an irritated frown that wrinkled his forehead in another reminder of a puzzled basset hound. Harley took the chair he indicated with a wave of his hand and looked idly around the office while he conversed in monosyllables.

It was a large office, in stark contrast to the other tiny cubicles. Not that office space was a high priority, as most of the employees drove the vans or busloads of tourists and didn't require desks. Tootsie, as office manager, scheduler, and receptionist, had the second largest workspace. Rhett Sandler, in the other office, did payroll and accounts receivable. Harley thought he had the personality of a doorknob, but since he was in charge of handing out the money, she'd never said that aloud. Apparently, he did a good job, and at least he didn't embezzle funds like the last guy had.

"Yes. No. Not at all." Penney leaned back in his chair with a loud squeaking sound and swiveled to stare out the window.

From the two-story buff brick building that housed Tour Tyme, his view consisted of tree tops and the edge of a huge Taco Bell sign. Poplar Avenue separated the building from Taco Bell, an often perilous crossing of endless traffic. But Harley's reward was always a hot bean burrito and maybe nachos. Depending on money and appetite.

As the conversation continued, Harley began to fidget. Sunlight from the corner windows gleamed on Penney's balding head, highlighting the fuzz that sprouted like random weeds. In contrast, his thick, busy eyebrows bore a striking resemblance to animated caterpillars, going up and down in a rhythm matching his terse responses. Overlarge ears bent slightly forward at the tops, really looking like dog ears. Elementary school must have been hell.

Finally he hung up the phone, linked his fingers together atop his desk blotter, and gazed at her with a riveting stare that only increased her discomfort.

"So," he said finally, "quite a weekend for you."

"You could say that."

"Indeed. There are many things I could say."

This didn't sound at all like a congratulatory interview. She nodded. "I'm sure you can."

Penney seemed determined. After an awkward pause, he said, "I trust your parents are doing well now."

An unsubtle reference to the fact her father had recently been a murder suspect.

"They're very resilient," she replied.

An understatement. She didn't think her mother had batted an eye, but then, Diva had complete faith in her own psychic abilities even when others were skeptical, and she had predicted a good outcome, so perhaps that was understandable.

"Perhaps next time, you'll request authorization before you borrow company property," Penney said then, and Harley felt some sort of explanation was necessary.

"I should get the stun gun back this evening. It was part of the investigation, but not a vital part, so I'll bring it back in tomorrow, as good as new."

"And, um, ahem—the stun guns are only for emergency use, Miss Davidson. I trust you are fully aware of that? And they're not to be used on paying tourists unless the situation is dire."

"I've only had to use it once, and the circumstances were what I considered pretty dire. He was drunk and terrorizing the other passengers, and he nearly caused me to wreck. It was the only way I could control him."

Penney's caterpillar brows lowered slightly. "Yes, though the insurance company was not especially impressed, it did seem necessary in that instance. And he did have a criminal record."

He clasped and unclasped his hands, and Harley had the distinct impression he wanted to say something else but didn't know if he should. She waited. Sunlight slanted through windows to heat the room, backlit the fuzz atop his head, and made her squint. Finally he nodded again.

"New rules are being implemented, and we are requiring all employees to take a short course in safety per our insurance company's request. You'll be notified of the dates and times, as will our other drivers."

Oh, that'd make her popular with the other drivers.

All in all, it wasn't exactly the kind of reception she'd expected. A little more excitement would have been nice. Appreciation, perhaps. Not that she was too surprised by his reaction. She had experienced something similar from Bobby Baroni, who hadn't been quite impressed about her participation in the capture of jewelry thieves the police had been after for months. His reaction had been more along the lines of . . . irritation. But as a detective in the homicide division of the MPD, Bobby wasn't easily impressed. He'd been that way when they were kids, too. It took a lot to impress him. Unless you were a stripper with a 36DD cup.

Tootsie looked up when she went back into the reception area. "From the expression on your face, I'm guessing you didn't get a bonus."

"Unless you want to look at a required safety course as one, no. Not that it matters. I still have the Crimestoppers cash as a bonus." Harley slumped against the edge of Tootsie's desk. "Being famous isn't all it's cracked up to be."

"So I see. Don't worry. Fame never lasts."

The lobby of The Peabody Hotel on Union Avenue in downtown Memphis always teemed with tourists in shorts and tee shirts. They crowded around the elegant marble fountain in the center, taking pictures of the ducks that paddled around and around. It was also a meeting place for the business lunch crowd, and it took Harley a few minutes to find a seat that wasn't so near the fountain that she'd get splashed or elbowed by a fanatical tourist with a Nikon. It seemed somehow fitting that the hotel's custom of keeping plain mallard ducks in the fountain had begun with a drunken hunter. The Peabody had made the fowl their mascots and sold everything from duck-shaped mints to duck shoehorns in the gift shop. The one thing *not* served on any menu in their restaurants and delis, however, was duck. They limited duck to the ones treated royally in the marble fountain during the day, and in a palatial duck house at night. A marketing tool that was a huge success. The Peabody liked to advertise that it was the "Meeting Place of the South." Probably true. At any given time you might see Hollywood actors or Saudi sheiks in the lobby.

Subdued lighting, plush carpeting, lots of gold gilding, hanging crystal chandeliers, and marble-topped tables surrounded by comfortable chairs and cushioned couches made waiting in the lobby easy, if not timesaving. Aunt Darcy was late as usual.

A perky waitress bounced over to take her order, and she asked for a Coke. Aunt Darcy arrived at the same time as the Coke, and she ordered a gin and tonic as she kissed the air beside Harley, then took a chair next to her. She wore an exquisite red silk suit that complemented her slender frame, fair features and short blond hair. Gold gleamed at her throat and wrists, equaled only by the flash of diamonds on her left hand. A drift of Chanel wafted above the round marble table, but it was quickly eradicated by a cloud of cigarette smoke as Darcy lit up.

"You don't mind, do you?" she said, and before Harley could say yes, went on, "I'm just so nervous. It's so trying. I had no idea you'd be of any use at all, but when I read the article this weekend, I knew at once that you were the answer. It has to be kept private, you see, and I didn't want to risk dragging in outsiders. You know how people can be, I'm sure, always talking and saying things, because they're jealous or envious or just spiteful. Well, on top of everything else, I surely don't need that, Harley, and so decided that I'd just get you to fix it. You can find out if it's true, and if it is, why then you can just get that friend of yours, the Italian boy, to make him stop and everything'll be just fine after all. Don't you think?"

"Uh . . . "

"I knew you'd agree. Now, don't you say a word to Mama about this, because she'd never understand, especially when she told me I shouldn't have a partner at all, that I should keep it all in my own name and hands, but you know how it is nowadays, with the economy and all. I swear, I don't know what the world is coming to with all those Republicans in Congress. It's just a shame, is all, a dreadful shame. We've been Democrats all our lives, and even with that scandal—well, he was still better than a Republican, don't you think? Though it *was* such a nasty business with that cigar and all, and so unnecessary. Maybe—oh well. Not that it matters. This isn't about politics."

"Well," Harley finally got in, exasperated that a woman who talked so slow could say so much so quickly, "what *is* it about, Aunt Darcy?"

"Why, sugar, it's about illegal smuggling. Didn't I say? Someone is smuggling illegal goods into my shop, and I think my partner is behind it."

Two

It had started out to be such a nice day. She'd felt so good when she woke up, being famous and richer by a few bucks. Solving a crime and snagging a hot guy just made things so much better she hadn't even cared that she still had bruises and scratches from her ordeal. How quickly things could go to hell.

"Aunt Darcy," she said patiently, "you need a private investigator. Or a cop. I'm a tour guide. It's not at all the same thing."

"Don't be silly. It's in all the papers. Of course you investigate things, just like that woman on cable television—the book writer. What's her name? Oh, it doesn't matter. You were able to solve the jewelry thefts and caught the man who murdered that elderly woman, and I'm sure if you can do that, you can do a simple thing like find out who's smuggling things into my shop. I could lose everything, Harley, if the police found out about this. Just spy on Harry and tell me if he's in on it. I think he knows who's doing it and just won't tell me."

"And Harry would be—?"

"My partner. Harry Gordon." Darcy took another puff of her cigarette, a long brown thing that smelled vaguely like cloves and reminded Harley of the pot her brother Eric smoked. "Harry's supposed to be a silent partner," her aunt continued, "but he's been coming in to the shop a lot more the past year, and then—well, I just found it this past weekend."

"Found what? Drugs? Weapons?"

Darcy blinked, her long lashes batting over eyes that seemed an unnatural turquoise. "No, nothing like that. Illegal imports. Endangered animal skins. Ivory. Things like ancient artifacts that I know can't be legal. Statues. Vases. Some kind of powder. It isn't drugs. It just isn't legal. Powdered rhinoceros horn or something like that. The federal government banned these things, and I don't know who is doing it or how they're getting them through Customs. But if my clients found out I was involved in any kind of illegal business, I'd be bankrupt in a week."

The waitress brought Darcy's gin and tonic, and she held up two fingers to indicate another one as she pulled the first one toward her.

"So you see, don't you," Darcy continued, somehow managing to smoke and talk and drink in almost the same breath, "why it must be kept very, *very* quiet?"

"Aunt Darcy—"

"I'll pay any expenses you may run into, of course. And I'll buy your lunch. Order anything you like."

"It's not that I don't appreciate your confidence in me," Harley began, "but—"

"Listen here, Harley Jean Davidson, we're family. Family always sticks together. If you can help find out who killed some strange old lady, you can certainly help me find out who's trying to ruin my business!"

It was the strangest thing about Aunt Darcy; just when you thought she was three bricks shy of a full load, and a wilting violet to boot, she turned into Raging Bull.

Harley groaned. "Fine. I'll see what I can do, but don't expect miracles."

The frown that had briefly distorted Darcy's face vanished, and her smile was serene and reassuring. "Now, sugar, I know you'll find out who it is. Come to the shop tomorrow and I'll tell you everything you need to know. You can do one of those stinger things, like the police."

"Sting. Stinger is a drink. And no, I don't—" She paused. Aunt Darcy had stopped listening so there was no point in even trying. The waitress delivered her aunt's second gin and tonic, and she scooped it up. How did the woman suck down so much gin and not fall out onto the floor? If *she* drank like that, she'd end up paddling in the fountain with the ducks.

Aunt Darcy glanced at her watch. "Oh, I've got to run, Harley. I'm supposed to meet a client at their house in Harbor Town. A new job, very expensive. Remember now, not a word to anyone. If it got out, I'd be ruined."

Kissing the air beside Harley, she left in a flurry of clove cigarette smoke and lingering perfume. Harley got stuck with the check and no lunch. Sixteen dollars for a Coke and her aunt's two gin and tonics? That was too pricey for her budget, but it wasn't the waitress's fault and she left a tip as well. Twenty bucks to listen to some ridiculous story that would prove to be just a mistake.

It wouldn't be the first time her aunt had thought someone was trying to ruin her business. Last year, she'd been convinced a rival design shop was stealing her clients by telling lies about her all over town, and she threatened to sue for libel. That had turned out to be a mistake. And the year before that, there'd been the disagreement with furniture manufacturers—well, no point in dredging all that up now. She'd go just to keep peace. And to recoup her twenty dollars.

After stopping at Taco Bell to pick up brunch, she crossed Poplar to the office parking lot with only one near crash. There was a parking space in the shade and she grabbed it. Leaving her car's windows down would be an open invitation to steal it, but parking in the sun meant the temperature inside might reach a hundred and fifty degrees in the summertime. Even though it was still relatively cool, no point in taking unnecessary chances. Toyotas, especially older ones like hers, were prime targets for chop shops, one of Memphis's major business attractions for budding young entrepreneurs.

Air conditioning inside gave her a spurt of energy. If she ran up the stairs to the second floor instead of taking the elevator, it might work off some of the junk food she'd eaten lately.

By the time she reached the Tour Tyme offices, she was out of breath. Staggering into the reception area, she hung over Tootsie's desk for a moment, gasping for air. He didn't look up.

"You're still on call. I didn't put you on the schedule since I didn't know when you'd be back. There's a Graceland run," Tootsie said. He'd filed his fake nails into a perfect oval. "You can take that tour if you want. Tourists from Nevada. What do you think of this color?" He held out his nails for her to inspect. He'd changed colors already, a deeper shade of purple.

She leaned forward as the black dots in front of her eyes faded. "Nice. Perfect Plum?"

"Claret Craze. I went to Stein Mart on Sunday and found a gorgeous dress in a deep claret. Very Jennifer Aniston. Do you think my hair would look good cut like hers?"

"This year's cut or last year's?"

"Last year." He tugged at the end of his pony tail, soft auburn strands curling around his palm. "I've been thinking of cutting it a little shorter, since every so often I like to go as Cher. She can be a refreshing change, but I have to wear wigs and they get hot."

"Keep it long," Harley advised, "it's more flexible."

"Right. It's a mystery to me how you can know about nail polish colors and hair lengths when you so obviously don't apply it to yourself."

Inspecting her nails—or where they'd be if she didn't bite them—she said reflectively, "Cami has never given up hope I'll turn into a girly-girl. She keeps me updated. If I had polished nails they'd have to be in bubble gum flavor. Or bean burrito."

Tootsie ignored the last. "So Charlsie's van broke down. How about a one o'clock pickup at the Radisson? Only four women from up in Michigan, but they want to go to Victorian Village."

"Great. I like going to the Village."

She took the log book down the hall to catch it up since she hadn't entered her mileage or time last week. There had been other things on her mind, like finding her parents after King, their neurotic dog, had been abducted and the neighbor responsible for the dognapping was murdered. Of course, the police had immediately suspected her father had killed the neighbor, so he and her mother had gone on the run. And then there was Harley's narrow escape from jewel thieves and psychotic murderers when she tried to get evidence to clear her father. That still made her shiver when she thought about it. Why had she thought changing jobs would eliminate the stress in her life? It'd obviously followed her. But at least being a tour guide was less stressful than working in marketing for a corporate banking firm whose managers talked like drill sergeants to their employees. It'd do for now. She looked at it as a working vacation. And time to decide what she really wanted from life.

Here she was, closer to thirty, unmarried, with no kids or mortgage or even a steady boyfriend, drifting through life as aimlessly as a dandelion thistle in the wind. Diva said she was a late bloomer, but her mother had no expectations for Harley other than that she be happy in whatever she chose to do. It was a simplistic view of life that often bumped up against the harsh corners of reality.

But then, that was how Diva was, an idealistic dreamer with a proclaimed connection to the psychic world that was uncannily accurate at times. Enough to validate her beliefs in her own abilities, anyway. Harley wasn't always so sure. There were the times Diva was right on the money with a prediction or warning, or even just a certainty about someone. Like last week, when she'd been so sure Bruno Jett was connected somehow to their dog's disappearance. It'd turned out that he was, though indirectly. And Diva had been sure all would turn out well in the end, which it had, but not without a lot of stress. And panic. But both those predictions could be explained away as coincidence.

Then there was her warning about the Chinese pug . . . that one was harder to explain away. Diva couldn't have known that Harley would almost be hit in the head with a heavy ceramic pug. It was just that kind of obscure thing that made Harley wonder if her mother really did use a sixth sense at random moments. Practicality demanded Harley apply rational explanations to the unexplainable. There were times, however, it was impossible. Diva often defied logic.

When the phone rang, Harley wasn't surprised to hear her mother on the other end say, "When Darcy asks you to help her, consider it carefully. It will set you on a different path."

"Aunt Darcy already asked. I didn't fully agree, but I didn't refuse. And how'd you know about it?"

Ignoring that, Diva said, "It's your choice, Harley. Just be sure it's what you want to do."

Diva's low alto vibrated softly in her ear, and Harley toyed with the impulse to ask her advice. Then the moment passed, and she said only, "I'll be sure."

It was a lie, of course. She'd been roped into it with cords of familial guilt, lassoed by a master. Jewish mothers had nothing on Southern women, and a Southern Jewish mother was a force to be reckoned with. She should be grateful, she supposed, that Aunt Darcy was Methodist. Otherwise, there was no telling what Harley might have agreed to do for her.

Just checking out shop inventory or shipping manifests couldn't be too bad. Nothing more complicated than a few boring hours on a Tuesday afternoon when she'd rather be doing anything else. Then she'd present dear Aunt Darcy with a bill, including the twenty dollar charge for drinks at The Peabody.

Life had its perks. She'd try to keep that in mind while she went through the motions of finding Aunt Darcy's imaginary smuggler. Really. She'd probably just forgotten she'd ordered fake zebra skins or bath powder and imagined the worst. It was probably due to the gin she kept hidden in bottles for a little pick-me-up. A wee nip here, a wee nip there, and by the end of the day she'd pickled her brain. It was amazing no one had caught on in all this time, but if they had, it was one of those things that went politely unmentioned in the family. Like inherited insanity. Most of the time she thought her entire family was nuts. It was uncomfortably close to the truth.

But this was nothing like her last foray into thievery and flying bullets. This would be quick and easy. And profitable. Her favorite things.

Time to get back to work and put the weekend's ordeal behind her. She finished logging in her time for last week, then took the elevator down two flights to the ground floor and parking lot where her trusty little '91 silver Toyota waited in the shade. Good transportation, one of those cars that were fuel efficient and comfortable. Best of all, it was paid for.

First, she decided as she juggled the keys and brown backpack she used as a purse, she'd replace her broken cell phone. That was imperative. It was her link to the world.

Poplar Avenue was busy as always, traffic snarling up on occasion, and she shoved the car into second gear and shot through an orange light at Perkins, clicking on her right turn signal just before reaching the cellular phone store.

By the time she left, she was nearly two hundred dollars lighter and thirsty. She'd stop for a Coke first, then sign out the van by noon to make her Radisson pickup on time. Tour Tyme housed the company vehicles in a rented garage off Poplar, not far from the main offices. The size vehicle used depended on the size of the tourist group. No point in wasting gas.

After picking up the van, she headed downtown to the Radisson to pick up her group. They'd be waiting for her in the open-air lobby divided with walls of old brick. Victorian Village wasn't far from downtown and the river. It was a remnant of life in the nineteenth century. A few houses had been donated to the city and kept up with city funds as a reminder of what life had been like over a hundred years ago. Somehow, the incongruity of the tree-shaded elegance in a tiny pocket right next to Juvenile Court never quite registered with city officials or visitors. Still, the three-story homes held an aura of times gone by, of what it was like to live without modern amenities if you were a wealthy family. None of the hovels from the Pinch District on the river had been restored, she'd noticed. That area had been settled by Irish immigrants in the early- to mid-eighteen hundreds, called Pinch or Pinch-back for the look on residents' faces and their sunken bellies, a pinched look of hunger and deprivation. Her ancestors had probably been among them at one time. Fortunately for them, not on the nearby slave block, however. A historical marker was the only remnant of the auctions of human beings that used to take place near a backwash of the Mississippi River. A lamentable part of Memphis history.

It was a nice afternoon, and the women from Michigan were a fun group that enjoyed the sights and made Harley laugh. They were there to enjoy themselves, and had no qualms about saying what they didn't like. The Magevney House, furnished in period pieces and with an elegance visible despite the under-funding in recent city cutbacks, was always a favorite. There were even delicious rumors of lingering ghosts, and the women were disappointed they didn't make an appearance during their tour.

Afterward, Harley took them back to the hotel across the street from the Redbirds' new baseball stadium. She gave them advice on which sights she thought they'd be more interested in seeing, which Blues clubs on Beale Street they'd enjoy, and reminded them to get to the lobby of The Peabody Hotel before five if they wanted to get good photos of the ducks marching from the marble fountain up the red carpet rolled out to the elevator that would take them to their penthouse home for the night. Then they could go on the roof to see the ducks basking in their twenty-five thousand dollar cage complete with oil murals on the back wall, elaborate beds, a wading pool, and plenty of food. The ladies liked that suggestion best, and Harley left them buying more film in the gift shop.

It was after six by the time she left the van at the garage and the keys at the office, and the car wash would be closed. She'd intended to wash away any traces of King's brief travels left in the back seat of her Toyota while her parents had been cruising around town avoiding the police. Removal of the dog's hair and potent canine fragrance would have to wait.

It was a fairly short drive from the Tour Tyme garage down Poplar Avenue, one of the main thoroughfares in Memphis, to Kenilworth Street. Her apartment was an upstairs flat in a renovated brick house across from the zoo, convenient to peacocks, monkeys, and Overton Square, a fading intersection of restaurants, quirky shops, and a New Orleans style hotel.

Harley parked in back of the apartment house on a pea-gravel slot that ended in a railroad tie bumped up against a gigantic oak tree. The other residents had garage space, but one of them would have to move or die for her to get one. That was all right. Her Toyota was built to last.

A wide hall with a tiled foyer led to all the apartments. The spacious staircase in the middle rose to the second floor and her apartment on the north side. Two doors opened off the foyer into downstairs apartments, and a door under the staircase led to the basement laundry room. All the conveniences she needed, plus indoor plumbing. The last hadn't always been handy in her younger years.

Lugging her backpack by one of the straps, she tackled the stairs at a run. Exercise of any kind helped keep her in shape, particularly since bean burritos had a way of adding a little fat if she didn't watch it.

Even with her apartment still showing signs of being ransacked, looking more like the bottom of a trash barrel than her usually neat, free-of-kitsch refuge, it was good to be home again. The cupboards in the kitchen had been emptied out, drawers dumped on the floor, couch cushions tossed, and her mattress dragged off the bed. There had to be something that would take out the smell of the olive oil spilled everywhere before it turned rancid in the heat. She'd already scrubbed it off the floor, but it had left a definite residue. She'd cleaned up the bath powder dumped in the bathroom, refolded towels and put them away, but it needed deep cleaning and she didn't feel like it. Especially since Morgan would show up at any moment.

She opened the French doors leading to the balcony and turned on the ceiling fans to circulate fresh air. White sheers in front of the open doors fluttered in the breeze that brought in the fragrance of newly mown grass and the lemony sweet scent of magnolias in bloom. It also allowed in the faint roar of lions and snarl of tigers from the Overton Park zoo across the street. It was a simulation of the African delta that she rather enjoyed most of the time.

By the time Morgan arrived, she'd managed to vacuum the living room and replace books on shelves, restoring a good portion of the former order she craved. If she wasn't a neat freak, she still preferred things tidy. A rebellion against her childhood, Tootsie had once told her. He loved to psychoanalyze everyone, including himself. Self-analysis would certainly be a pip in his case, with multiple-choice reasons for Tootsie's preference for women's clothing.

"Hey you," Mike said, coming in her apartment door with Taco Bell sacks and smelling delightfully of hot peppers and cumin. "I brought extra nachos."

"Yum. I smell sour cream, too. You can stay."

"You're so easy."

When he grinned like that, her heart did a little flip. Relationships had never worked out for her, and she didn't know if this one would, either. After all, they'd had less than a happy start, what with her thinking Mike was a jewelry thief, and him thinking she was mixed up in the thefts herself. It'd only been a week since they'd hooked up. *You need to keep your distance*, logic warned again. But when had logic ever done anything for her?

"Only for a man who brings me extra nachos," she said. "I've got the plates ready on the coffee table. Beer or Coke?"

"Coke. I'm on duty in a little while. Late shift."

"Oh." That was a bummer. "Another sting operation?"

His shrug indicated unwillingness to confide details. That was the thing about cops who worked undercover. They could be damnably tight-lipped when they wanted to be.

The bean burrito with extra sour cream beckoned beneath the paper around it. It was a staple in her diet. Halfway through the flour tortilla and beans, she looked up at Morgan. Damn. He looked good enough to eat, too. Six-two with dark hair and killer blue eyes, he had a body like one of those naked marble statues that were popping up in Memphis gardens—perfect. And the tight black tee shirt and snug black jeans displayed his potential. He'd gotten a haircut. It barely touched his collar in the back. His face was all hard angles and planes except for his mouth. It had a sensuality to it that promised a woman all kinds of delicious things without him saying a word. A small scar right below his bottom lip showed white against the color of skin no one could get in a tanning booth or lying on the beach. Oh yeah. Definitely delicious stuff. Any man who could give her the shivers just by looking at him had to be lethal.

"So, how was your day?" he asked when they'd polished off one Taco Bell sack and started on the other one. "Find any bodies?"

"You really need to get over that. It's not like I make a habit of it."

"God, I hope not. So, get a raise?"

"You've gotta be kidding. I hope you brought the stun gun back. Penney is more irritated about unauthorized use of it than impressed by anything else."

Morgan didn't look surprised. He rarely looked surprised by anything, probably a sideline of his job, to look like he'd seen everything.

"Yeah, it's in my car."

She licked a glob of sour cream off her fingertips. "Don't suppose you can fix my tickets after all, can you?"

"Harley—"

"Never mind. Just thought since I was instrumental in capturing jewel thieves, the MPD might want to overlook a couple of minor traffic offenses."

"Another time. So, what's your next plan?"

"As soon as I finish off these nachos, I'm going to finish cleaning. Care to help with the heavy stuff?"

Morgan stood up and stretched, an intriguing sight. What a body. Hard abs, great pecs and lats—oops, there went that flutter in the pit of her stomach again.

"So where do we start?" he asked. "Looks like you've got a lot done in here."

"The bedroom. Whoa, sport. Don't get excited. My mattress and box springs came off the frame again and I can't get them back on right by myself."

He grinned, and something dark and sexy glittered in his eyes. "Oh yeah, we'll fix it and then test it."

"I thought you were on duty."

"Always. I may have to frisk you for contraband." He moved close, ran his hand over her tee shirt, and gave her a wicked leer guaranteed to summon goose bumps and anticipation. "Committed any crimes lately?"

"I've been bad," she whispered when she could catch her breath, "*very bad.* Arrest me, copper."

"My pleasure, lady. And yours."

That was one of the things she liked best about Morgan. He always knew what to say.

Three

"This is the fabric room," Aunt Darcy said, sweeping out one arm to indicate a large room on the second floor of the shop. "We have swatches and textile books in here for our clients to use in choosing new drapes and furniture. Our designers work here a lot."

"And is this where you found the, uh, illegal stuff?"

"No. I just wanted you to see it. You haven't visited since we expanded and remodeled. It has grown a lot in the past year, and we run a multimillion dollar business now. Letting Harry in has its upside, but now . . . I just don't know. Someone is smuggling in banned goods, and he's the only one who has complete access to our overseas connections. He takes trips abroad to choose new items, visit wholesale suppliers, things like that."

Harley glanced around the spacious room with long windows allowing in the morning light. Built-in shelves housed huge fabric books, and other slots held bolts of material. Light wood floors and white painted walls gave the room a clean, open feeling.

The old two-and-a-half story Victorian house, built by a cotton merchant in the nineteenth century as an out-of-town getaway and weekend retreat, had gone through quite a few incarnations over the years since the heirs had sold it. Boarding house, whorehouse, children's home, restaurant, and thrift shop had done some damage. Aunt Darcy had bought it as a labor of love fifteen years before, and she'd opened her design shop after some extensive and expensive renovations. Of course, the prime real estate that had once surrounded the house had long been sold, and now traffic went up and down a major thoroughfare only a quarter mile away. Designer's Den sat on a side street that ended in a cove, flanked by an accounting firm, a beauty shop, and an empty building. The aluminum siding was a tasteful blue with white trim, and the parking lot in front had crushed seashells that matched the trim. In the back, a huge storage area and cargo doors were a recent addition, some of it utilizing what had once been the servant's quarters. An impressive operation.

"So where did you discover the items you think may be illegal?" she asked, and her aunt flashed an annoyed frown.

"I don't *think* they're illegal. I know they are. Real zebra skins, an endangered species of elk, and ivory *objets d'art.* Also, there's powdered rhinoceros horn and Cuban cigars."

Okay, the last she knew was definitely banned.

"Where did you find them?" she asked again, and Darcy led her back down the stairs.

"I found things packed in various crates," she said, "tucked into armoire drawers, antique chests, and wrapped in carpets."

Keys clinked as she unlocked a set of double doors that led into a cavernous storage area. Huge carved armoires, teak chests, rolls of carpet, oriental vases, statues, and greenery reminded her of the import warehouse where she'd nearly met her doom hiding from a jewelry thief. No fertility gods that she could see, however, a small disappointment.

Darcy crossed to another locked room, a small area more like a walk-in closet. Inside were several animal skins that looked like the real thing, a huge jar of some kind of powder, and a wooden case with *Havana* stamped on it. The cigars, no doubt. Yep. Looked like illegal goods.

"I hid these here so I could show them to you," Darcy said. I don't know what to do with them."

"What's in the jar?"

"I'm sure it's powdered rhinoceros horn. I think people use it as a kind of aphrodisiac or something. I read that in *Cosmo.* Here. Take some and get it tested, will you?"

"Tested? And who do you suggest I get to do that? The neighborhood drug runner?"

"Don't be ridiculous, Harley. You have connections."

"I don't have connections. I just know people who know people who have connections."

"Good. Now here." She'd put some in a tan envelope. "See what you can find out about it."

"Just for curiosity's sake, how does Harry explain this powder? I mean, he's got to call it something on manifests or invoices, or explain it somehow."

"I haven't seen invoices for these things, but he does order a lot of French bath powder."

Harley carefully took a sniff of the envelope. "Well, it does smell nice."

"Maybe to another rhinoceros. It's atrocious. Honestly, it seems you'd have inherited *some* sense of style or good taste from the Eaton side of the family."

Ignoring that, Harley asked, "So how do you figure Harry's involved? I mean, why do you suspect him of the smuggling?"

Taking a deep breath, Darcy said with unusual venom, "He's a bastard. I should have listened to Mama and Daddy, but it was just so tempting—he put a lot of money into the shop. That's how I was able to expand and remodel. At first, he was a silent partner. Then he started going on buying trips, sending back furniture and accessories from places like England, France, and Italy that were quite suitable. Not long after that, we got in some shipments from Russia, China, and Colombia. Not expensive antiques, just things that I'd call junk. We argued about it, and Harry insisted that there's a market here for it."

A bitter smile twisted her lips. "I'm afraid he was right about that. I was amazed at how well and quickly some of the most awful pieces sold. So I kept quiet, thinking that this was just a new trend, or he just knew a lot of people with bad taste. Then we started getting shipments like this one, only I never thought to actually look inside the trunks and armoires when they were delivered. Harry took care of all that, said he had a certain clientele that preferred the more kitschy stuff. He'd brought in his own designer—a perfectly wretched woman—and she handles all those clients. When one of the clients called and said his furniture was late, I uncrated one of the carved chests from Colombia and found the Cuban cigars. I started looking around then, and found this other stuff. These skins are illegal, Harley. And there's more. Look."

Darcy opened a wooden chest. Straw chaff drifted to the floor as she lifted a beautiful figure of what looked like a dog holding a scepter.

"This is an Egyptian god, a jackal holding an ankh, probably carved five thousand years ago. It should be in a museum, Harley, and in that other crate are ancient Mayan statues. I'm afraid they're stolen, and I'm convinced Harry is responsible for smuggling them into the country. I'll lose everything. Everything!"

Her voice had risen slightly, and Harley put a hand on her arm. "If he has, you can prove you didn't know anything about it. After all, you're going to report it."

"Report it?" Darcy blinked. "You mean—to the police? Oh no,

I'm not! I'm not about to have my name in the paper like that. Why, I'd lose every one of my clients. No, no, you're going to prove that Harry's responsible, and then we're going to confront him with the proof. I thought maybe you could get that Italian boy to come with us, just as leverage. Muscle, I think I've heard it called. You know who I mean. The Mafia guy."

"Mafia—*Bobby?* He has the weight of the Memphis Police Department behind him, Aunt Darcy. Bobby won't involve himself in anything underhanded. I know. It's a shame, but that's the way he is. He will, however, advise us on how to press charges and keep it as quiet as possible. Listen—if you wait and the police somehow get involved, then you'll be under suspicion and it will be in all the papers anyway."

Darcy's eyes narrowed. She looked positively ferocious, kind of like a thwarted possum, with bared teeth and glittering eyes.

"There is no way this side of hell that I'll risk everything I've worked for like that. *No.* You get the proof, and I'll take care of Harry."

That was Aunt Darcy. A velvet steamroller. Iron fist inside the lace glove. Oh yeah. It was a family trait. Even Diva had her inflexible core. It seemed to be a female characteristic inherited from Grandmother Eaton, and her mother before her. Nana McMullen was one hard lady, but with none of the velvet. Now in her mid-eighties, Nana was all steel and stubbornness, age stripping her of any need for pretense at courtesy or gentility. A scary old lady. Apparently, Aunt Darcy had inherited a wide streak of her grandmother's stubbornness.

"Okay," Harley said, "I'll see what I can find out. But why haven't you been able to find out anything? Don't you keep records?"

"Of course we do. But Harry keeps separate records. You'll have to find where he hides his books and get them for me. He's got a desk here, but he keeps that kind of thing in his home office, I'll bet."

Oh boy. "Uh, that might be classified as breaking and entering."

"I have no idea how to classify it. I just want his ledgers. Get them for me. I'll pay you well."

"How well?" Okay, so it was a little crass to shake down family, but Aunt Darcy had the bucks and spent freely when she wanted. Besides, she still owed Harley twenty dollars for their drinks at The Peabody.

"Five thousand dollars if you get me those ledgers." Aunt Darcy said it without a blink, her blonde hair unturned. Her face relaxed back into the pre-possum mode, looking unlined and pleasant again.

"Five *thousand* . . . okay. I'll do what I can."

"As quickly as possible, please. We're expecting another shipment, and Harry's supposed to be out of town until next week, so be at my shop Thursday afternoon at two. That will be the perfect time to see what's coming into the shop. Just watch out for his helper. Sherry something. Brown hair. Annoying voice. Very bourgeois. She hovers like a vulture."

"Won't she think it's strange that I'm visiting?"

"I've already thought of that. You'll be here consulting with me as a designer to redo your apartment." Darcy smiled. "Now see, sugar? You'll do just fine."

Not bad. Maybe Darcy wasn't as scattered as she'd once thought. And that was a little scary, too.

"You sure you want to get mixed up in that, baby?" Tootsie frowned, pushing away from the filing cabinet to roll his chair back across the floor to his desk. "Your aunt needs to go to the police."

"Yeah, I tried to tell her that. I think once there's proof either way, she can be convinced." She heard the doubt in her own voice and sighed. "Or whatever. She's willing to pay me five thousand to find out what's going on and get her his books."

Tootsie whistled softly. "Wish I had a generous relative."

"She's not generous. I think she's desperate." Harley frowned. "Could you get me a background check on Harry Gordon? I'm supposed to go back to the shop and pretend I'm remodeling my apartment so I can see what's coming in, and maybe get my hands on his books. While I don't really think he's dumb enough to keep incriminating records anywhere close by, it will at least satisfy Aunt Darcy if I make the effort."

"Sure, I'll do what I can. But be careful. Your family has a way of getting into trouble without trying."

"Don't I know it." She raked a hand through her hair, then remembered she'd put extra gel on it to hold it in place. It felt like porcupine quills. Spiny and sticky. That made her think of the rhinoceros powder. She pulled out the envelope Darcy had given her.

"Can you get Steve to test this, see if it's some kind of bath powder or if it's drugs or something?" Steve was a cop and Tootsie's significant other, but despite their long, monogamous relationship,

Harley had never met him. He always seemed to be working. Harley had once suggested that he was Tootsie's imaginary playmate, much to his amusement.

She held out the tan envelope. "Aunt Darcy's convinced it's an illegal substance used in voodoo rituals. What do they do with powdered rhinoceros horn? Never mind. I'd rather not know."

Tootsie's smile was wicked. "Sure, I'll have Steve test it. Preferably, on me."

"Tootsie—"

"Oh, all right. You want this done on the quiet, I presume."

"Of course. Will Steve keep it quiet even if it's illegal?"

"No. But he will let you report it yourself. You know how cops are. Prone to be law-abiding."

"An unfortunate side-effect at times."

Tootsie lowered his voice. "I've got a bad feeling about this one, Harley. Sure you want to do it?"

"No, but it'll keep peace in the family if I at least try. Besides, what can happen in a design shop?"

By one-fifty-five Thursday, she'd returned to Designer's Den, located off Poplar almost in Germantown, the elite town that blended into the city limits of Memphis with hardly a blink. Poplar Avenue stayed the same, except that in Germantown, the roadside speed limit signs also listed speed limits for horses. Germantown was a Mecca for the horsey set.

It was one of those June days Shakespeare had written about and Memphis was famous for—blue sky, warm breeze, the sweet fragrance of flowering plants in the air. Along with loads of pollen to irritate the noses of the allergy prone.

Harley parked her car on the side, off the crushed seashell parking lot bordering the rear drive, and stared at the huge truck nosed against the back loading area. It had no logo, nothing to designate it as a shipping firm or delivery van, just a plain white-sided truck. That was rather odd. Didn't most delivery firms like to advertise? Maybe she'd go in the back way and see what was up.

It was blacktop back there. The white van used by Designer's Den to deliver furniture to clients was parked against a line of hedges. Behind it was a Mustang convertible, sporty and blue and definitely not Aunt Darcy's. She had a sensible—and expensive—four-door white sedan, one of those with all the bells and whistles. It also defiantly bore a row of Obama-Biden 2008 stickers on the back bumper. When the presidential elections came around again, Aunt Darcy would replace them with whatever Democratic candidate ran against the Republicans. She could be counted on for party loyalty, no matter what the scandal or platform. Of course, there were plenty of rattling skeletons in both party closets that often sent Harley's father, Yogi, into a rant against the government and Big Brother, so Harley avoided all family political discussions. It could turn ugly quickly.

A rather florid, tall man with iron-gray hair and piercing blue eyes stood with a clipboard near the cargo doors, and he seemed startled to see her.

"The entrance is in front, miss," he said, but she ignored him and climbed up the three steep steps to the cargo bay.

"Oh, I know, but I thought I might find Darcy Fontaine back here. She's supposed to meet me, didn't she tell you? Are you one of her employees?"

"No." His eyes narrowed slightly, but the polite smile remained fixed. Ah. This would be Harry Gordon, who obviously hadn't left town. "You'll find Mrs. Fontaine in the *front* of the store. I'll be glad to escort you there," he said.

"Oh, don't bother. I know where it is. My, what a lovely chest. Is it French?"

"Portuguese. And it's an armoire. Really, I must insist that you leave this area. Insurance requires that we not allow anyone back here where there might be an accident."

While he spoke, he took her firmly by the arm, his fingers digging into her biceps with iron determination. It was almost as if he was afraid someone might see something they shouldn't. Maybe Aunt Darcy was right after all, though it did stretch the imagination to think it would be anything more than a few Cuban cigars. And how did he manage *that?*

"I'm a customer," she lied as he escorted her toward the double doors leading into the shop, "and Mrs. Fontaine said to meet her back here to look at a new shipment."

He sliced her a quick, hard glance from those bright blue eyes that were cold and hot at the same time. "Really. Then I take it you're interested in Portuguese armoires and Grecian urns? If not, you'll find styles more to your taste up front, Miss—"

It was an open invitation to provide her name. She could almost hear his mental wheels clacking.

"Davidson. And you are . . .?"

"Harry Gordon."

As suspected. She smiled. "And I do like Grecian urns, as a matter of fact. I'd like to look around for a few minutes before we discuss anything, however." Not an entire lie. She picked up a vase with ugly, primitive looking figures on it. "This is nice."

Moving closer, he took it from her hands and carefully put it back in the straw-filled box at the bottom of a carved chest. He closed the lid. "These are a new shipment not yet catalogued. Look, Miss Davidson, you'll have to wait until we've inspected our shipment."

"Then perhaps you should speak to Mrs. Fontaine, since she said I could browse through everything as soon as it got here. Get first pick, you know, before anyone else can try to buy it out from under my nose. Like this pretty jewelry box." She picked up an item still in a crate, with straw clinging to it. The carved images in white bone looked Celtic, snakes and dragons all twisting around in sinuous loops.

His florid complexion went redder, and for a moment she thought he might turn purple. He reached over to pluck it out of her hands, then excused himself with a harsh mutter and stormed toward one of the delivery men working in the truck. There was a brief, low discussion during which he handed over his clipboard, and then he went back toward the front of the shop without another word to her.

Well, he'd left the clipboard, but unfortunately, it was in the possession of a large, burly man with a single eyebrow and low forehead. Primitive man at his best. Maybe brashness would work, as subtlety would be lost on this guy.

She strode toward him, whipped out her tour guide ID in an arc that she hoped was too swift for him to catch, and said, "Yes, I'll go ahead and look at that now, please. Thank you."

Reaching for the clipboard, she was elated when he looked surprised and uncertain and held it out. Then he seemed to recover and snatched it back, scowling at her.

"No," he said in a heavy accent she couldn't place, "no' allowed."

"Of course it is. I want to see what's on that bill of lading. You're familiar with Customs? Immigration?"

The last word caught his attention and he blanched. Harley kept her hand out, an eyebrow arched and her foot tapping impatiently. It was easy to see his internal struggle as he stared at her with the same look she'd seen on moose heads mounted on walls—a glassy-eyed, stunned sort of resignation.

Oh yes, she thought as the clipboard in his hand quivered closer to her outstretched fingers and success, *give it to me . . .*

Of course, nothing was ever that easy.

"Julio!" boomed a voice, startling the man into almost dropping the clipboard and making Harley jerk in annoyed surprise. Harry Gordon strode back into the delivery area with Aunt Darcy in tow.

Just a few more seconds and it would have been hers, Harley thought with a surge of exasperation at her aunt's abominable timing. Aunt Darcy's expression was caught between anger and fear. She looked like a trapped ferret. Her eyes darted between Harry and Harley, and her lips stretched back over her teeth in a grimace. Darcy could have at least called to warn her that Harry would be here, dammit.

"Miss Davidson," Gordon said flatly, "you've no business back here at all."

"Of course I do. I want to look at some unusual furniture, and I was told you have quite a few unique items coming into the shop today."

His eyes narrowed. He wasn't fooled one bit, and his lowered brows conveyed skepticism as well as irritation.

"Then wait until it's all unloaded and inventoried. Your aunt will show you into the shop for now."

Apparently, Aunt Darcy had told all. What a nitwit. How did she expect Harley to skulk around the shop if Gordon was suspiciously watching her every move? Honestly!

"I'm sorry," Darcy muttered when they were at the front of the shop standing by a table holding glass globes and crystal figurines, "but I goofed and said you were my niece. I'm just so upset. He came back early and this shipment came in late . . . and now the other merchandise that I showed you Monday is gone. I kept it locked away, but it's all disappeared."

"Super." She picked up a small glass globe with faint multicolored transparent swirls in the center, lovely and elusive. Diva would love it for her séances and palm readings. She shook it. "So now that he knows I'm family and his suspicions are probably on high alert, I'll come back after six."

Darcy frowned. "But we'll be closed."

"Yes. I know." When her aunt still didn't get it, she said, "*After* hours he'll be gone and I can do some snooping."

"Oh." Darcy reached out, took the glass globe from her, and set it gently back onto the table. "If you think that's best. What time shall I meet you here—oh wait. That's no good. I have a Junior League meeting tonight. A charity auction."

"If we give him too much time, whatever he's bringing in now may be gone. We need hard evidence, something to hold over his head. We can use it as leverage to get his records. Or his resignation."

"Well, I suppose I could give you a key," Darcy said slowly and obviously reluctantly, "if you bring it back to me tonight."

"I'll see you at Grandmother's Saturday for lunch. Why not then?" It was Thursday night and she had plans with Morgan for later, something deliciously wicked if she was lucky.

"Oh all right, I suppose I can trust you. You *will* be careful, won't you, Harley? I mean, if he should find you in here he'd know I suspect him, and then it could get really ugly, or he could somehow say I'm involved in it when I'm not, really, except that it did seem too good to be true that we could sell all that awful stuff he imports at such a markup—"

"Aunt Darcy. I'll be careful. I'll need a camera to take pictures of the stuff he's brought in, do a little snooping and see if I can find his ledgers or invoices, though I doubt he lets any of it far from his sight. He probably keeps it in a safe at his house."

"I'll give you my camera," Darcy said, "but be careful with it. I use it for clients' homes, and don't want it broken."

"Are you sure you want to do this? It'd be easier to call in the police, you know. If he's smuggling, they'll put him in jail."

"It'd also ruin my reputation. Clients will think I'm unreliable, that somehow I'm mixed up in all this as well. If at all possible, I want to keep this quiet. Just please get me some proof that Harry's smuggling. Then I can make him go away."

"That might be called blackmail or extortion," Harley said slowly. "I'm not up on all the laws, but it sounds dangerous. Harry doesn't look like the kind of guy who'd take it well."

"I should have listened to Mama and Daddy," Darcy said again, and Harley couldn't argue with that.

It was nearly eight when Harley let herself into the shop, using the borrowed key Darcy had made her swear she'd guard with her very life. Ready to punch in the alarm code, she saw that it hadn't been set, and paused. Definitely odd. But then, Aunt Darcy was so rattled by all this, she may well have forgotten to set it.

Waning light lent a musty gloom to the shop lit only by a few lamps here and there. It was quiet and still. Thick carpet underfoot gave way to the muted gleam of light oak floors in the next showroom, crowded with brocade couches and chairs, tall armoires, lamps, statues, tables, more chairs, and dozens of pots of greenery. No canned music filtered through hidden speakers; the only sound was the hum of the central air conditioning.

Moving quickly through the showrooms to the back, Harley paused when she heard a loud thud, like the slamming of a door. Her heart pounded, and air constricted her lungs as she froze. Meeting up with Harry Gordon would *not* be the highlight of her evening. The parking lot was empty except for the big store van out back, but it stayed there all the time. No one should be here, but an uneasy feeling of being watched prickled the back of her neck and made her reach for the Mace can she wore clipped to the waistband of her jeans. No point in being stupid.

The camera slung around her neck clinked softly as she moved forward, taking slow steps and trying not to bump into anything expensive. It was darker here, lamps on low providing spotty light, and suddenly her breathing sounded far too loud in the smothering gloom.

This was silly. No one was here. It was after hours. She was just jittery. Luck often went in the other direction when she started snooping. Still . . . she came to an abrupt halt when the thud sounded again, louder and closer. A door?

Oh no, this was getting too weird. Every instinct in her body shrieked at her to get the hell out of Dodge. She'd never pretended to be brave. Or noble. Just needy. She'd just have to find another way to get the proof for Aunt Darcy—and a fat check in return.

Backing up, she bumped into a tall cabinet and glass clinked loudly. She looked around, but nothing looked familiar. She was lost in a maze of dimly-lit showrooms and furniture. An Exit sign had to be somewhere. Let's see, she'd been standing by a table in the front showroom earlier in the day, looking at glass globes and thinking how Diva would like one of them for her séances or palm reading. That would be—which way? So many damn rooms in this sprawling house now that it'd been renovated, the original two-and-a-half stories altered to a rambling structure that somehow managed to still look artistically cluttered.

She stepped through an open door and found herself in yet another furniture-crammed showroom. Afghans were draped over love seats and fringed ottomans; paintings hung on the walls and were stacked on the floor leaning against chairs and each other. Great. She should have left a trail of bread crumbs to find her way out.

Light slanted into the room to her right, and she moved that way, rounding a corner to see an open door to the cargo area banging in the wind. Relief and a crazy urge to laugh hysterically eased her tension. It was only a door left open. What a wuss she'd become.

She moved to the door, peered out, and saw taillights leaving the parking lot. A white car very similar to Aunt Darcy's Lexus squealed onto Massey Road. That explained the alarm not being set. But it didn't explain why Darcy was here when she was supposed to be at her Junior League meeting. Or where she'd parked the car and why she'd carelessly left the back door open. Maybe she'd just forgotten something. Not that it really mattered. The rear parking lot was empty except for the white van. Maybe she'd go ahead and look around instead of giving in to the jitters.

The double doors to the back storage area were open, and she approached cautiously in case Gordon had shown up as well. For a place that was supposed to be empty, Designer's Den sure was busy.

It was darker inside the storage area, and she reached just inside to find a light switch. It tripped a bank of fluorescent lighting overhead, and she paused a few steps inside the doorway. At first glance, everything looked the same. The big Portuguese chest and a stack of crates stood to one side, and some packing straw lay littered on the floor as if someone had been interrupted in unpacking. No motion or sound intruded on the heavy silence, but she still felt a chill shiver down her spine. It was the same kind of chill her great-grandmother would say meant someone was walking over her grave. Not a nice thought. What little courage she'd mustered promptly disappeared. Time to hit the trail.

She turned around to hit the light switch again, and bumped into Harry Gordon.

"Oh shit!" she yelped, leaping backward. "You scared the crap out of me. I didn't hear you—hey, are you all right?"

Harry Gordon didn't answer. He just stared beyond her, his bright blue eyes faded and opaque. His mouth sagged open, and his face was gray as putty—and as unanimated.

Something wet and warm smeared her palm and she looked down, staring blankly for a moment at the bright red stuff like ketchup. Then she looked up at Harry Gordon again. The tip of some kind of animal horn protruded from his chest and, apparently, was all that held him up.

Oh boy. She'd known meeting up with Harry Gordon wouldn't be pleasant. She just hadn't thought it'd be fatal.

Four

"How the hell do you do it, Harley?" Mike Morgan shook his head in disbelief. "You're a magnet for murder."

"Oh, gee thanks, I appreciate your comfort, but really, it isn't necessary." She gulped a big swig of hot coffee he'd brought her, still shivering with reaction despite the night's heat.

She'd called Mike first, and he'd called in the police. Harry Gordon still hung from an elk horn in the storage area, waiting for the coroner to finish his investigation. Macabre.

Mike peered down at her. "So why are you here alone? I thought you told me you had to do something with your aunt tonight."

"No, you never listen. I said had to do something *for* my aunt tonight. This was it. Oh no, not murder—I was just checking on some stuff for her."

"What kind of stuff?"

"What, are you working homicide now?"

"Practicing." He shifted position, moved closer, his voice dropping. "These aren't hard questions, Harley, but someone's going to ask them. Better be ready."

"I am ready. Ready to leave."

Morgan smiled and looked at something beyond her. "Too late."

She didn't have to look. She knew who it had to be. Bobby Baroni. She turned and put on a bright smile when she saw him stalking toward her. Bobby was tall, well-built, and Italian to the roots of his black hair. His parents were third generation Americans, his grandparents still spoke in their native language at home, and his great-grandparents had never learned English at all. They hadn't had to, living downtown near the river in what used to be the Italian quarter of Memphis, selling pasta and pastrami to mostly Italians but a surprising number of Irish as well.

"Hi, Bobby!"

"Shit, Harley." He didn't look happy. In fact, he looked distinctly grumpy. He gave her a look from his dark eyes that was both wary and professional. Bobby never let friendship interfere with his duties as a homicide detective. Unfortunately.

"Why is it," he began, flicking his gaze from her to Morgan and back, "that I always seem to find you near murder victims lately? If I didn't know better—and I'm not sure I do—I'd think you were some sort of aberrant serial killer."

"Isn't that redundant? I thought all serial killers were aberrant."

Bobby's eyes narrowed. "This is no time to try funny, Harley. How'd this happen?"

"Hell, *I* don't know!" she said indignantly. "He was dead when I got here, hanging off that elk horn like a winter coat." She couldn't help a shudder. A sick feeling sat in her stomach.

"Did you give a statement yet?"

She nodded. "To that officer over there. You're not going to make me give it three or four times again, I hope."

"As many as it takes, Harley." He wrote something down in his little spiral notebook, then turned to Morgan. "You called this in. Were you with her?"

"No. She called me, hysterical—"

"I was not hysterical!" she protested, but both men ignored her as Mike kept talking.

"—because she'd found the vic. I told her not to touch anything, to wait outside in her car with the doors locked, and then I called it in."

"Yeah. Well, let's run this down again, Harley. You said you were doing something for your aunt—what?"

"Uh . . . I have her camera." She held it up when he looked at her. "I was taking pictures for her. Of furniture. Stuff like that."

"Right. I'll just keep it for a while, if you don't mind. Give it to that officer over there. I don't suppose you'll tell me why you're here after hours? Why she didn't do it herself?"

"She, uh, had a meeting." No way was she going to tell them Aunt Darcy had been here.

"A meeting. Why is taking pictures of merchandise so important she'd send you to do it? You've never gotten along that well with her. Why so buddy-buddy all of a sudden?"

The bad thing about Bobby was that he remembered too much, and knew too much about her family. It could be damned inconvenient.

Not wanting to lie to Bobby, but knowing the truth would only be worse without proof, she said, "Well, we're not exactly buddies, but I was, uh, looking at some of the new stuff that just came in. You know. Unique stuff for my apartment."

Bobby just looked at her. He had a way of ferreting out the truth that was quite annoying, but she held firm. He didn't believe her, she could see that, so he just waited for her to blurt out everything she knew. This time, it wasn't going to work. Darcy was family, and blood was thicker than water. Even thicker than friendship, although she felt queasy about it all.

"At wholesale," she added when he kept staring at her.

"Wholesale?" he finally said in a frankly disbelieving tone. "Your Aunt *Darcy*? Has she had a recent brain transplant? She's never given wholesale to anyone, not even her own mother."

That was true, dammit. She'd gone too far. Why had she added the last? Bobby knew that Darcy Fontaine believed in profit even at the expense of her own family. She'd just remodeled Grandmother Eaton's kitchen and only gave her a five percent discount. Hardly wholesale.

Fortunately, a female shriek distracted Bobby, so she was saved from having to give a plausible explanation. That could wait until she'd actually talked to Aunt Darcy to find out why she'd been here and if she'd seen her partner impaled on an elk horn.

"Harry! *Oh God no, not Harry!* Please, you've got to let me see him . . . *noooo!*"

The shrieks rose in volume until Harley's eyes throbbed and she winced. Two uniformed policemen were trying to contain the plainly hysterical woman struggling to get through their barrier to the warehouse.

"Do you know her?" Bobby asked Harley, and she shook her head.

"Never seen her before in my life, but I don't think I'll forget that voice. It grates like fingernails on a chalkboard."

Bobby's faint smile told her he agreed with her assessment, but he only said, "Come to the precinct in the morning to give an official statement."

"So," Morgan said while Bobby walked toward the crime scene in the warehouse, "why were you here again?"

"I already told you—"

"Yeah, and I don't quite believe you."

Indignant again, she said, "I have never lied to you!"

"Maybe not, but you have an annoying habit of not telling me the entire truth. So technically, it's the same thing."

"Not quite." She really hated it when he got technical. He was so often right.

"Oh yeah. *Quite*. You went to Catholic school. Isn't there a sin of omission as well as a sin of commission?"

"How should I know? I slept through catechism classes, and I've forgotten everything I had to learn anyway. Look, thanks for coming to my rescue. I feel better now. Think I can go?"

"Better ask Baroni about that. He's the primary on this one."

"Chicken."

"Oh no, I'm not about to lay the egg. Let Baroni handle you. I've done my rescue bit for tonight."

Her brow arched. "That mean we won't be having a late dinner in bed?"

"Hey, I said I'm not into any more rescue, but I'm not crazy. We're definitely on for a late dinner in bed." Reaching out, he snagged her arm, pulled her against his hard chest, and bent his head, kissing her until little lights exploded behind her eyes and she forgot they were in the middle of a crime scene. Then he let her go, grinning when she breathed a long sigh and stood unsteadily for a moment. "Your place. I'll be waiting on you."

Still groping for equilibrium, she said, "Yeah. Later."

"I'll bring dinner. No, *not* Taco Bell. Branch out. Try new things."

She blinked, but the protest went unuttered. He was already walking away anyway. Wow. The man curled her toes.

The screech that split the air curled her hair.

Jerking around, she stared at the woman still fighting the police to get a glimpse of Harry Gordon. Dark hair that frizzed into some kind of curly mess flopped in her face so that Harley couldn't get a good look at her, but she definitely made herself heard.

"Harry can't be dead, I just talked to him," the woman screamed, and Harley saw that the officers had finally gotten her to stand up instead of sag between them, though they still had to support her. She seemed so genuinely distressed that Harley knew Harry Gordon had to be more to her than a fellow employee. The woman's shrieks were so loud she had no trouble hearing her, even across fifty feet of parking lot illuminated by strobe lights and security lamps.

"Ma'am," one of the cops said to the woman, and Harley thought she recognized Officer Delisi, who had questioned her just last week after Mrs. Trumble's death. "You need to calm down. If you want to help us, you've got to answer some questions. Did you know the deceased well?"

Nodding and shuddering, the brunette indicated her willingness to comply, but she looked up at them through her lashes, a swift assessing glance that caught Harley off-guard. It was so—so calculated. Hm. Maybe she wasn't as grieving as she seemed. Had the officers even noticed?

"Sha-ree Saw-say," she said when asked her name, then spelled it "*Cheríe Saucier.*" Harley thought it sounded like a topless dancer's stage name. Still, the petite brunette wore clothes no dancer would wear, an expensive line Harley recognized from shopping with Tootsie. The simple lines of the pantsuit were elegant, Dolce & Gabbana at odds with her K-Mart navy pumps.

If there was one thing she'd learned from Grandmother Eaton, it was that a true lady paid scrupulous attention to her footwear, even if she couldn't afford expensive clothing. Still, this was the twenty-first century, not the era Grandmother Eaton obviously preferred. Etiquette rules of the past no longer applied. Even the ironclad rule about not wearing white before Easter and after Labor Day had been abused in the past few years. Yet her adolescent lessons were difficult to ignore, so Harley regarded the woman curiously as she walked to where the woman and officers stood.

It was no surprise to hear her say she worked closely with Harry Gordon, that he'd hired her as a designer and consultant. This was the woman Aunt Darcy disliked so intensely and had called a "wretched woman." She could see how they'd clash. Darcy Fontaine could spot a female fraud a mile away and had no doubt pegged Cheríe Saucier the moment she'd laid eyes on her. Oh yeah, she was willing to bet there had been some interesting fireworks a time or two.

Which reminded her—why had Aunt Darcy returned to the store? And what had she really meant when she'd said, *"I'll take care of Harry"*? No. Not Aunt Darcy. She might be a ruthless pest and one of those annoyingly determined women, but she wasn't a murderer. It'd be too untidy. Besides, Harry had been impaled on a horn, and it took strength to do that. The heaviest thing Aunt Darcy lifted was a bottle of gin.

Well, Saturday was lunch at Grandmother Eaton's, and she intended to ask her aunt some of those questions.

"You need to talk to Darcy Fontaine," Cheríe Saucier spat at one of the officers, and the calculating look in her eyes belied her previous hysteria. "She had a huge fight with Harry earlier today."

Uh oh. This didn't bode well for Aunt Darcy. Harley sidled closer to eavesdrop, earning a narrow glance from Officer Delisi.

"I heard her tell him she'd kill him before she'd let him ruin her business," Cheríe added, to Harley's dismay. "And she would, too. The woman is a total bitch. I wouldn't put anything past her."

"Funny," Harley piped in, "she says the same thing about you."

That earned her a longer stare from the closest officer, an unfamiliar face.

"It's true," Harley defended Aunt Darcy, though God only knew why, since she had the sinking feeling there was a lot more to this than dear old auntie had confided in her. "They hate each other, so I wouldn't be taking Miss Saucer's word as gospel."

"*Saucier*," Cheríe snapped, emphasizing the last syllable as *say*, and Harley just smiled. If that was her real name, Aunt Darcy was a Republican.

Glaring at Harley, Cheríe ground out, "And every word is true. They had a huge fight and Darcy Fontaine threatened Harry. I was standing behind the door and I heard her."

"Snooping? Besides, that's hearsay, isn't it, officer?"

"Look, Miss Davidson, if you've already given your statement, you need to go home now. We'll call you when we need you," the officer replied, and she saw on his little brass name tag that his name was Logan.

"Certainly, Officer Logan. Uh, have we met?"

He grinned. "Not officially. But I know who you are. And I'll take that camera."

"Oh." No doubt half the police force could recognize her now. That could turn out to be a huge drawback. "I'll just be running along then," she said, and gave him the camera. With a last glance at Miss Saucier, who'd crossed her arms over her chest and narrowed her eyes, she went to find her car and try to get out of the now crowded parking lot. Vans and police cruisers littered the lot, looking ominous and final. A television crew pulled up beside the coroner's van, and she recognized one of the Channel 3 reporters. She walked a little faster, and crushed seashells crunched under her feet. Her Toyota seemed miles away, but she got to it before the reporters saw her. She felt safer once she was inside with the doors locked. Cameramen turned on more lights to add to the surreal image of electric fireflies.

This looked really bad for Aunt Darcy. Should she call her? Try to warn her? What if the police were already there questioning her? Well, only one way to find out.

Her new cell phone lay on the car seat, still plugged into the charger. She punched in the number of Aunt Darcy's cell phone and waited. Two, three, four rings, then the automatic system came on to invite her to leave a message. She hung up and dialed her house, but no answer.

For several moments, she just sat there. Aunt Darcy should answer her phones. She rarely let the system take messages. Unless she was avoiding someone.

Harley got a really bad feeling in the pit of her stomach.

After going to the police station the next morning to give her official statement, Harley felt a need for a distraction. Family usually provided that in spades. She hadn't yet broached the subject of the luncheon at Grandmother Eaton's tomorrow with Diva. It could go either way.

Cami—Camilla Watson, her best friend since junior high and partner in many youthful crimes—said it was because Diva had never forgiven Grandmother Eaton for disapproving of Yogi. Ancient history now, but the rift between them remained. It wasn't that they never spoke, it was just that they spoke to one another like acquaintances instead of mother and daughter. Maybe one day they'd settle it, but for now, family reunions and holidays were the only times they saw one another.

Unlike Cami's family, who got together once a month for "First Sunday," an excuse for a decadent feast and gossip. Some of which centered on Cami's friend Harley, who had coaxed her into quite a few pranks and adventures in their younger years. The next First Sunday ought to be a real pip after their last adventure. Cami's mother had probably come close to fainting when she learned that Harley had involved her daughter in the chase of jewelry thieves. No doubt, it'd be a while before Harley was welcomed at First Sunday again, especially if Mrs. Watkins knew that Cami had ridden around town on the back of a motorcycle, been hit in the head, and locked in a trunk.

Harley smiled at the memory of Cami dressed up like Lucy Liu, wearing a black leather jumpsuit her pervert of an ex-husband had bought her, and a football helmet. It had reminded her of the fun they'd had as adolescents, riding around late at night, smoking cigarettes and rolling yards, all the innocent stuff kids did when trying rebellion on for size. Of course, last week had been less innocent and a helluva a lot more dangerous.

Now she'd found another body. There was no explaining this macabre change in her daily routine.

Maybe she was in mid-life crisis. Only four more months and she'd only be three years away from thirty, and here she was with just one serious relationship behind her—two if she wanted to count George Goldfish, now freed in the Audubon Park koi pond. Of course, her on and off relationship with Bobby Baroni through the years had been more friendship than anything serious, despite the fact they'd tried out the physical stuff a long time ago. She loved Bobby, but only as a friend. Besides, he was dating an exotic dancer at the moment, a really hot blonde who went by the name of Angel.

And she had Mike Morgan. A shiver dispelled some of the heat inside the car. Oh yes. He was definitely a distraction. A hold-on-to-your-panties-this-is-gonna-be-good kind of distraction. He made her want to swear off panties altogether.

Why did she have to go and get sidetracked by an undercover cop? She knew all about those guys, having heard from Bobby how unstable they were, prone to dangerous mood swings when they were working on a case. And as a homicide detective who often worked out of the West precinct, Bobby should know what he was talking about.

But that hadn't mattered once she met Mike. From the first, he'd flipped her switch. She still wasn't sure how long it would last, but it was a great ride for now.

She bought a Coke and headed for her parents' house. Since everything that'd happened, she felt the need to check on them just to be sure they weren't in any kind of trouble or causing any kind of trouble. Either was always possible.

The section of Memphis her parents lived in was an older part, houses built back when the University of Memphis was called Normal State. Like everything else in the city, the area had gone through some radical changes over the years. The neighborhood melded from single-family houses in the thirties through the fifties, to boarding houses and rented rooms in the sixties with hippies and beaded curtains and incense, and flowers painted over bright blue and yellow walls and porches. A few of the original residents had held out during the era of free love and *Jesus Christ Superstar*, among them her father's parents. City buses still designated the area as Normal on the banner over the windshield, though it'd been anything but normal during the sixties. Now a few head shops and tattoo parlors, tucked in next to pizza parlors and Laundromats, served as reminders of days gone by, and still turned tidy profits, of course. Head shops and tattoo parlors were obviously timeless. She turned off Highland onto Douglass.

Vanna, her parents' puke-green Volkswagen van that was decorated with Picasso-style body parts, sat in the driveway. Good. They were home. Wind chimes tinkled a welcome on the front porch, and the house was quiet, save for Elvis music coming from the direction of Yogi's workshop. He loved Elvis and still mourned his death every year at the annual candlelight vigil held at the Graceland mansion. Yogi had also been known to grow long sideburns and don a wig and white jumpsuit in honor of the King. For that reason alone she tried to avoid her parents during the month of August. Childhood memories of abject humiliation still had the power to bring a surge of heat to her face.

But despite that, and an early childhood living in California communes with her parents, it always felt good to come back. It was home. Safe. Comforting. There were good memories inside the two-story bungalow where her bedroom was still much as she'd left it. Improvements had been made over the years to the house. Yogi had made stained glass panes to fit the transom over the front door, and the thick concrete pillars out front had been repainted a bright white a few times, but the neat yard of grass and orderly flowerbeds like other houses on the street had long given way to Diva's style of gardening. Spring and summer brought pretty weeds mixed with daffodils, irises, and wild roses that ran rampant over the fence and around the huge oak tree shading the house. Soon they'd cover the walkway that went from the city sidewalk just beyond the jagged teeth of the unpainted pickets, all the way up to the generous front porch. Since an unfortunate incident that had involved her father's dog, an order of cheese being delivered down the street, and the mailman, their mail was now left in a box attached to the outside of the picket gate. It was best that way.

To her surprise, her brother wasn't asleep on the couch as usual, but then she remembered that Eric was probably in class at the university. He'd managed to get an art scholarship, and their grandparents subsidized any odd expenses out of a college fund set up when he'd been born. She had attended college for three years as well. Another mistake. She should have stuck it out, but at twenty it'd been hard to believe that. Still, she wasn't doing too badly now for a college dropout. Not if one considered being a tour guide driver as fulfillment of a lifetime dream.

Really, she needed to get herself back on track just as soon as she figured out what track she wanted to be on. All roads, she'd discovered, do not necessarily lead to Rome.

Diva appeared in the kitchen doorway, smiling as sweetly as if she'd never disappeared with Yogi and the dog for three days and made Harley crazy with worry. Little bells attached to the hem of her multicolored skirt tinkled a light tune as she walked, and her tunic top was tie-dyed to match. With her white-blond hair pulled into ponytails on each side of her face, she looked in her late thirties instead of fifty-one. Harley did a mental comparison with Aunt Darcy, who was so sophisticated in tastes and appearance, but looked older and harder instead of younger. Maybe it was the stress in Darcy's life, for Diva rarely let anything bother her for long.

A ceiling fan stirred wisps of hair to frame Diva's face as she said, "You're almost in time for lunch, Harley. I'll have your father pick some more greens for you."

Yuck. "No thanks. I brought my lunch. I appreciate the offer, though. How's Yogi doing?"

Moving gracefully back into the kitchen with Harley trailing behind, Diva waved her to a chair while she returned to the sink. Shiitake mushrooms, bean sprouts, and water chestnuts were washed and in a metal colander. A rack of spices scented the air as Diva worked.

"He's fine. A little worried about King, but Dr. Hezel assured him the hair would grow back eventually."

Harley propped her elbow on the counter and her chin in her palm. "I take it y'all took King to the vet already."

"Oh, of course. You know how your father feels about that dog. King must have been someone important to him in a former life. They have such a connection, a bond that goes beyond just mutual affection."

"Right." Harley had her own opinion about King's former life. She was certain he'd been a hit man for the mob, or perhaps even a drug kingpin. The dog had lamentable tendencies toward a life of crime. "So, have you thought any more about my suggestion that you put your money in a bank instead of a pickle jar?"

"Yes, Harley. We have." Diva deftly chopped mushrooms into a bowl with the bean sprouts and water chestnuts. "Yogi feels it best to continue as we are for now. You're so kind to worry about us, though. We simply cannot allow money to become the most important thing in our lives. You saw what happened when we got greedy."

"You didn't get greedy, Diva. Yogi accepted an offer of work. That's hardly the same thing." Harley plucked a water chestnut from the bowl. It was cool and crunchy. "Add some soy. Really, I worry that one day someone's going to think you've got a lot of money stashed and rob you."

"If someone needs money that bad, they have only to ask. We freely share the gifts we've been given. Will you please hand me the bamboo shoots?"

Harley found them in a small carton on the counter and passed them to her mother, trying again. "Last time, King was kidnapped. Next time, it could be you or Yogi or even Eric."

A tiny little frown puckered Diva's unlined brow. Hope rose. Perhaps mention of one of them being kidnapped would work after all.

"Your father's been very despondent since the police were here. Perhaps you'd speak with your new friend and see if he can do anything about returning the plants?"

Harley blinked. "Diva, forget the pot plants. They're illegal. Morgan was doing us a favor by not busting all of us for them, and so, I might add, was Bobby, who's always known you grow pot in the backyard next to the tomatoes. I'm sure you have seeds somewhere. Plant more."

There were times she wished her parents would grow up and enter the twenty-first century instead of holding onto a way of life that was long gone and had probably never existed like they thought it had anyway. It had occurred to her more than once that she understood Grandmother Eaton's frustration with her oldest daughter.

Turning wide blue eyes on her, Diva gazed at her until Harley began to fidget. It was that look that always made her feel two years old again, pinned by the sudden realization that her mother knew everything she was thinking.

In a familiar husky alto that worked so well in séances and tarot card readings, Diva said, "Harley, we're happy the way we are. We'll never be what you or my mother wants us to be. It's all right. Everything will be fine."

"You always know what I'm thinking."

Diva smiled. "You have an open, free spirit. It's easy to see what you're thinking. I could do it even without my gift."

She didn't doubt that. "Nevertheless, it'd make me feel better if you'd at least take some precautions."

"Harley, I want you to be careful of the plots. They may hurt you."

Plots? The back door leading from the screened porch banged and Harley had just enough time to brace herself before a black, white, and pink dog launched himself at her with great glee. Large bare spots in his coat testified to his recent dognapping, but he was in good shape for a dog that had been held captive in a storage closet.

"Down, King," she said, without a prayer he'd listen, and tried to pet him at the same time as she tried to fend off his exuberant greeting. Panting and slobbering, the dog leaped about, his toenails clacking against the tile floor and wood cabinets. Part Border Collie, part Mexican jumping bean, King had no sense of decorum whatsoever. When she finally got him to stay down by putting her hand atop his head and holding him between his ears, brown streaks of dirt from his paws stained her khaki jeans. One of the hazards of petting him.

"You really should get him some obedience classes," she said when Yogi beckoned the dog closer. King promptly leaped up and licked her on the mouth before abandoning her for Yogi.

Spitting and scowling, Harley wiped her mouth with a dish towel. Yogi seemed oblivious to King's bad habits. He smiled serenely and stroked the dog's ears and blotchy fur.

"He's perfect the way he is."

"Not even in the Big House. Seriously. You should look into dog training. I talked to a nice lady at Border Collie Rescue, and she gave me some good advice for high-energy dogs like King. He needs a high fence to keep him contained, and lots of exercise, like throwing a Frisbee, or jogging, or—"

"King gets plenty of exercise." Tilting his head to one side, her father smiled. He could be so endearing, with his generous paunch covered by a tee shirt saying *Ban War—Free Love*, and his knee-length ragged shorts that were frayed at the hem. If not for the gray streaking his brown hair, which was pulled back into a ponytail on the nape of his neck, he could almost be the poster child for the era of the Flower Child. "Are you staying for lunch, Harley? I can pick some more greens."

She sighed. "No. Thanks. I brought my lunch."

"Then I could pick some for you to take home for dinner tonight."

"Uh, Mike's bringing takeout later."

"Mike—oh. You mean Bruno?"

"That was his undercover name. The sting operation's over so he's using his own name for the moment. Until another sting or undercover project, I guess." She tried not to think about that. Maybe it was time to throw herself into the breach before she lost her nerve. "Hey, by the way, Diva, Grandmother is giving a luncheon tomorrow. She'd like you to come. It's a girl thing."

Diva paused in cutting up celery. She stared out the kitchen window for a moment, then turned with a faint smile. "I suppose Darcy and the girls will be there. Yes. Well, this weekend Yogi and I have the big flea market at the fairgrounds. You know, the first weekend of every month is the really big one. Yogi has several of those windmills to sell. You've seen the ones that look like the Eiffel Tower? And my trolls and rabbits . . . and I still have so many crystals left. Would you please see if the police will return our supplies? They shouldn't need them now."

"So, that's a no, right?"

"Well . . . " Diva gave one of her airy gestures that could mean almost anything and smiled vaguely. "We're just so busy, you know."

"Right. I'll tell Grandmother."

"Give them my best. And Harley? You'll be just fine. Darcy needs some life lessons, and this is all karmic energy being recycled."

"Uh hunh." That was so Diva, no mention of the murder, just her observations on karma. "So what'd I do this time to get bad karma?"

"It's not necessarily bad karma. There are lessons in good karma as well." She smiled. "I know you don't like talking about it. That's all right. You'll be fine."

"Glad to hear it." She only stayed a few more minutes, then made her excuses and left. An afternoon in the company of a tour group seemed preferable to the vague feelings of guilt that nagged her. On the way to her car, she waved at Mrs. Shipley across the street, who acted as the self-appointed neighborhood sentry.

"I see you've found another body, Harley Jean," Mrs. Shipley called out with a cheerful wave. "So much excitement . . . you be careful now, you hear?"

"I will, Mrs. Shipley, I will." Sadie Shipley resembled a bright tropical bird, dressed all in yellow and blue, looking like something out of a Disney cartoon with her hair frizzed out in a bad dye job and her makeup applied with a trowel. But she had a good heart, even if she was the neighborhood busybody. There were worse things to be.

Saturday luncheon at Grandmother Eaton's yawned before Harley like a prison sentence. She was caught between a longing to be anywhere else and an urgent desire to talk to Aunt Darcy, who still hadn't returned her calls. The desire to find out what was going on won out.

She dragged herself out of bed at nine Saturday morning, leaving Morgan asleep. She was glad it was her day off, but not glad she'd agreed to play nice with her cousins. It was a long-standing conflict that had started the summer she'd moved back to Memphis. The details were fuzzy in her mind now, but it had something to do with a boy. Hormones had gone berserk that year.

"I'd like to be a fly on the wall," Morgan remarked while she was getting ready to go.

She looked at him in the bathroom mirror, a gob of hair gel in each palm slowly turning to stone. "So would I. Unfortunately, I have to show up as myself."

"That has distinct advantages." He leaned against the doorframe, his arms crossed over his chest. His slow smile made her tingle down to her toes again, an event that seemed to happen far too often lately.

Feast or famine seemed to be the pattern of her love life these days. Feast was much more enjoyable.

Famine seemed preferable to the cuisine Grandmother Eaton served, however—the kind of dishes popular in quaint little restaurants, with sprigs of greenery atop tiny mounds of shredded fish. Thank God for Taco Bell. A person could starve if they had to depend on her grandmother or Diva for decent food.

"It looks delicious, Grandmother," Harley's cousin Madelyn said primly, and gave Harley a look that obviously meant she was supposed to agree.

"Are those orchids?" Harley asked instead, inspecting the tall bouquet gracing the middle of the dining room table. It looked like a dozen orchids had been tucked into a tower, studded with silvery leaves. Silverware sparkled, crystal gave off delicately colored prisms of light, and long tapers had been lit. Curls of silk ribbon drifted across exquisite china plates. She had to hand it to Grandmother Eaton, she sure believed in setting an elegant table.

Grandmother Eaton looked very pleased. In her early seventies, she looked younger even though her hair was silver-white. She'd dressed in a linen suit for the occasion, and wore jewelry at her throat and wrists as if they were going out for a meal at Chez Philippe instead of eating in her own dining room.

"Thank you, girls. Yes, those are indeed orchids. Aren't they lovely? Janet said the tower effect would be perfect. I'm glad you like them, Harley."

Madelyn lifted her brow at Harley, then exchanged a glance with her sister Amanda that plainly conveyed her disapproval of their cousin. They reminded Harley of two blonde poodles, one starved-looking, and the other obviously well-fed.

She rolled her eyes and asked, "So where's Aunt Darcy?"

It was the perfect opening for a discussion of what had to be on all their minds—Harry Gordon's murder. She waited expectantly.

"Darcy called to say she'll be a little late," Grandmother Eaton said after a moment of awkward silence. "All that . . . trouble, you know."

Trouble. A nice term for an ugly death.

"Yes," Harley said, "I'm the one who found the *trouble*."

Grandmother Eaton regarded her solemnly. "Yes, dear, so I understand. Dreadful thing. Just dreadful. Youth is so resilient. You look remarkably calm, despite what had to be an extreme shock. Perhaps that's why you chose such an . . . *interesting* . . . ensemble to wear. Linen would have been so much cooler, but denim and cotton are acceptable under the circumstances, of course."

Censure oozed from her grandmother, but Harley chose to ignore it. She'd known when she put on a tee shirt and jeans that not dressing up would cause comment. She'd dug through her closet but just hadn't found a suitable skirt and blouse. Much as she hated it, a shopping trip to the mall loomed in her future. She'd take Tootsie with her. Then it'd be bearable. It was always fun watching sales ladies' faces when Tootsie tried on silk blouses or evening gowns. Or high heels in the shoe department.

Madelyn and Amanda wore nice skirts and blouses, of course. Suck-ups. Madelyn was tall and skinny, Amanda shorter with curves that bordered on plump. Their clothes came from Macy's, their personalities from Elvira, Queen of the Night.

"So," she said to distract from her fashion *faux pas* and direct the conversation back to the murder, "is Aunt Darcy at the police station giving her statement?"

Amanda made a muffled sound, and Grandmother Eaton nodded. "Yes, I believe she is downtown. She'll need our support when she arrives, and perhaps it's best that we not mention the unpleasantness."

Unpleasantness was another obvious synonym for grisly murder. Harley nodded agreement.

"I imagine Aunt Darcy will be stressed enough. What with having her partner murdered, then being grilled by the cops and all."

"Grilled?" Madelyn looked startled. Her eyes widened, and she blinked long lashes that reminded Harley of a Daddy-longlegs. False lashes must be in fashion again. "Why would Mama be *grilled?*"

She pronounced Mama in the French way, with the accent on the last *ma*, and Harley rolled her eyes again. That college graduation trip to Paris must have left a lasting impression after all.

"Because Harry Gordon was her partner, and besides the murderer, Aunt Darcy was the last person to see him alive," she pointed out.

Madelyn's eyes narrowed and her mouth tightened. "Really. You don't have to be nasty, Harley. Besides—we don't know at all who the last person to see Harry alive was. And neither do the police."

"True. But they will. Trust me on that. The MPD is very efficient."

Madelyn looked rattled, and her mouth went so flat it nearly disappeared. Harley lifted a brow. Maybe Cousin Maddie knew something she wasn't telling. Could it be . . . ? No, no, Aunt Darcy wasn't a murderer. Bitchy, uppity, snobbish, yes, but not murderous. Still, the police might very well have another point of view on that subject, so maybe it'd be best not to rule Darcy out completely just in case they found out she'd been investigating Harry for smuggling.

"Don't worry, Maddie," she said, "I'm quite sure you can give Aunt Darcy a great alibi since you're living at home. You saw her come in Thursday night, didn't you?"

"Why would you assume I'm always home?"

"Because you don't usually go out until later, after a hard day of getting manicures and pedicures. Unless you've actually gotten a job?"

Madelyn glared at her. Amanda, who had finagled a job as a designer in her mother's shop, put her hands on her less than thin hips and defended her older sister.

"Don't be mean, Harley. Madelyn is still coping after . . . after everything."

"You mean her divorce from that idiot? I thought she was still celebrating, not coping."

"At least I've been married before, and am not an old maid like you," Madelyn snapped.

"Old maid? Who talks like that? It's the twenty-first century, Maddie, and liberated women even have the vote these days. Of course, living in that ivory tower of yours, you probably think getting married is the only option women have. There are others, I promise."

"You mean like working for minimum wage baby-sitting tourists? Fine career choice *you* made, Harley. I'm so impressed. Why don't you just admit you aren't capable of doing anything else?"

This wasn't going at all the way she'd intended, Harley realized, and sucked in a deep breath to keep the familiar irritation from taking control of her brain and tongue. No point in reverting to fourteen again. Now she needed answers, not a squabble.

"Maybe I'm not living up to my potential," she said, and saw Madelyn's eyes narrow in suspicion, "but I'm only trying to help Aunt Darcy right now. Believe me when I tell you that the police are going to ask you a lot harder questions. And you better be prepared to tell the truth, because a lie will only make things worse."

"Worse? For whom?" Madelyn's eyes darted to her sister, and Harley once more got the feeling there was something going on they weren't telling.

"For anyone dumb enough to lie to cops," she said bluntly.

Madelyn immediately fluffed up like an irate chicken. It wasn't an attractive look for her. She had one of those long, thin patrician noses, and it quivered like a bird's beak.

"I'm getting tired of you accusing me of lying!"

"Why won't you answer a simple question? Were you with Aunt Darcy Thursday night? Can you give her an alibi for her whereabouts between six and nine?"

For a moment Harley thought her cousin would refuse to answer, then she blew out an exasperated sigh and said, "No, I wasn't with Mama Thursday night. She went to a Junior League meeting, however, so she has plenty of people who can give her an alibi."

Harley didn't mention seeing Aunt Darcy's car leave the parking lot of the shop at a time that'd be certain to incriminate her. There had to be a good reason for it. She hoped.

"Girls," Grandmother Eaton interrupted with a definite edge in her voice, "do hush. I believe Darcy has arrived at last."

A slight commotion in the entrance hall preceded Aunt Darcy's arrival, and Harley heard Janet, Grandmother Eaton's British housekeeper, ask Darcy if she'd meant to leave her car door open like that.

"No," Darcy said over her shoulder, sounding harried and looking frightful, "go out and close it if you like. Mama, I need a drink. Something strong. Quick!"

Amanda had already started toward the liquor cabinet, and Harley just watched as Darcy staggered across the entrance hall and to a dining room chair, flopping into it. Her hair stuck out at odd angles, and she had dark circles under her eyes. She wore a rumpled blouse and dark slacks, and absolutely no jewelry. Grandmother Eaton looked frozen in place, and Madelyn stared at her mother with something like shock on her face.

Harley blinked. This Aunt Darcy bore only the faintest resemblance to the impeccably garbed woman she usually saw. Her hands shook, her bare lips quivered, and until she'd downed three fingers of bourbon, neat, she didn't say another word.

Silence sounded loud in the dining room. They all waited like eager beagles, gazing at Darcy Fontaine as she held out her glass for more bourbon. Amanda obliged.

Darcy raised the glass in her hand, shaking only slightly. "Gestapo. That's what they are down there, Nazi officers! I've never been so thoroughly humiliated in my entire life. I'm calling a lawyer." Her gaze moved around the dining room and lit on Harley. Then her eyes narrowed. "Your friend Bobby is the first man I intend to sue!"

It was obvious she was expected to say something in return, so Harley asked, "Was he rude to you?"

"Rude? *Rude?*" Her voice rose shrilly on the last word. "He practically accused me of murder!"

That wasn't unexpected. Bobby was usually pretty quick on the uptake, and he no doubt asked her if someone could vouch for her whereabouts when her business partner was killed. It wasn't an unusual question, Harley thought, but of course, Aunt Darcy wouldn't acknowledge that.

"I'm sure he doesn't suspect you, Aunt Darcy," she said in the most reasonable tone she could manage, "he just has to eliminate everyone who didn't want to kill Harry."

That reassurance apparently wasn't as soothing as she'd meant it. Aunt Darcy sat up with a jerk, spilling some of her bourbon.

"Well, I never said I didn't *want* to kill Harry!"

Harley stared at her. "Great. I hope that isn't a confession."

"Really," Grandmother Eaton said rather shakily, "you shouldn't say such things."

"My thought exactly. Aunt Darcy needs to watch what she says." Harley glanced at her cousins, who were staring at their mother with something like dread and fascination. Time to find out just where she'd been that night, but not in front of them. She put a hand on Darcy's arm.

"I think we need to speak privately, Aunt Darcy."

She half-expected her to refuse, but instead her aunt nodded brusquely. "Yes."

Harley followed her into the kitchen, then out onto the sun porch. Bright squares of light gleamed on the tile floors, and the air smelled faintly of flowering plants she couldn't name. But her grandfather no doubt could. His new hobby since retirement gave him far too much free time.

Darcy turned with her back to the light, arms crossed in front of her as if she was cold. "I didn't kill him, Harley, but I'm glad he's dead."

"Well, let's not bother with small talk. Okay. What did you tell the police?"

Waving an impatient hand, Darcy turned to look out the glass windows into the wooded grounds beyond. "The truth, of course."

"Uh hunh. All of it?"

"All they need to know."

"Yeah, well I hate to be the one to tell you this, but if you lied or left out important stuff, it's not going to look too good for you."

When her aunt turned back to look at her, Harley was struck by how vulnerable she appeared. There was a panic in her eyes that Harley had never seen there before, not even during her most dramatic tantrum.

"Harley, if I told them everything it'd look so much worse than it is."

"So letting them find it out on their own is going to be better? Look, Aunt Darcy, they're not stupid. And they have a way of getting to the truth that can be very unsettling if you're not expecting it. I can talk to Bobby for you, explain that you were frightened and that's why you didn't tell him you were at the shop right after Harry was killed, but that you didn't have anything at all to do with killing him, and he can—"

"What on earth are you talking about, Harley? I wasn't at the shop Thursday night."

"Aunt Darcy, I *saw* you. Or your car, anyway. You were leaving the back way as I came in the front way."

Darcy went pale. Her eyes widened, and for a moment she didn't say anything. Then her words came out in a choked whisper. "You . . . saw my car? Oh dear God. This is—what am I going to *do*?"

Just as Darcy collapsed in a boneless heap on the tile floor, the British housekeeper Janet appeared in the doorway to announce that lunch was served. Harley looked up at her.

"Better keep hers warm. She's a bit indisposed at the moment."

The unflappable Janet nodded. "Shall I ring for the doctor?"

"That might be good."

There were times, Harley reflected as she took a stuffed pillow from the wicker chair to put under her aunt's head, that she felt as if she were living in a very bad English play. All she needed now was a fussy Belgian detective to show up and solve the case. It'd certainly be preferable to the reality of her aunt being a possible murderer.

Five

"Stress," the doctor said, one of the few in Memphis who made house calls, which explained the shiny new red Porsche sitting in Grandmother Eaton's driveway. "Mrs. Fontaine just needs bed rest and quiet for a few days."

"So why are you giving her a shot?" Harley wanted to know.

He smiled as he filled a syringe. "It's a sedative."

"Got any extra?" She batted her lashes innocently when he gave her a startled glance. "It seems there's a lot of what she's got going around."

The doctor looked like he wasn't certain if she was serious or joking, and Harley didn't offer any reassurance either way. Any man who looked like an Abercrombie & Fitch model and drove an eighty-thousand dollar car could figure it out for himself. Where did Aunt Darcy find these guys? She was like a magnet for the Smart and Shallow.

Grandmother Eaton appeared in the doorway of the sitting room where Aunt Darcy had been taken and announced that she'd made arrangements for the girls to escort their mother home, once the doctor had finished. "Unless you think it best for her to remain here?"

She didn't sound like she considered that a good thing, and the doctor agreed. "No, Mrs. Eaton, I think being in her own bed would greatly improve her frame of mind."

Harley thought not being a murder suspect would be a better improvement, but no one asked and she didn't voice her opinion. Grandmother Eaton had things well in hand, it seemed, as usual. A strong woman, usually unflappable, and though none of them would ever admit it, that trait thrived in both her daughters. Even Diva had her own brand of strength, although she called it *chi* or inner serenity or some other kind of nonsensical term that Harley thought was the same thing when you got right down to it. It just all meant coping with the unexpected.

But now she couldn't help wondering if Darcy's way of coping had included removing the source of her problem. She'd never seemed homicidal, but then, maybe the unexpected had happened and she'd seized the moment. It was possible. Unpalatable, but possible.

Harley didn't say anything while Madelyn and Amanda got their mother loaded up in her own car, just watched from the doorway as Darcy was eased into the back seat with a pillow behind her head and the sedative relaxing her facial muscles so that they sagged. She looked her age.

Right before Madelyn closed the car door, Aunt Darcy glanced up and caught Harley's gaze. Her features tightened briefly, her eyes glittered with a determined, hard light, and she gave a slight shake of her head that could mean anything. Interesting.

"I'll call my lawyer," Grandmother Eaton said when the car pulled away, and Harley turned to look at her.

"Why?"

"It never hurts to be prepared. They've questioned her twice now. Well. Since you and I are the only ones left for luncheon, shall we eat in the sitting room? I'll have Janet bring us in a tray."

Harley thought of the shredded fish. "I'm not that hungry, Grandmother."

"Neither am I, but we should eat. Perhaps fresh strawberries and cream cakes?"

Harley smiled.

After the delicious ripe strawberries and English-style cream cakes, Grandmother Eaton asked, "What do you think of all this business?"

"I'm afraid to think. It could get nasty."

Grandmother nodded. She looked elegant and beautiful in a refined, dignified sort of way, much like a queen, Harley had thought as a child. Most of the time there seemed to be few similarities between her and her two daughters, except that her white hair had once been blond and her eyes were blue. Diva, with her fey, will-o-the-wisp personality, and Darcy with her determined, often brash manner, bore no resemblance to quiet, cultured Isabel Eaton. Of course, Nana McMullen was in that gene pool, too. Grandmother's mother happened to be a tiny forceful woman with no regard for tact. Maybe it was true that family traits often skipped a generation.

Since she was thinking of her great-grandmother, Harley asked, "How is Nana doing?"

Grandmother Eaton did the polite equivalent of an eye-roll, that delicate lift of one eyebrow and slight smile that could mean almost anything. "Mother is doing just fine now that she's moved into an assisted living facility. It gives her an . . . outlet . . . for her favorite activities."

Harley figured that meant Nana was still drinking warm beer she hid in the laundry room. Or flirting with other octogenarians who'd suffered through the Great Depression, World War II, and rockabilly music.

"I'll have to go visit her sometime," Harley said. "Once all this stuff with Aunt Darcy is resolved."

After taking a sip of tea from a fragile china cup so thin it looked like it might break at any moment, Grandmother said, "Darcy should be prepared for all contingencies. I do wish she'd listened to me about that man. He seemed a very unpleasant sort. A ruffian. Not at all . . . proper. I offered to advance her the money to expand if she needed it, but she's so determined to do things her way. Just like Deirdre." She smiled faintly. "That's not a criticism of either of them. Over the years I've come to understand that just because they're my children, I don't always know what's best for them. People have to go their own way when they're adults. Make their own mistakes, suffer their own consequences. It's personal growth. I've done my share of it. But it's much more difficult to watch your children make mistakes that might ruin their entire lives."

Harley shifted uncomfortably. Was she talking about Diva marrying Yogi? Because that subject was off the table. Yogi might have his flaws, but he was a good person and a wonderful father.

Fortunately, Grandmother didn't go there. She leaned forward and patted Harley on the knee. "You're a very bright young lady, and I know you'll do well when you find your direction."

"I hope so. Where's Granddad?"

"Playing golf, of course. Any excuse will do, but a luncheon with 'gabbing females' as he puts it, gave him the perfect out. I'll let him enjoy his day, and won't burden him with this new development until he gets home. He worries so, you know."

Janet came to the sitting room door and said, "It's Miss Madelyn on the phone, Mrs. Eaton, asking for you. Her mother is having some kind of difficulty."

Probably out of gin, Harley thought unkindly, then felt slightly ashamed. After all, "she was family." That phrase was used to excuse everything from insanity to criminal activity. It was an acceptance of the quirks of one's blood kin, the final apology and explanation to strangers.

"Talk to Aunt Darcy, Grandmother," she said. "I need to leave anyway."

After saying good-bye to Grandmother, she left by the back door. It felt more comfortable than the austere front entrance. The Eaton house was one of those older homes in East Memphis, a stately Colonial with a triple garage and wide driveway on a wooded lot that was at least a half acre. It was a quiet neighborhood where many families had reared children and sent them off to college, and where grown grandchildren now visited. It didn't seem conducive to the kind of lifestyle Diva preferred, even now. Aunt Darcy may have thrived here, but Diva would have felt stifled.

There was certainly nothing stifled about her mother now. The years had freed her to be herself. Just as Harley was free to indulge in extracurricular activities.

Luckily for her, Morgan was still at her apartment. Just what she needed, a few uncomplicated hours with a man guaranteed to give her cold shivers and hot flashes.

Bright and early Sunday morning, Harley showed up at the Fontaine household with a box of Krispy Kremes and a hopeful smile. Fortunately, Amanda met her at the door. She was much easier to cajole than Madelyn.

"Hi, Mandy," Harley said, and breezed past her into the entrance hall. Last time she'd been here, the house had an Oriental theme. This time, it was English Victorian. Lace. Cabbage roses. Prints and chintz. Good lord. Aunt Darcy took furniture from the shop, left the price tags on, and in a pinch, sold it if a customer wanted it badly enough. Apparently, current trends leaned toward frou-frou. The room was crowded with ornate accessories, tablecloths, fringe, and lots of Tiffany lamps. It was Diva with reasonably good taste. A nightmare, in Harley's opinion.

Amanda said, "What are you doing here? And don't call me Mandy. Harley *Jean*."

"Point taken. I brought doughnuts for Aunt Darcy. They're Krispy Kremes. Two dozen."

Amanda looked intrigued. And hungry. Harley pried up the box lid so the sugary scent of warm doughnuts wafted toward her. She knew she had her when her cousin's eyes glazed like one of the crullers and a tiny bead of drool escaped one corner of her mouth.

"I'll take them to her," she offered, and Harley smiled. What an innocent.

"That's all right. I don't mind. I'll take her up a few and leave the rest down here for you and whoever else would like one."

Two minutes later, Harley was on her way up the wide staircase to the second floor. If she played it right, she'd have some time alone to find out just what the devil was going on. She didn't buy for one minute that fainting act her aunt had done in Grandmother Eaton's sunroom. It had to have been a cop-out, a distraction. Now it was time for some truth.

"Hello, Aunt Darcy," she said when she edged into the darkened room that smelled like clove cigarettes, and heard her aunt mutter something that sounded like "shit!" under her breath.

"Who let you in?" Darcy demanded irritably. "I said I didn't want to be disturbed."

"Amanda. I brought you some doughnuts. Krispy Kremes. I know you like them."

That wasn't quite true. The doughnuts had really been a distraction for Amanda and/or Madelyn, as well as an excuse to get up the stairs. She had no idea if Aunt Darcy liked them.

"I never eat pastries this early."

"Just as well." Harley set the plate on a table crowded with pictures of strangers in frames with curlicues and bows. One price tag read $125 for a small framed sepia tone reproduction of a man in a bowler hat. It couldn't be a relative. He looked too respectable. "I didn't come here to feed you anyway. What were you doing at the store when Harry Gordon was murdered? Did you have anything to do with it? And if not, did you see anyone else there?"

Darcy drew the coverlet up over her head. "Go away," came the muffled reply, but Harley ignored that and reached over to jerk down the covers.

"Look, you can lie to the cops if you want, you might even get away with it for a little while, but they don't give a damn about you or me or even Harry. They just want the truth, and you can believe me when I say they generally get what they want. If you're hiding anything, they'll know it. Now I can help you if you'll let me. You just have to be honest."

Bleary eyes glared at her. Somehow Darcy's hair was neat even though she was lying down and had pulled the covers over her head. Hardly a hair out of place. Amazing, and probably due to industrial strength hair spray. Proper hygiene was the first sign of recovery, so she must be on her way to putting the ordeal with the cops behind her.

"Harley, you're fired. There's no need for you to concern yourself with me or Harry any longer. He's dead and my problem is over. I'll still write you a check, just *go away!*"

Unperturbed, Harley shook her head. "Hunh uh. Your problems are just beginning. And I have no intentions of going away, though I will take your check. One hundred ought to cover it for my time and expenses." She paused for a brief moment of regret, the fading vision of five thousand dollars creating an actual cramp, then she said, "It seems to have escaped your notice, but you're a suspect in a murder case. Think about it. You're probably the last one besides the murderer to see Harry alive. You were at the shop when you said you weren't. You have no alibi, and—"

Darcy shook her head. "Wrong. I do have an alibi. I was at the Junior League meeting, just like I said."

"Aunt Darcy, the police check these things. They'll talk to the Junior League. You have to know that."

"Let them." Darcy's chin stuck out in mulish stubbornness. "I was there. You must have seen a car that looked like mine. It wasn't my car, and it wasn't me. I'm not the one who's got it wrong, *you* are."

Harley frowned. Maybe she was wrong. But it had certainly looked like Aunt Darcy's car, right down to the Obama-Biden stickers plastered across the back bumper.

"You've still got that white Lexus, right?"

Darcy hesitated, then nodded. "Yes. There are probably thousands in the city of Memphis. I can't have the only one."

"I'm sure not. And you're probably not the only one with a white Lexus who voted for Obama, either, but it's too big a coincidence that a car that looks just like yours, with four bumper stickers just like yours, was in the parking lot of your shop at around the same time Harry Gordon was murdered. Sure you didn't just drop by, maybe saw Harry already dead, then ran out of there?"

"Positive."

"So you're going to stick with that story."

"I'm sticking with the truth. Now go away, Harley. You're giving me a headache."

Harley thought it might be the gin in the small water glass beside her bed that was giving Aunt Darcy a headache, but she didn't say it. "Sure. On my way out now. Let me know when you come to your senses. I figure that'll be right around the time you're arrested for murder."

Darcy went even paler, though Harley hadn't thought that possible. Still, she only pressed her lips more tightly together and reached for the water glass with a shaking hand.

"All right, if you must know, I wasn't at the Junior League meeting the *entire* time. I was . . . with a man."

"A man, as in not Uncle Paul?"

Darcy nodded, looking so miserable that Harley believed her. Well. That was interesting.

"You should tell that to the police, Aunt Darcy. They'll keep it quiet if they can, and no one has to know, but it will help clear you if—"

"No!" Aunt Darcy sounded quite fierce about it, and color finally lit her face. "And don't you dare say a word to anyone, do you hear me? I'll deny it if you do."

"Fine, it's your funeral. I hope that's not a prediction."

When she got to the door, Harley turned to say, "By the way, that powder you had me get tested? It was French bath powder, just like Harry said. Are you sure he was smuggling?"

"Yes. I know he was, even if I can't prove it. Believe me or not, I don't care."

This was really strange. Darcy usually had a strong survival instinct. Why hadn't it kicked in?

She was still puzzling over Darcy's lack of survival instinct when she stopped by Memphis Tour Tyme to retrieve her paycheck from Mr. Grinder, the security guard. Office employees didn't come in on the weekends or holidays; only the drivers worked, and days off rotated. Most tours were already scheduled, and any emergencies were handled by either Mr. Penney or Tootsie. Since Tootsie's car was parked in front of the building, it was likely that one of the vehicles—or drivers—had broken down. She parked her Toyota next to Tootsie's car. He had a four year old Acura that still looked new. He took excellent care of his cars. Mr. Grinder had an old Chrysler that had seen better days.

Last week she and Cami had scared Mr. Grinder half to death when they'd snuck in to borrow a stun gun for their investigation of jewelry thieves. It'd given him the most excitement he'd had since World War II. Near ninety if he was a day, and looking remarkably similar to a dried apple doll, his hands still trembled and he had a nervous tic under his left eye. She hoped the gun he wore on his arthritic hip wasn't loaded. It looked way too big for him to manage.

He sat behind a small desk that held a console, a stack of magazines, and a thirteen-inch color TV. On the small screen, George Stephanopoulos smiled at one of his usual political guests, and the sound was turned off. The best way to listen to any politician.

"How are you, Mr. Grinder?" she asked loudly since he sometimes forgot to turn up his hearing aid, and he nodded.

"Yes, that's right. It's a nice day." He unlocked the top desk drawer and held out her paycheck with fingers cruelly twisted by arthritis. "I'm sure you've come by for this."

"Thank you. You're always prepared."

"Yes, my hair's thinning a bit on top." He took off his cap and smoothed a hand over the white wisps that clung tenaciously to his pink scalp. "Still got a way with the ladies, though."

"You're a rascal, Mr. Grinder," she said, and apparently he heard that and seemed pleased by it.

"I sure am." He clacked his false teeth together in what may have been an invitation, so Harley took the elevator up to the second floor to find out what Tootsie was doing.

Tootsie looked up at her with a lifted brow. "What's up, baby?"

"Name it. You still have on makeup. You look like a raccoon. Good show last night?"

"Great show. I vamped it up, did my Cher routine and sang *Gypsies, Tramps and Thieves*. I rocked. You should have come."

Harley sat down in Tootsie's office chair to watch him connect wires to the older model computer on the desk. "I was a little busy. Life's been crazy since Thursday night."

"Honey, life's always crazy for you."

"Now, I don't know why you'd say something like that."

"A murder in a design shop, guy hanging off moose antlers, what d'ya think?"

"Elk horns. He was hanging off elk horns." Harley stared glumly at Tootsie. "What are you doing here? I thought you were usually off on Sundays."

"Hooking up the DSL. The ogre thought it was time we stepped into the twenty-first century. Not that this dinosaur of a computer will help that much. Not enough RAM or gigs."

"Uh huh." Her interest in computers rated pretty low. RAM and gigs meant goats and pitchforks as far as she was concerned. She barely listened as Tootsie rambled on about memory and software for a few minutes. Then he looked up at her.

"So what are you doing here? I already gave your runs to Charlsie. She's doing Graceland and Tupelo today. A fan club from England."

"I came by to get my paycheck. I was a little distracted Friday and forgot to pick it up." She leaned forward in the chair. "Darcy's mixed up in the murder. She was there."

Tootsie plugged in a wire then ran a hand through his hair to shove the long strands out of his face. "Think she did it?"

"I don't know. She says she has an alibi, but I saw her car leaving the parking lot right before I found Harry. She told the police that she was at her Junior League meeting." Darcy's affair would remain a secret for now. She had to have some standards.

"Maybe she was."

"Maybe, but how many cars like hers in Memphis still have a Kerry-Edwards bumper sticker? Most people don't continue to advertise that they voted for the losers."

"So, maybe someone else was driving her car."

Harley looked at him. "Damn. Of course. That makes sense—you're a genius, Tootsie."

"Only pointing out the obvious, baby." He smiled a little when she made a rude comment. "You're too close to it. Darcy's your family. My advice, let the police handle it."

"Now you sound like Bobby and Mike."

"Both reasonable men."

"Both cops."

"Not necessarily a bad thing."

"You only say that because the imaginary Steve is a cop."

Tootsie grinned. "That doesn't make it less true, baby."

"You know, you're at your most annoying when you're smug."

"Not at all. I can be far more annoying. Now move out of my way so I can see if I've got this hooked up right."

Harley rolled close to the file cabinets while Tootsie played with the computer. It made sense. If Aunt Darcy hadn't been in her car, someone else had to have been. But who? It'd have to be someone she trusted, because she'd never loan anyone else her car. That left only a very few possibilities. Starting with Mandy and Maddie, the gruesome twosome. Her bet was on Madelyn. But then . . . she hadn't even considered that her uncle might figure into this. Maybe because he seemed like a timid mouse most of the time, one of those mild-mannered men who seemed to fade into the background except when he was expected to ante up some money. Darcy almost couldn't be blamed for having an affair, but Harley had always thought Paul a really nice guy. Not that she had any qualms about investigating him. And that made her wonder—could Harry have been Darcy's lover? Was that what she was hiding?

"Got it," Tootsie said, and she looked over as the monitor popped up a home page.

"So do I," Harley said, and stood up. "Keep my schedule flexible this week, okay? Just in case."

"Sure. Crimestoppers must pay more than advertised. Unless you've come into money and don't need our paltry paychecks."

Harley made a face. "Unkind of you to remind me, but if I clear Aunt Darcy, I'll take her entire check so fast she won't have time to reconsider."

"So what happened to the five thousand for investigating Harry?"

"Harry being dead and all, I can't take the entire thing for just a few days' work. I charged her a hundred instead. But if I can keep her out of jail, it's worth at least five thousand, don't you think?"

"That's one of the reasons I love you, Harley, you have scruples."

She shuddered. "Don't say that. You'll ruin my reputation as a bitch. Life is much easier when people hesitate to cross you."

"Don't I know it."

"If I didn't know better, Tootsie, I'd swear we were separated at birth."

He made a wry face. "Except that I have much better taste than you."

"I happen to like shabby chic, thank you very much. You're into elegance. I'm into the right price. In fact, I think I'll hit my favorite secondhand clothing store after I talk to a few lucky people I like to refer to as suspects."

"You frighten me, baby."

"That's what Morgan says."

"He should know."

"Yeah, but he keeps hanging around anyway. He's just a sucker for punishment, I guess."

It always gave her a warm feeling to think about Mike Morgan. She could blame it on the summer heat, but denying it didn't change it. The man tickled her libido in the best possible way. It probably wouldn't last. She knew she wasn't that good at relationships. There was no reasonable explanation for that. Except maybe it had something to do with her early life, when they'd moved around a lot and she'd learned that most people were only temporary. Either they had moved on, or Harley had moved on with her parents, traveling around California from commune to commune, or someplace on a whim, the freedom of the seventies giving way at last to their more stable life in Memphis. While she'd spent nearly half her life here, the mark of the first fourteen years had left more of an impression, it seemed. Maybe there really was something to that theory that the first five years of a child's life molded the rest of it. She hoped not. Living out of a van and eating dried seaweed really wasn't that appealing.

Heat struck like a closed fist when she stepped out onto the parking lot where her trusty Toyota waited in the shade of a tree. June was one of those months that could be hot as a furnace or quite pleasant. Sometimes it turned out to be both. In the same hour.

Crossing Poplar Avenue on a Sunday was a lot easier than during the week, and she made it into the Taco Bell parking lot across from the office building with only a few annoyed honks from other drivers. Memphis drivers were notoriously impatient, ignoring Southern hospitality in favor of a two-second head start at stop lights. Southern hospitality obviously did not extend to the perils of Poplar Avenue.

It didn't take long to get her food, and she pulled back onto Poplar and headed toward her apartment. She needed a little quiet time to think. And plot her next move.

Tootsie's suggestion made sense. Aunt Darcy had to have loaned her car to someone. It made a lot more sense than another identical Lexus with an identical row of bumper stickers just happening to be in the parking lot. So now there were more possibilities, the list of suspects a bit longer than before. That was good for Darcy, bad for the police.

When she pulled into the driveway shared with the other tenants, someone darted in front of her and she had to brake hard. Sarah Simon. It was a rare sighting. Normally, Sarah stayed in her apartment and peeked out her windows through closed drapes. Now, she scuttled like a crab to get out of the way before getting hit.

"Hey, you okay?" she called, but Sarah ran all the way back into the building without looking over her shoulder. She had short auburn hair, and loose clothes that looked like pajamas flapped around her legs. Sarah lived in the apartment below hers, and as far as Harley knew, only came out on Groundhog Day. Strange girl.

The red brick house held four apartments and five tenants: the Spragues on the second floor next to Harley, Sarah Simon right below her, and Mr. Diaz below the Spragues. She didn't know his first name, but he had a really nice CRX that he parked in the garage. It was a mystery why there were only three parking slots in the garage for four apartments, but as the last tenant to lease, Harley parked under the oak tree. At least it was shade on hot summer days.

Even with the ceiling fans and floor fans on, it was warm in her apartment. Harley opened the French doors and windows to get a cross breeze, took off her tee shirt and put on some shorts with her sports bra. Then she went out to sit on her balcony to eat. Bean burritos and nachos with cheese spanned three of the major food groups: vegetables, grains, dairy. Not bad. One day all this junk food was going to catch up to her, but right now, she ate pretty much what she liked. Diva's dire warnings of obesity and rickets, among various other sinister diseases, couldn't fight the lure of Taco Bell.

Just across the green expanse of lawn in front of her apartment building, the Overton Park Zoo had a Sunday crowd. Cars rolled slowly through the park, bikers and walkers and picnickers enjoyed the day, and the occasional shriek of a child drowned out the peacocks. But not the diesel engines of an occasional city bus or the irritated blast of a car horn. Ah, summertime was nigh.

She propped one foot on the wide white-painted concrete rail of the balcony and leaned back in her chair to finish off her second burrito. Her neighbors were home; she heard their New Age music seeping through the walls. The Spragues. They hated her now. All because of that unfortunate incident in the laundry room when one of the jewelry thieves Harley had been pursuing had mistaken Tammy Sprague for Harley and bopped her on the head. Tammy was all right, but apparently carried a grudge. Ah well. No big loss. They hadn't been that close anyway.

It occurred to her as she started on the nachos that while it was quite possible she'd mistaken Darcy as the driver of the Lexus, she'd been sure she'd caught a glimpse of blonde hair before it'd sped away. That meant it could be Madelyn or Amanda. It all happened so quickly, and there'd been no reason to be suspicious of anything at the time. If Darcy, who by her own admission wasn't the most compassionate person in the world, was covering for someone, it had to be family.

Harley thought about that some more. She really needed to talk to her cousins, and she needed to do so separately. That wasn't always easy since Madelyn had come back home to live. She and Amanda could close ranks quickly, even though they didn't always get along well when left on their own. Madelyn could be cruel, poking fun at her sister for being what she called "fat" when she was really only healthy. Harley had learned a long time ago not to defend Amanda, after a memorable afternoon at a family reunion when they were all teenagers. It had ended in a hair-pulling, nail-scratching brawl that Harley had won, even if barely. All the adults took sides, except Diva. And Nana McMullen. Diva had been disappointed in the unnecessary violence, and Nana McMullen had enjoyed the entertainment. Scary old lady.

As she was pondering her misspent youth and the mystery of the cheese to tostada ratio always being off by a few chips, her phone rang. She went inside to answer it, bare feet padding over the wood floor that still bore faint traces of flour residue despite being scrubbed several times.

It was Cami, her partner in crime.

"You won't believe this," Cami said before Harley had a chance to say Hello, "but I'm on the horns of a moral dilemma."

Harley rolled her eyes and licked melted cheese off her fingers. "Uh hunh. Funny you should mention being on horns."

"You've got to stop finding bodies, Harley. It isn't healthy. Now listen—this may shock you, but Bobby has been calling me."

"It'd be a shock if he didn't. I saw the way he looked at you. So what's the dilemma?"

"He has a girlfriend."

"Angel of the topless dancer variety. Why is that a dilemma? Bobby never dates one person for very long before he moves on. That's a warning, in case you missed it."

"No, he's more than dating her, Harley. She *lives* with him."

"Still?"

"Affirmative." Cami blew out what sounded like a sigh, and added, "What should I do?"

Harley grimaced. "I really don't like getting mixed up in other people's love lives. I'm not good at it. Hell, I'm not good at my own, so I'm the wrong person to come to for advice."

"You're doing all right. Bruno—I mean Mike—seems like a great guy."

"He is. So far. But it's only been a week. It could go south at any time now. My record on long-term relationships is six months, but that was with George."

"George? I don't remember you dating a guy named George."

"I didn't date him. He was my goldfish, remember?"

"Oh yeah. The koi you liberated in the Audubon Park koi pond."

"I think he still remembers me, though, unlike most of the other men in my life."

"Men don't forget you, Harley. They may cross the street when they see you coming, but they don't forget you. Now, back to my problem. What should I do about Bobby?"

"Run the other way. He has commitment issues. Unless you just want a good time in bed, he's probably not the guy. Besides, he's allergic to pet hair and you have a zoo at your house."

"I adopted two of the cats out this week. I think it's going to work out great for them."

"Uh hunh." Harley wasn't that big on cats. They'd always seemed like such sneaky, evil creatures, skulking about to leap out from dark corners to massacre unwary birds. And bare toes. That reminded her of the one cat she had liked, one of Cami's rescues, a contrary beast that had seemed less repulsive than most. She'd never met a blue-eyed cat before, and he'd reminded her in a way of Morgan. Must be the arrogance.

Cami was saying, "I have this stuff I spray that eliminates the animal dander so people with allergies can visit. It works really well. Bobby hardly sneezed at all last time he was here, and his eyes didn't swell up and turn red, and his nose didn't run . . . "

"Last time? How many times has he come over?"

There was a brief silence, then Cami said faintly, "Four."

"Four times? In a week? Cami, you've been holding out on me."

"We haven't really talked."

"That's true. I've been busy. And it sounds like you have, too."

"Not like you think. I mean, we haven't slept together or anything. And he doesn't stay long, usually. He just comes over and we sit out on my deck and have a beer or wine, talk about things."

"Things? What kind of things?"

"Sometimes he talks about cases he's worked on, but mostly we talk about personal stuff. You know. Things we did when we were kids, old girlfriends—my ex—what we want in life. Stuff like that."

It sounded serious. Harley got alarmed. The only thing she'd ever known Bobby Baroni to take seriously was his job. Cami might get hurt, and she didn't need another disappointment.

"Hey," she said, "I'm about to go check out a few family alibis. Wanna go with me?"

Cami sounded surprised. "Are you involved in this case, Harley? Bobby said—"

"Keep in mind that Bobby thinks like a cop. It's a flaw or a virtue, depending on which side you're on. So. Go with me. I just want to be sure my cousins are telling the truth about where they were when Harry Gordon was killed."

"The gruesome twosome?"

"Those are the ones."

"Are they still obnoxious?"

"They don't spit anymore as far as I know, but other than that I can't see that they've changed that much."

"I have to be back at work at eight tonight. I'm on split shifts. Can I make it home in time to get ready?"

"Sure. This shouldn't take too long."

Harley should have known better.

Six

Cami wore a cute halter top and pair of shorts, and she'd dyed her hair blonde again. She drove her little green Saturn and had the sunroof open, so she had on a baseball cap and sunglasses.

"You look like a duck," Harley said by way of greeting. "Now I feel overdressed in my cutoffs and tee shirt. Do you remember where they live?"

"Thanks for the compliment. Out off Massey Road, right?"

"I'll guide, you drive. Got another hat?" She smiled when Cami pointed to the back seat.

When they arrived, Amanda was in the kitchen. The empty box of Krispy Kremes still sat on the counter near the island sink, and her cousin sported a thin layer of glaze around her mouth. She looked guilty of something, but Harley wasn't sure if it was gluttony or lying.

"Hey, Mandy. What's up?"

"Why are you back so soon? Mama's asleep, and—"

"Not to worry. I just thought of a few things I'd like to ask you, that's all. You remember Cami, don't you, from my old neighborhood?"

Looking defensive, Amanda crossed her arms over her ample chest and nodded. "Yes, of course I do. How are you, Cami?"

The niceties over, Harley jumped right in. "So where were you Thursday night? Say, between the hours of six and nine?"

For a minute, she thought Amanda was going to keel over right there on the kitchen floor. She sucked in air, her eyes got big, and she went so pale she blended right into the white pickled color of the cabinets.

"Why . . . do you want to know?"

"Use your imagination. Look, I'm just trying to help out Aunt Darcy. The police intend to solve the case, and they have a tendency to ask unpleasant questions. If they haven't already asked you this, they will. Trust me. They just move at their own speed for their own reasons. If I can, I'm going to make sure all of you are above suspicion. Now. Where were you?"

"Here." Amanda's chin came up, and her round, pretty face took on the expression of a petulant mule. "Just like I told the police. Right here. All night."

"Great. So you have proof of that, right? Someone who saw you and can verify that?"

Amanda blinked. Her lower lip quivered slightly, and a flake of glaze dropped to the front of her blouse. "No. As a matter of fact, I don't."

"Aunt Darcy saw you? Madelyn, maybe?"

"I . . . I was here alone at that time."

Ah, so the lovely and bitchy Madelyn had lied. Not surprising. It had been her best subject in school.

"Really, Mandy? All alone, huh. Maybe you made some phone calls, talked to someone who can say you were here?"

"No. I watched TV. One of my favorite shows. And don't call me Mandy."

"Mandy suits you. It's cute. Friendly, in a puppy dog kind of way. If I were you, I'd go with it. Well, while I'm sure you aren't involved in any way, you better be prepared for some in-depth police questions when they get back around to you. I assume you already gave a statement of some kind to them?"

Amanda nodded. "That night. When they came to talk to Mama."

"And she was gone when the police came."

"Oh no, she was back home by then. Madelyn had Mama's car, so she picked her up at the meeting and brought her back. They were both here the rest of the night."

"Ah. That's good. Thank you, Mandy. You've been a great help."

And now I know who was in Aunt Darcy's car at the shop . . .

They found Madelyn playing tennis on the courts behind the house. Paul Fontaine had built them a few years before when Darcy flirted with getting physically fit. Apparently, she now had activities of a different physical nature, so a lawn service kept weeds from sprouting in cracks in the asphalt, and that was usually the most action on the courts.

"What a surprise, Maddie, to find you out here playing tennis in the heat," Harley said, and smiled when her cousin shot her a sweaty grimace. "You don't usually do anything that gets you into a lather unless it involves wine, a man, and Mr. Bubble."

Madelyn's partner, a tanned, tall, athletic type who looked as if he regularly made the society pages, caught the tennis ball and bounced it off the court a few times. He seemed to be a bit uncomfortable. As he should be. He had at least twenty years on Madelyn, maybe more.

Wiping her face with an embroidered terry towel, Madelyn stalked toward Harley where she stood in the shade of a flowering crepe myrtle. Her fair skin was flushed and damp, and her crisp tennis skirt hadn't lost its snap in the heat. Neither had her tongue.

"What the devil do you want?"

"Do I need a reason to visit my cousin?"

"You're not here to visit. You want something. Get to the point, Harley."

"What a suspicious nature you have, but you're right this time. I do want something. Like the truth. Where were you Thursday night between six and nine?"

"At home, just like I told the police."

"Wrong answer. You were in Aunt Darcy's car. Why? Where's your car?"

Madelyn's eyes narrowed. "How do you know that? And what difference does it make to you where I was and what I was driving?"

"Let's just say, inquiring minds want to know. Besides, the police might be interested to learn that you lied to them."

"You wretched little sneak! You wouldn't!"

Harley smiled. Madelyn hissed a few nasty words that singed some of the leaves on the crepe myrtle, then she glanced toward the Memphis version of actor George Hamilton before she turned back to say through clenched teeth, "We'll talk about this in private. Give me a few minutes."

"To think of a reasonable lie?"

"To get rid of Trey so we can conduct *family* business in private!" Her glance at Cami left no doubt that she did not include her in the family, then she pivoted on an expensively shod foot of spotless white leather and stalked toward the bemused Trey.

Harley looked at Cami.

Cami shrugged. "Guess I'll go talk to Mandy for a while."

"Distract her with food and she might say more than she wants."

"I'm watching my carbs. But maybe she'll say something interesting."

"You're on a diet? Why?"

Waving a hand dismissively, Cami muttered something about

fitting back into her size four jeans as she walked off. Harley watched her for a moment. There might be more between Cami and Bobby than she'd thought. That could be interesting. Or disastrous. With Bobby, it was a toss-up. To the despair of his stereotypical Italian mother, Bobby had commitment issues. He'd never married, nor expressed the least interest in having a long-term relationship. Instead, he had the habit of choosing totally unsuitable women so that friends and family were relieved when the relationship finally ended. The only exception had been Harley, but that'd been when they were still teenagers and it'd never been serious, just an experiment both had decided to end quickly. It had turned into a friendship they both maintained without much effort. Most of the time, it worked well. On occasion, Bobby irritated her into avoiding him, and vice versa.

But Cami was different. She was vulnerable. Her ex-husband Jace had done a number on her and destroyed any self-esteem Cami had left. For a while, Harley had thought she wouldn't recover from the divorce. The menagerie that Cami kept, as a volunteer animal rescue worker in the spare time she had from her job at the telephone company, had temporarily convinced Harley that her best friend had lost her mind. Then she'd decided it was just Cami's way of coping with being alone. Surrounded by needy dogs and cats was more than enough companionship for anyone. She hoped Cami didn't get too emotionally involved with Bobby. He was much better as a friend than a boyfriend.

"Lord, Harley, you look like you've been trawling racks at the Salvation Army. But then, you usually do. Don't you own decent clothing?"

Madelyn, of course. Harley turned around. "How nice of you to notice. That won't work, though. I still want to know where you were Thursday night and why you were in your mother's car instead of your own."

"You've always been too damn nosy. Too bad you and your hippie parents didn't stay in California with Charles Manson."

"Well, I did learn a lot from dear old Chuck, so don't push it." Sometimes Madelyn could be a real bitch, but not even she could really believe Diva or Yogi would ever have even known Manson. If she was working this hard to distract Harley, she really did have something to hide.

"I liked it better when we saw each other once a year," Madelyn said, and Harley nodded.

"So did I. Now. Answer my questions and I'll go away. It's very simple."

"If you must know, I borrowed Mama's car because one of my tires needed air and I had an errand to run."

"That errand would be . . . ?"

"I visited a sick friend in the hospital."

"Right. Every cheating husband's favorite excuse. What friend in what hospital?"

Madelyn's lips tightened and the end of her nose actually twitched. "Margaret Meade at Baptist East."

"You do know I'll check that out, don't you? So will the police if you tried this crap on them."

For a moment something flickered in Madelyn's eyes and Harley could have sworn it was fear. Then she shook her head and looked toward the house. Heat shimmered up from the tennis courts, and Madelyn gripped her tennis racket with white knuckles.

"All right. Fine. I didn't visit anyone in the hospital. I . . . I went to see someone. A man."

"A married man, by chance?"

Madelyn looked back at her, then nodded. "Yes. He's married. And I have no intention of telling you his name."

"Fine. Save that for the cops. They always find out the truth."

To her surprise, Madelyn collapsed on the grass beneath the crepe myrtle and put her face into her palms. "What am I going to do?"

Not entirely unsympathetic, Harley said, "Tell the truth. It can't be worse than the lies you invent."

"Oh yes it can," Madelyn said, her voice muffled by her fingers and the leather half-gloves she wore to protect her palms. "You just don't know."

Exasperated, Harley said, "Dammit, tell me!"

Madelyn looked up at her. "I was with Harry Gordon right after the shop closed Thursday night."

Oh boy.

Harley plopped down on the grass in front of Madelyn. "Yeah, you're right. It's worse."

"What am I going to do?" she asked in a kind of a wail that frightened away some birds.

"That depends. Did you kill him?"

"No!"

"Then you can tell the truth when the cops ask you. If you lie—

and they have a way of finding out that kind of thing—they'll wonder what else you're lying about. Did you meet Harry at the shop?"

"Yes. We'd had an argument and I went there to end it with him. We quarreled, because he threatened to tell Mama—I don't want Mama to know, Harley. Promise you won't tell her."

"Okay, I won't, but you should. It's going to come out, you have to know that. Let her hear it from you first. And why don't you want her to know? I thought Harry was single. Did you just lie about seeing a married man?"

"Yes. I lied about that. Mama decided she didn't trust Harry. You know how she can get, Harley. She gets these ideas and you just can't convince her she's wrong. She thought Harry was stealing from her, or some such nonsense. Besides, she always said Harry was bourgeois, and she'd never have liked me seeing him."

"So you and Harry had, uh, a thing going on, right?"

Madelyn looked irritated. "Do I have to draw you a picture?"

"No, that's all right. I'm not that into porno. Was it serious between you?"

"I don't know if you'd say *serious*, but we did enjoy one another's company exclusively."

Harley thought about Cheríe Saucier and her hysterical fit when she'd learned about Harry. "Did Harry and Cheríe have anything going?"

"Who?"

"Cheríe Saucier. You know. She worked with him."

"Oh. *Her*. No, of course not. Harry would never be interested in her, though she didn't know that."

"Did Harry know that?"

"Know what?"

"That he wasn't interested in Cheríe. She sure seems to believe differently."

"I'm sure she does. She's an opportunist, a nasty little thing."

"Did she know about you and Harry?"

Madelyn's eyes widened. She put a hand up to her throat, fingers pressing against her windpipe as she drew in a sharp breath. "Do you think—could she have killed Harry because of . . . of me?"

"She seems to think Aunt Darcy killed him. Or so she told the police."

"That vicious little bitch! Mama could no more have killed Harry than I could."

And that, Harley thought, was precisely the problem. Both Darcy and Madelyn seemed quite capable of removing any obstacle in their way. But murder? Fortunately, it seemed unlikely either of them could have hung Harry off an elk horn even if they'd wanted to. That'd take a certain amount of upper body strength, and Maddie was limited to tennis rackets, and Darcy to gin bottles. No, neither of them could have killed him. Surely, the police would recognize that.

Harley got to her feet and brushed pine mulch from her bare legs. Her cutoff jeans were worn and comfortable, her tee shirt cool if not fashionable. She held out a hand to help her cousin, but Madelyn ignored it.

"I trust this will remain confidential, Harley," she said in that haughty way she had, and Harley just shook her head.

"Not a chance. Even if you don't have a decent sense of self-preservation, I feel a family obligation to keep you out of jail. Besides, it's embarrassing and inconvenient to visit the Big House on holidays. So come clean with the cops or I'll do it for you."

"You sneaky little toad! You promised!"

"No, I promised not to tell Aunt Darcy you've been banging the help. I said nothing about keeping quiet to the cops."

She left Madelyn still sitting under the crepe myrtle and went back up to the house, where Cami and Amanda were sharing a bag of fried pork rinds. When she lifted a brow, Cami grinned.

"No carbs."

"Gross. Say good-bye, Mandy. Cami, you got your cell phone with you?"

Cami produced it from her purse and followed Harley out of the house to the Saturn. "I thought you got a new cell phone."

"I've bought several new cell phones recently. I'm going to have to start figuring them into my monthly budget if they don't stop breaking."

With a nervous glance at her cell phone, Cami started the car while Harley punched in a few numbers. Tootsie answered on the third ring.

"Hi, gorgeous," Harley said cheerfully, and heard him laugh.

"Okay baby, you must want something. What is it?"

"A little more of your magic. You know, the way you have of coming up with all kinds of info when no one else can."

"Spoken like a true brownnoser. Do I want to hear what you're going to say next?"

"This won't hurt at all. I just need to know all you can find out about Cheríe Saucier. Yeah, I know. I'll spell it for you."

Tootsie said he'd get back to her with the info in a little while, and Harley hung up and stuck the cell phone back in Cami's purse.

"Where to now?" Cami asked, squinting against the bright sunlight coming through the windshield. "Somewhere respectable, I hope."

"Sure. We have a little time to kill, I guess. Let's check out the shop. The cops ought to be done by now, and maybe we can find something they overlooked."

Cami gave her a quick glance. "You sure about that? How do we get in?"

Harley smiled. "I still have my key. Aunt Darcy never asked for it back."

Yellow tape swagged around the back where Harry had been found. Cami parked under a line of hedges where they weren't easily seen from the road.

"Why is it we always seem to be breaking and entering these days?" she muttered as they made their way around to the front of the shop, and Harley grinned.

"I have a key. It's only breaking and entering when we break before entering. I don't think there's any law against unlocking and entering."

"Good thing. I've got a bad feeling about this."

"You never have bad feelings around the right thing." Harley unlocked the door and pushed it open. "You need to think about what you and Bobby are doing."

"I thought you liked Bobby."

"I do. He's the brother I never had."

"You have a brother," Cami pointed out.

"Yeah, but Eric . . . well, Eric is just Eric. Bobby, I can talk to about stuff. If it isn't about art or music, talking to Eric is like talking to one of your cats. Kinda twitchy."

"You bonded with Sam. He's a cat."

"But Sam is a cool cat. Even better, he's *your* cat. Ah. Here we are."

Harley found the light switch and the alarm. It wasn't set, but that wasn't unexpected. The cops had no doubt left it that way, and it was unlikely Darcy had come back to set it.

"Do you know where we're going?" Cami asked as Harley led the way to the back, and she nodded.

"The office is back here. Harry had a desk in a little alcove, and it's probably still there. I hope the police weren't looking at manifests and things. Maybe they were more concerned with actual evidence, fingerprints, stuff like that."

"Did your aunt tell them about Harry smuggling?"

"I don't know. If she didn't, then we've got a very short opportunity to find out what we can about him before they figure it out. Once the cops know about the smuggling, there's the motive for her to murder Harry. But I figure he had to have accomplices that got greedy, or maybe he didn't pay his connections."

"There are really pretty things in here," Cami remarked as they passed through one of the showrooms. "I had no idea it'd be this nice. Look at that—that's an antique armoire."

Harley recognized it. "It's Portuguese. It's just in, and already in the showroom." The piece had ornate curves that flowed in intricate patterns, the top two doors open, two drawers below closed. Perfect for smuggling in animal skins, European antiquities, valuable paintings, or whatever else smugglers could steal. The most likely possibility was one of the smugglers had killed Harry. There was no honor among thieves, and he'd seemed like the type to cheat when he could. Maybe one of the deals had gone bad. But she had to find some evidence to prove that.

It was quiet, not even the air conditioning making noise as they skirted couches, tables, floor lamps, elegant vases and curio cabinets on their way to the back. Harry's desk was in an alcove in the big room where he'd met his grisly end, not something she really wanted to think too closely about at the moment. Their footsteps were muffled by the thick carpet underfoot, and only Cami breathing through her mouth like a panting dog made any sound.

The only light came through a tall window at the end of the room; it was filtered by a big potted tree that looked remarkably real. Harley paused, fumbled for the light switch, and the bank of overhead fluorescent lights hummed into use. She deliberately ignored all reminders of a dead body and police investigation, and steered straight toward the alcove where an antique desk fit against the wall.

Cami stopped short, staring at the smears of graphite dust left by the Crime Scene Unit, to the chalk outlining the empty space where the elk horns and Harry had hung. Her voice sounded shaky.

"Is this . . . is this . . .?"

"Yep. Don't look. It was pretty nasty."

The drawers of the antique desk were locked, but she had expected no less. Fortunately, she'd been foresighted enough to arm herself with another metal pick for recalcitrant locks. Yogi made them by the dozens, apparently expecting lots of locked doors in his life. Probably due to long experience.

It took her a few minutes, but she got the top drawer open, and that in turn freed the other drawers. Apparently, the police had been clever enough to get there first. The top drawer was completely empty. The second and third drawers held only color brochures of exotic places like Majorca and Prague. No wonder they'd been left behind. Hardly affordable on a policeman's salary.

Disappointed, she stood there a moment, just staring at the desk and trying to think where else Harry might have hidden his illegal manifests. Maybe he didn't really have manifests. It'd be foolish, given his occupation as a smuggler. Aunt Darcy could be wrong about that. A second set of books would be too risky. But how else would he know what was coming in, how and when? He had to keep some kind of list or schedule. And what did he do with the smuggled goods?

Drumming her fingers atop the gleaming surface of the desk, only slightly marred with remnants of fingerprint dusting powder, she considered her next move. A search of Harry's house would probably be impossible. Despite her recent dip in the detective pool, she was notoriously cowardly. It was the closest she came to a religion since her days as a student in Catholic school. Going from the complete freedom of her early life in communes to the restricted discipline of well-meaning nuns could have been more traumatic if she hadn't actually yearned for some kind of structure in those days. She'd even briefly flirted with the idea of becoming a nun, until a fling with Bobby Baroni in the back seat of a Ford had proven her lack of real commitment to the vocation.

"What now?" Cami asked as she plopped her purse on the desk, and Harley shrugged.

"I don't know. I guess I thought something would jump out at me, or the police would have left behind something important." She'd dropped the little metal pick, and bent to retrieve it from the carpet. A faint gleam under the desk's kneehole caught her attention, and still bending down, she reached up under the desk to find the source. Her fingers grazed something metal and sharp. She pressed it, and a soft click sounded. What the—? Going to her hands and knees, she wiggled her way under the desk to investigate. A small door had popped open. Her heart raced with excitement. The missing manifests, perhaps?

No. It was a tiny compartment hardly big enough for a button. But it did hold a key. She pried it loose from the tape holding it to the opening, and scooted out from under the desk. With a grin, she held it up so Cami could see. "*Voila*!"

Cami didn't look impressed. "Walla what?"

"That's French for *Looky what I found*. Never mind. It's a key. Now we just have to find what it fits, and I bet we find the missing evidence we need to prove Harry's a smuggler."

"How is that going to help? He's dead. The police are looking for his killer, not illegal imports. Besides, didn't you just say that'd give your aunt a motive?"

"Cami, Cami, you can be so shortsighted. If we find the evidence, we find the motive. If we find the motive, we find the killer. See how simple that is?"

"So what if it really is your aunt? I've always thought she had the personality of a serial killer."

"The only thing Aunt Darcy is capable of killing is a bottle of gin," Harley said, though she wasn't completely sure that was true. She slid the key into the pocket of her cutoffs, then retrieved her metal pick and looked around the storage area. Evidence that the police had done a thorough investigation showed. Furniture was pulled from the wall, rugs unrolled and clumsily rolled back, graphite residue was everywhere, and file cabinets had been left partially open. Aunt Darcy would have a fit when she saw the disarray. They had that much in common. Both liked things tidy.

"So now what?" Cami said, looking around with her hands on her hips. "I think we've done all we can do here."

"First, I'm going to see if this key fits anything here, which I doubt since that'd be far too easy, then we'll go. No point in pushing our luck."

Cami looked agreeable, and wandered over toward a stack of rolled carpets against the far wall. Harley tried the key in the desk locks. It didn't fit, not that she'd thought it would since it looked more like an old fashioned door key, then tried it on all the shop's closet and Exit doors. It didn't fit any of them. Of course not. There would have been no reason to hide it. Maybe to Harry's house? A lock box in a bank?

"You missed this door," Cami said when they went back to the storage area and Harley pocketed the key again.

"What door?"

Pulling back a roll of carpet, Cami pointed to a small door built into the wall. It was barely visible, looking like part of the wall unless you looked really close. Then the outline could be discerned in the wainscoting. The wallpaper design hid it very well, but there was a definite keyhole right beside the white painted molding.

Harley inserted the key. It turned with a metallic click of tumblers and the door swung open. A musty smell wafted out from a narrow flight of stairs that led down into pitch darkness. She left the key in the lock and stood there indecisively.

"What is it?" Cami wanted to know. "Another storage room?"

"I don't know. Storm shelter, maybe. But isn't it odd that it's hidden like this? Why is it disguised?"

"Let's look inside, Harley. I'll wait here."

Harley shot her a wry glance. "Right. You're really brave as long as it's not you."

"There might be bats in there. I don't like bats."

"What if there are spiders? I don't like spiders."

They stood there for a moment, staring into the void that beckoned. The hair on the back of Harley's neck stood up without the benefit of gel. She had no idea why. All of a sudden it just seemed risky to be doing this. Despite the stuffy air and possibility of finding smuggled goods, she shivered.

"Harley? Maybe you shouldn't."

"Yeah. Still . . . it seems a shame to have found this door and not at least see where it goes. Doesn't it?"

"Uhhh . . . "

"This is silly. It's a door. It's probably the basement, though I didn't know there was one. And I can't imagine why the entrance would be hidden. Or why the key was hidden under Harry Gordon's desk. Or why I'm talking out loud instead of just going on and getting this over with."

Dredging up her flagging courage, Harley stepped into the stairwell. To her relief, there were no cobwebs, just cool concrete walls as she gingerly made her way down the steps, feeling for a light switch along the way. *You'd think they'd have had the good sense to put a light switch in here close to the top,* she was thinking when something bumped into her. She screamed. Cami screamed. Then Harley realized Cami was right behind her on the steps.

"Damn, Cami! You scared the crap out of me!"

Cami's teeth were chattering. "I didn't want to stay up there by myself. Sorry."

"Tell that to my stomach. It dropped to my toes. Let go of my shirt, please. You've got skin."

Cami released her shirt, but she stayed so close to Harley that they could have been wearing the same shoes.

Finally Harley reached the bottom of the stairs, and stood indecisively. Except for the thin light coming through the open door, it was dark as a grave. That thought made her shiver again.

"Isn't there a light down here?" Cami asked plaintively.

"*I* should know? You're the one who found the door."

"Maybe the light's upstairs. That'd make sense. To have the switch up there, I mean."

"Right. It would. Go check."

"No! I mean, maybe both of us should go."

Cami sounded shaky. Somehow, that made Harley feel better. Being scared alone was never a good thing. Having company in terror made it bearable.

"Okay. We'll both go. If you'll, uh, just give me room to turn around here . . . "

They'd made it three steps back up when the light from the opening flickered, and both of them looked up. A shadow blotted out the light, then grew bigger as the door began to close.

"No," Harley yelled, "stop!"

She charged up two more steps with Cami clinging to her back like a baby possum, and got almost to the top just as the door slammed shut with a solid thunk. Everything went black as pitch.

"Oh, help," said Cami.

"Oh, shit," said Harley.

Seven

Harley felt her way up the last step and tried the door. It didn't budge. There was no knob, no release catch. Just smooth wood.

"Dammit all," she said irritably, "another self-locking door. Why do they make these things? Hey! Is anyone out there? Hey!" She pounded on the door until her hand hurt.

Cami's voice came from close by, sounding really faint. "Harley?"

"Yeah?"

"I have to pee."

Harley leaned against the locked door and sighed. "Of course. Well, give me a minute to find the key—uh oh. Never mind. I'll pick it. I still have my pick. Thank God for a father with a slightly criminal turn of mind. He likes being prepared for all emergencies."

"Good." Cami's teeth chattered, a weird sound in the velvety blackness that swallowed them. After a moment, she said, "Think this is how Jonah felt?"

"Jonah who?"

"You know. The guy swallowed by a whale."

"Good God, Cami." Harley felt along the wood, fingers tracing the lintel and frame, down one side, then the other, feeling for the lock. There had to be one. If there was one on the outside, there was one on the inside. That's the way it went.

"Of course, there would have been the ocean," Cami said in a reflective tone, "and ribs. A tongue. A heartbeat. Whales are mammals. It would have been warm in there."

"Not to mention halitosis from all the dead fish. Cami, you're scaring me. Get a grip. You're regressing back to junior high."

"Junior high?"

"Sister Mary Margaret. All those Bible stories she used to tell us. Third period. Right before lunch, remember?"

"How do you remember things like that? I have trouble remembering what I ate yesterday and you remember what period we had lunch in junior high school."

"I can't remember what I ate yesterday. I only remember Sister Mary Margaret because she made the stories interesting. And she didn't tell on me when I snuck out early on the days they had chocolate cake in the cafeteria."

Cami laughed. It was a nice sound. Harley smiled in the darkness. At least one of them felt a little better. She didn't want to scare Cami, but she couldn't find the lock. There had to be one. How could there *not* be one? Locks on doors generally went all the way through. Anyone who built a storm shelter or basement and didn't put a lock on the inside was just asking for a lot of trouble. Unless . . . no, that was ridiculous. Why would Aunt Darcy be involved? Yet she'd never mentioned the basement as a possible place to look for stolen goods.

Damn, she hated what she was thinking. And even more, she hated what the police would think when they found out about the smuggling, which they would if they hadn't already.

"Harley, did you find it yet?"

"Not yet."

"If you don't hurry, there's going to be a wet spot on these stairs."

"Yeah, well if I don't get it open soon, there'll be two wet spots."

Damn. Where *was* it? She scraped her knuckle against something hard and her heart leaped. A quick investigation with her fingertips discovered no lock, only some kind of metal plate over where it should be. By now her fingertips were bleeding and she regretted, not for the first time, her lack of fingernails. One more reason to stop biting them.

"Cami, you've got nails, don't you?"

"Nails? Like what you hammer?"

"No, fingernails. Something to pry off this metal plate. It's covering the lock."

"Oh God . . . "

"Now don't panic. It's not like we're in the wilderness. We're in the basement of a design shop that usually has at least a half dozen employees and plenty of customers. We'll be fine."

Cami was fumbling in the dark, her hands making slapping sounds as she searched for the plate cover. After a few moments, she said, "I'd have to have a screwdriver to pry off this thing. It's fastened pretty firm."

She sounded remarkably calm. Harley nodded, then realized Cami couldn't see her. "It's okay. We'll just have to think of something else."

"Yeah? How fast? I really gotta pee, Harley."

"Me too. Maybe there's a toilet down here somewhere. Or we could just go scratch in the dirt like one of your cats, I guess."

Cami made a funny sound. Harley wasn't sure if she was laughing or crying. It was a toss-up. She could relate. At the moment, she felt like doing both. She'd never thought the complete absence of light could be so—well, *dark*.

To keep from continuing that line of thought, she said, "Well, as long as we're stuck here for the moment, why don't we explore our options. Let's see what's down here. We need a crowbar or screwdriver. We may even find another door or a window."

"Right." Cami didn't sound too convinced, not that Harley blamed her.

They cautiously made their way down the narrow steps again, holding on to each other just in case. Once they reached what felt like the bottom, Harley—who was in front—fumbled along the wall, fingers skimming over a surface that seemed to be concrete block. It was cool and dank. There were probably spiders down here as big as dinner plates. She shuddered.

I should have known better than to unlock secret doors. That kind of thing never turns out well. What was I thinking? I've watched more than enough horror movies. When will I learn? Now Cami is going to get hysterical and I'll have to calm her down.

"Harley?"

"Yeah?"

"You do know you're thinking out loud, don't you?"

"I am?"

Cami's grip on her shirt tightened. "Yeah. I can't promise not to get hysterical. I've seen too many horror movies, too. I don't like this."

"Well, one thing's for sure. We're the only ones down here. If there was anything hiding, it would have already started up the chain saw."

"Is that supposed to make me feel better?"

"It doesn't?"

Whatever Cami might have answered to that remained unsaid as Harley tripped over something on the floor and went down like a felled oak. Cami screamed. The sound bounced off the walls and seemed to reverberate like a snare drum assault. Harley rolled away from what felt like a bolt of material.

She got to her feet, brushing grit from her palms, then followed the sound of screaming to reach Cami and give her a brisk shake.

"Hey! It's all right, Cami. Damn, it's hard to believe such a big sound comes from such a small woman. Before you get too hysterical, it's possible we can find some kind of light down here. After all, it's a storeroom."

Cami's teeth chattered loudly. "H-h-how do you know that?"

"Because I tripped over some bolts of material or a rug. Big, bulky, soft. We can use it to wrap up in if we get cold. First, I'm going to see if I can find a light. Matches, anything. There must be some kind of light switch down here somewhere. Maybe one of those that you can turn on and off from either switch, y'know?"

In answer, Cami's teeth chattered more loudly. Harley felt a twinge of regret for involving Cami the last time and this time, too. Cami wasn't cut out for this. She'd led a sheltered life, apple of her parents' eye, still at the same job she'd gotten right out of high school, the only bump on her smooth road the divorce from Jace. In just two weeks, there'd been more excitement in Cami's life than in their past fourteen years combined, Harley was certain. Except, of course, for adolescent pranks, none of which measured up to being kidnapped and threatened by career criminals.

"Just stay right here, Cami. Sit down on this rug or whatever it is. I'm going to see what else is down here. Or feel what else is down here, since I can't see a damned thing."

She helped Cami sit down, not as easy as it might seem since there was absolutely no light at all. She'd always heard the other senses got sharper if one was compromised, but maybe that took time. The only sharp thing she felt right now was foreboding.

There were some kind of shelves on the wall, and she cautiously felt her way along. Only a few shelves, maybe three, holding what felt like glass vases, stone statues, and unrecognizable objects. She found a weird-shaped glass thing, kind of oval, smooth with a wooden base. It had a switch of some kind.

A flick of the switch turned on a blue and red light. Ah. A lava lamp. The sixties styles had come back, but this couldn't have been here since the days of Nehru jackets and free love. Real lava lamps were scarce. Diva and Yogi had one in their bedroom, possibly a holdover from their younger days, but more likely a flea market find since they'd lived in a van in the late sixties and early seventies.

"Hey, we have some light," Cami said, and sounded much more cheerful.

"This must mean there's electricity down here. I have high hopes there's a better light somewhere. And maybe a phone—hey! Where's your cell phone?"

"In my purse."

"And your purse—"

"Is on that desk where you found the key. I feel like Alice in Wonderland down the rabbit hole, regretting how I got here and quite positive I don't like it," Cami said sadly.

"It's not forever. We have lava light, so we're bound to find even better surprises."

"I don't like surprises. Not lately. I think I've lost my interest in excitement. It makes my stomach hurt."

"Cami, it's my fault for dragging you into this."

"You didn't drag me. I came willingly enough. Damn. This rug has really uncomfortable lumps in it. And it's not very pretty."

Cami was peering at the rolled up rug where she sat, a big long thing with tasseled fringe and a distinctly unpleasant odor. Mildew, most likely. Harley wondered why anyone would put a valuable rug down here in the basement to rot.

"Maybe we'll find a chair, though it's not as big down here as I thought. Kinda narrow for a store room or basement. It must be some kind of storm shelter."

Swirling red and blue light waltzed over the walls, not much, but better than none at all. No electrical cord tethered it to the wall. Great. Battery powered, which meant it'd probably run out sooner than she liked. Shelves held dust and suspicious small pellets. If mice could get in here, that meant it wasn't completely airtight, which Harley considered a good thing. She sneezed. Dust scattered, and she sneezed again.

"Gesundheit," Cami said. "Find anything?"

"Dust and doody. Mouse doody. Your cats would love it here."

"Probably not. They prefer rooms with a view."

"So do I. Unfortunately, there doesn't seem to be any windows down here. Or another door. I had hope, but there you go."

"Harley? Do you think someone deliberately shut us in here?"

Harley hesitated before answering. That shadow had looked suspiciously like a silhouette right before the door slammed shut. But she could be mistaken. She probably was mistaken. Now that she thought about it, she was certain she was mistaken. Who would have locked them in here and why?

"No," she said, "I don't think so. The door just closed by itself."

Maybe.

"I still have to pee, you know," Cami said then. "No toilet down here, I suppose?"

"Not unless you want to think of this as one big litter box. I think I see a mop bucket in that corner if we get desperate."

"*Omigod . . .* "

Cami sounded suddenly horrified, and Harley peered at her in the thick shadows, just able to see her leap up from the floor. Blue and red glowing lava lamps didn't put out much light.

"You don't *have* to pee in a bucket, it's just an option. What is it? Cami? You okay?"

"I don't know . . . this rug feels funny."

"It's old and probably mildewed and falling apart."

"No, it's not . . . not that. It's lumpy." Cami's teeth were chattering again.

"A few lumps shouldn't scare you so bad. Probably just dead mice. Come on, Cami, I know this seems bad, but it's not like we'll be stuck here forever. Even if we end up here overnight, someone will be here early in the morning and let us out."

"I have to be at work at eight tonight, remember?"

"Oh. Well. You might have to consider this a personal day."

"It's not what I consider it that counts. I have supervisors, you know. It's not like it used to be. Everything's so automated now, and there are layoffs all the time . . . I don't need this on my record, that I didn't even call in."

"I'm sorry, Cami. I really am. It's my fault if you get written up." Harley looked down at the rug. Hair on the back of her neck prickled. She had no idea why. It was a prickling she'd had before. It never meant anything good.

She looked back up at Cami. "When you say the rug is lumpy, what do you mean?"

"Weird. Like . . . like there's a couple of rugs wadded up inside. Or table legs."

Harley didn't say anything for a moment. She didn't like what she was thinking. It had to be her overactive imagination. The past few weeks had been nerve-wracking. Now she had this stupid premonition that reminded her of Diva's obscure prophecies. Next thing she knew, she'd be putting up a card table alongside Diva and reading tarot cards at flea markets. Ridiculous. Really it was. Still . . . there was something in that rug that wasn't supposed to be there. She just knew it. She thought of Harry Gordon and the stuff he'd been smuggling. Weapons, maybe?

"Well then," she said briskly and loudly as if trying to convince herself, "let's just see what's making you uncomfortable. No telling what they put down here and forgot about. It's probably just junk."

Harley grabbed hold of the edge of the rug, fingers digging into ratty wool and damp fringe, and she tugged at it firmly. It didn't budge.

"Give me a hand, will you, Cami? We'll just unroll it and see what's in here. It might be old lamps or something we can use."

Cami hesitated, then bent to grab the other end of the rug. They both tugged at the same time and succeeded in jerking it up. Something rolled free and brushed against Harley's leg. She jumped back. Nothing happened, so she took a deep breath and bent closer to investigate. Light from the lava lamp didn't provide enough illumination to see well, and she straightened to pull it closer to the edge of the shelf. Thin light wavered and danced over the floor and unrolled carpet.

For a moment she couldn't move, could only stare in horror.

"Harley?" Cami's voice sounded quavery and on the edge of hysteria. "Is that . . . is that—"

"A body? Yep."

While Cami stumbled toward the mop bucket in the corner, Harley stared down at the bloodless face and realized she recognized him.

Cami was right. They had fallen down the rabbit hole.

Eight

Harley roused from a fitful sleep when she heard a thumping sound. She and Cami were huddled together as far from the body as possible, up against the opposite wall that wasn't nearly far enough away.

"Cami," she said when the thumping came again, louder this time, "wake up. It must be morning. I hear someone moving around up there."

"God, I hope so. You don't think . . . it could be whoever put *him* down here?"

"There's only one way to find out. No, don't start that whimpering again. We don't have much of a choice. Unless you want to stay down here a while longer."

Shivering a little in the dank air, she went up the narrow stairs and started pounding on the door with both fists. After a few minutes of that, she heard someone say, "Oh my God . . . who are you? Are you behind the wall?"

"No, behind a door in the wall. There's a key sticking out—is that you, Amanda?"

"*Harley?*"

She could have collapsed with relief.

In what seemed like far too long a time when there was a key in plain sight in the keyhole, Amanda had the door open and Harley and Cami tumbled out into the storeroom. Light made them both squint, but Harley could still see that Amanda looked shocked and puzzled. But not speechless.

"How did you get behind that wall?"

"Just lucky. And it's a storage area. Call the police."

"Are you out of your mind? Why should I call the police because you got locked in a storage area? And how did you know it was there? I never knew about it, and I've been all over this shop." Amanda stuck her head into the opening and peered into the shadows. "What's down here?"

"A dead body." When Amanda jerked back and whirled around to stare at her, Harley said, "Which is why I said to call the police. It's my understanding that they generally like to be notified when one of those pops up."

Shaking her head, Amanda backed away, gazing at her in horror. "I'm beginning to think you're a serial killer, Harley."

"I'm beginning to feel like one. I've seen more dead bodies in the last two weeks than the coroner has, I think. Call the cops, Mandy. Please."

Cami had crossed the room to the desk where she'd left her purse, and Harley heard her angry exclamation. "Hey! Why did you do this?"

Amanda glanced over at her uncertainly. "Do what?"

"Empty out my purse like this. There was no need in that. Everything's scattered all over the floor, and now I can't find my cell phone. I need to call in to work . . . just look at this mess."

"I never saw your purse," Amanda said crossly, "I just got to work. It's all such a mess, so I came in here to see how much more damage the police have done. There's dust and yellow tape everywhere . . . we can't even open today. Probably not this week. We need a cleaning service to come in. Then we'll just hope we have customers."

"Mandy dearest," Harley said with a frown, "did you come in yesterday?"

"No. No one did. No one wanted to after—everything. Why?"

"Are you the only one here now?"

"Except for Madelyn. But she's in the main office. Mama isn't coming in today. She's still . . . resting."

Hung-over, was Harley's thought, but she didn't say it aloud. "And you're sure no one else came in yesterday? Just to pick up something, maybe?"

"No, no one else came in, Harley. No one *wants* to come here for anything right now. And it better be one of your sick jokes about there being another body."

"While that'd be nice, believe me when I say that spending the night in the dark basement with a corpse is nothing to joke about."

Amanda looked toward the door still standing open and blanched. A light dusting of freckles stood out on her nose. "Mama's going to have a fit."

"Just run along and call the police. I'll stay here to, uh, keep an eye on things. Not that he's going anywhere. He looked pretty stationary."

Amanda started toward the door, then turned around and looked back at her. "Is it someone we know?"

"I have no idea if you know him or not." That was true. But Harry Gordon had known him, and so had Aunt Darcy. It could turn out to be a real problem. Police were known to catch on to that kind of thing.

Of course, Bobby Baroni asked the expected questions right after he got through telling Harley that she was one step away from being incarcerated as a public menace. He said a lot of other things, too, none of them very nice, and one or two that were even downright nasty.

"One more time, Harley Jean," he said, his tone and the hard look he gave her indicating he was really pissed, "just what were you doing messing around here in our crime scene?"

"Obviously, finding a body *you* overlooked. Not that I was looking for one. I just seem to, uh, run across them lately. I'm not sure why. I've gone years without inconvenient corpses in my life, and now it seems every time I turn a corner, *bam!* There one is. Like finding a fly in my soup or something."

"I don't suppose you happen to know this particular fly?"

Bobby was writing in his little notepad, and looked up when she said, "As a matter of fact I do. His name is Julio."

"Know his last name?"

"No. I only met him once. He worked for Harry Gordon."

One corner of his mouth tucked in, but Bobby didn't say anything, just kept writing. From time to time, he glanced toward Cami, who sat all hunched up in a chair like she was cold. When he'd first come in, right behind several uniformed cops, he'd gone straight to Cami to see if she was okay and she'd started crying. Harley didn't blame her. She'd had a rough night. It'd been harder on Cami than on her. Maybe there was something good about having an early childhood that promoted self-reliance. It came in handy at times.

"So this Julio was a Designer's Den employee?" Bobby asked.

"No, I don't think so. Aunt Darcy didn't seem to know him well. I think he worked for just Harry. You'd have to ask her or the shop manager to be sure about that."

"I will."

She didn't doubt that for a moment. Bobby could be quite thorough and very untrusting. That had its good and bad points.

Police once more swarmed around Designer's Den, unrolling yellow tape, snapping on plastic gloves, and setting up lights down in the old storm shelter. Déjà vu.

When she went up to the front of the shop, Madelyn and Amanda were huddled in the manager's office, whispering. It struck her as odd they'd bother to whisper when no one else was around. She strolled in and perched on the edge of a desk. The room was decorated nicely, as it would be, of course, but nothing could disguise the fact it was an office. Four desks were placed according to principles of *feng shui*—Diva would be so proud—and the windows had expensive wooden blinds that matched the expensive wallpaper and lighting fixtures. Vases held tall skinny sticks that had been painted the same burgundy shade as the wall trim. Very nice.

"Hello, ladies," she said casually, and smiled when they both looked at her with tight lips. "What secrets are we telling in here? You don't happen to know anything about Julio, do you?"

"Who's Julio?" Madelyn asked sharply.

"You know. The dead guy with the blue face that I found in your basement."

"Oh. Him. That's not a basement." Madelyn shrugged when Harley just looked at her. "I think it's been closed up for years. Mama had the door boarded up long ago."

"Well, don't look now, but someone unboarded it. And obviously knew it was there. Who besides you and Aunt Darcy knew about it?"

"You don't think *I* had anything to do with this?"

"Again, as we've discussed before, dear cousin Maddie, what I think doesn't really matter that much. It's what the cops are going to think. Look, I know something's going on with you two. It's obvious as a rat in the Limoges sugar bowl."

Madelyn got a closed look on her face. Only Amanda showed any reaction, and she bit her lower lip and looked down at her feet, a sure sign she knew something she didn't want Harley to know. Fine. Amanda was the easy one to crack. Once she got her away from Madelyn.

"Maddie dearest, we'll continue this discussion later. The police want to see you."

"If they want to see me, they'll come and ask."

"I'm sure they will. Of course, if you're seen as uncooperative, they may ask you to go downtown with them. Last I heard, that could be a singularly unpleasant experience, but you go ahead and stay here.

Show your disdain."

"Really, Harley, the more I'm around you, the more I dislike you."

"Which justifies my absence from future family reunions."

As Madelyn took herself off with an irritated twitch of her mouth, Harley turned her attention to her cousin Amanda. She smiled to throw her off-guard.

"Maddie's never been the brightest bulb in the pack, has she?"

"She's the smart one," Amanda defended her sister. "And the pretty one."

"So you are—what? What's left, if Maddie's the smart *and* the pretty one?"

"Nice. I'm the nice one." Amanda sounded slightly bitter, then shrugged as if it didn't matter. Harley knew better.

"Well, if you don't mind me saying, I've always thought being nice was a bit underrated."

Amanda smiled. "So have I. But it's what I'm stuck with. So what do you want me to tell you now that you got rid of my sister?"

"I see they don't give you enough credit. You're much cleverer than Maddie. Okay, I want to know why you didn't answer the phone Thursday night if you were home like you said. It occurred to me, during a very long night spent in total darkness with a corpse, that you said you were home, but I called and no one answered the phone."

"I guess I didn't hear the phone ring. Maybe I was in the tub."

"And maybe you weren't home like you said."

"Harley, where else would I be on a Thursday night? Or any night? I have no social life. I'm always at home unless I'm at the shop or with a client. Read the appointment book. You'll see I have little time for anything but work or sleep."

For a moment Harley didn't say anything. She'd never really thought her cousin might be resentful of her life, but the tone of her voice bordered on an unfamiliar anger that she'd never have thought Amanda had in her. She'd always seemed . . . bland.

"Don't you get tired of that? You're what . . . twenty-six, twenty-seven now? Have you ever had a long-term boyfriend?"

"I could ask you the same thing, Harley."

"Yeah, but I'm not living at home with my mother and spending all my free time in the kitchen or watching TV."

"Running around with a transvestite is hardly a step up from watching *Queer Eye*, I'd think."

"If you're referring to Tootsie, he dresses much better than

Carson. And I'm willing to bet he's a better designer, too. His house is beautiful."

"I've always wondered if you're a switch-hitter."

"Ah, what a Maddie thing to say. Perhaps I've misjudged you, Mandy dearest."

"Most people do."

Harley didn't like the direction of the conversation. Who'd have thought Amanda could be so bitchy? Maybe she'd been around her sister too long. Or maybe it was stress. Or maybe it was like she'd said, most people had misjudged her. Whichever, Harley did some rapid mental adjustment and approached from a different angle.

"You know, the police think Aunt Darcy has something to do with Harry's murder. And now there's another body. This is liable to get worse quick. I'm worried about her, and you should be, too."

"Don't be. She has a solid alibi."

This wasn't the time to confess Aunt Darcy's extracurricular activities. "For *Harry's* murder, maybe."

That seemed to strike home. Amanda looked startled. Her eyes got so wide they looked like Blue Willow dinner plates. "Are you talking about Julio?"

"Who else? He's pretty dead. And he's in a storm cellar no one seems to remember being here. Also, he worked for Aunt Darcy. Or Harry, which is the same thing as far as the police are concerned."

"Oh God. Do you think . . . ?"

"Yes . . . ?" She waited for Amanda to make the connection, and just as she seemed to connect the dots, Madelyn stormed back into the office ranting about Harley making an ass of her by sending her off. Irritated, Harley waited for a break in the flow, then said, "I think it's time I run along now. You've both been very helpful."

The look her cousins exchanged didn't make her feel any easier, or contradict her feeling that they both knew a lot more than either had said. Damn. She really sucked at this investigation thing. She was more confused than ever now. And still had no answers that helped. The only bit of information that she hadn't known before, was that Amanda wasn't at all happy being the nice one who stayed home with a box of cookies and the remote. A lot of help *that* was in finding out anything.

She found Cami still in the storage room. Julio's body hadn't been brought up from the cellar yet—flashbulbs going off indicated that the crime scene unit were taking pictures and doing their thing down there.

Bobby was talking to another detective, and he glanced up when Harley went to sit down by Cami. For a minute, she thought he might say something to her, but he didn't.

"So, I noticed that Bobby was a lot nicer to you than me," Harley said, and Cami smiled.

"Not really. He's pretty mad. He said we're both crazy. And you're dangerous."

"Ah. How nice to be recognized for my talents. So, you ready to go?"

"I have been since we got here yesterday."

It took longer than either of them wanted to get away from the crime scene, but finally they made it out to the parking area and Cami's car. News teams were setting up again, vans with their logos crowding each other. They had to be scanning police radios to get here so quickly.

On the way to Cami's house, Harley reflected, "Amanda doesn't like staying home."

After a moment, Cami said, "You mean at all, or instead of having a boyfriend?"

"The last one. Funny, I never thought about her minding it. She always seemed happy. I guess she isn't really."

"Well, you don't see them very much. It's not anything you'd notice right off."

"No. I guess not. Sometimes I think I'm too self-absorbed. You know, just think about how I feel and not anyone else."

"That's not quite true. Besides, it's human nature to see things from your own perspective rather than anyone else's."

"Yeah. I guess so."

"Know what you need, Harley?"

"I'm afraid to hear this."

Cami laughed. "You need a pet. Something to take care of besides yourself."

"I have a pet. He comes by and brings food and pretty play toys."

"Right. Great sex is certainly fun, but it doesn't keep you grounded."

"I thought that was the point of it. You know, that feeling you get when it's really good and your eyes roll back in your head and all you can see is stars."

"And when he leaves?"

"I enjoy my solitude."

Cami was quiet for a minute, then she said, "After Jace and I divorced, I didn't do much except sit around the house and think how miserable I was. Then a friend of mine asked if I'd look after her dog while she went out of town. It was nice coming home to a house that wasn't empty. Even though it wasn't my dog, he jumped all around, wagging his tail and barking when I walked in, and it was companionship."

"I think you've carried it a little too far now. You're harboring a zoo."

"Maybe. Most of them are temporary, just waiting for a good home to come along. That's how I felt for a long time. Just waiting for someone to show up and rescue me. It took a while to figure out that I had to rescue myself first. I'm luckier than the animals. I have options. So do you."

"I'm happy," Harley protested, "a lot happier than I'd be picking up doggy doodles from the floor. Sometimes I'm gone long hours. I don't want anything I have to walk or that'll miss me."

"So that includes Morgan, I suppose?"

"Well, I don't have to walk him, and he's never hinted that he misses me that much, but I guess that includes him. What are you getting at, Cami?"

"Has it occurred to you that neither one of us is getting any younger and our biological clocks are ticking?"

"The only internal clock I have tells me when I've missed breakfast. Turn in to that Taco Bell up there on the right."

"There's no way I can eat tacos for breakfast."

They settled on the drive-through at a chicken and biscuit chain, then Cami dropped off Harley at her apartment and went home to feed her animals. Harley let herself in and thought how nice it was not to have to worry about feeding anyone or anything but herself. No nuggets on the floor to clean up, nothing but silence and solitude. Perfect.

The message light on her answering machine was blinking furiously, and she hit the button, then rummaged through the Mrs. Winner's sack for a biscuit while she listened. Tootsie had called three times and complained that she wasn't answering her cell phone and how did she expect him to give her the information she wanted if she wouldn't pick up. There were two calls from Mike Morgan, the last one a terse, "Call me when you get home" that indicated he'd talked to Bobby. Damn. That could get very inconvenient. The last call was a wrong number. A male voice that sounded foreign said, "Hello" a couple of times, then hung up. Foreign accents could be delicious and exotic. Maybe she should ask Morgan to pretend he was Russian the next time they played bedtime games. She returned Tootsie's calls first.

"It's Monday morning, do you know where your employees are?" she chirped when he answered the phone with his Memphis Tour Tyme spiel. "So what's up?"

"I could ask you the same thing. Mike Morgan called here looking for you."

"I have a feeling he knows where I am by now."

"So where are you?"

"Home. Just got here. You won't believe this—"

"Damn baby, I hate it when you start off a sentence like that."

"Right. Well, I hate spending the night in a dark cellar with Cami and a dead body."

Silence greeted that remark, and after a moment, she heard Tootsie make a wheezing sound. She smiled. It wasn't easy to rattle him, so she always counted it as a small victory when she managed to leave him speechless.

"So," he said after a minute, "I guess that explains why Cami never answered her cell phone either."

"It does. Shall I fill you in on the gory details?"

"God, yes."

It didn't take long. Then she asked, "What did you find out about Cheríe Saucier?"

"She died about eight years ago. Or at least, that was the only one I found."

"Hah! I knew that scrawny bitch was a fraud. Aunt Darcy is always right on the money when it comes to sizing up another female. Which makes her opinion of me a bit uncomfortable."

"So why did you want to know about her?"

"She worked with Harry Gordon. You know, it just occurred to me that Harry's dead and now the guy who worked for him is dead, and that leaves only Cheríe who might still know why. If I could talk to her, I might just learn something."

"Baby, your track record isn't so good. Leave that to the police."

"Well, I did pretty good last time."

"You almost got killed last time. This time, you've only spent the night in a cellar with a dead body. Think about it. You're still ahead."

"True. I'll think about it. I don't know where to find her anyway, so it's probably a moot point."

"Things have a way of happening for you, baby. Just when they shouldn't. That's not always a good thing."

"What did you find out about Harry Gordon?"

"Do you know how many Harry Gordons there are just in Tennessee alone, much less the rest of the US? I'm trying to narrow it down for you. It'd help if I had a birth date or his Social Security number. I'm trying to backtrack all references to Harry and designers, antiques, things like that at the moment. If I got paid by the hour, I could retire."

"You're an angel. A darling. Precious." No response. She sighed. "I'll give you a percentage of the five thousand."

"Now you're talking my language."

"So tell me about this dead Cheríe. Where was she from and what did she do? Maybe if I know something about her, I'll know something about the woman who stole her identity."

"I don't know if this is the same one, it's just the only logical one I could find. Not too much to tell. Her maiden name was Plotz. She married Luke Saucier in 1989, died in 1996 of cancer. Last mailing address was in Atoka, Tennessee. Left behind no children, two sisters, one brother."

"Sisters' names?"

"Anna Plotz Merritt, and Frieda Plotz. Brother's named Bernard."

"Do you think you could find out anything about the two sisters?"

"You're a pain in the ass, baby."

"I know. But you love me. So how'd you look as Liza?"

"Stunning. I suppose that's a not too subtle reference to the fact you gave me all those Minnelli-style clothes."

"Well, I do try to pay my debts."

Tootsie said something rude, then sighed. "All right. But you have to come to one of my shows. I want an honest opinion."

"Don't you get that from Steve?"

"Please. He's in love. He says whatever he thinks I want to hear."

"Not so very different from the boy-girl thing, I see. A pity. You'd think there'd be more advantages since you don't qualify for marriage."

"Why would you think marriage is an advantage?"

"It isn't?"

"Hardly." Tootsie laughed. "It's not like two guys together are conventional anyway. Why bother with a legal ceremony when you can pay an attorney to do things the way you really want them done? It doesn't change anything, just puts money in the pockets of all the wrong people. But I appreciate the sentiment, baby. Are you coming in at all today? This week?"

"Tomorrow. Put me down for something local. Right now, I want a hot bath and some sleep. I'm beginning to feel like a mushroom."

"A mushroom?"

"Yep, knee-deep in shit and left in the dark."

Laughing, Tootsie hung up. Harley thought about calling Morgan, then decided to get a bath first. She really did feel icky. And she'd need to feel human and awake when she talked to him, or she'd end up saying something she shouldn't.

Baths, Harley reflected as steam rose in waves that fogged the bathroom mirror and deep-cleansed her pores, were a necessary element of survival. Showers were just to get the dirt off. A bath was luxury. Especially with something sweet-smelling in the water, and all the water out of the hot water tank and into the tub. If she ever bought a house, it was going to have one of those big round Jacuzzis in it. A deep one, with lots of water jets.

She didn't leave the tub until the bubbles went flat and the hot water ran out. Then she wrapped herself in a sheet-size fluffy towel and wore it like a sarong. Not bothering to do more than finger-comb her hair, she padded barefoot into the kitchen and opened the refrigerator. She needed to go shopping. There wasn't much in there but some leftover Chinese, a bottle of wine, a beer, and a half dozen eggs. She opted for the Chinese. Mike had brought it, refusing to eat Taco Bell. The fried rice was really good, not too sticky, just enough seasonings so that a generous splash of soy sauce made it perfect. She piled it on a plate, heated it in the microwave, and went to the living room to eat. Twelve hours of fasting could hardly be appeased by one biscuit, even one with butter and strawberry jelly.

It took some work, but she finally got her apartment back the way she liked it. Tidy, no clutter, the white-striped slipcovers back from the cleaners, fitting snug on her fat chairs. She sank down in one of them, liking the way it seemed to close around her.

Cami was wrong. Harley didn't hear the ticking of her biological clock at all. Maybe she didn't have one. Or the batteries had run down. Whichever, she'd never dreamed of having kids and the mess that went with them. It wasn't that she didn't like kids, necessarily, it just wasn't a priority. Or even a remote desire.

When girls her age had baby dolls and played house under a tree, she was with the boys playing stick ball or skinny dipping in the nearest pond or creek, depending on where they'd parked their van. Sometimes they'd parked near a beach in northern California, a place that still seemed more like heaven than anywhere she'd ever been. Foamy surf breaking on black rocks, stretches of sand soft as sugar, air that smelled fresh and clean . . . a feeling of complete freedom that she hadn't had since then. The sixties era of free love and protesting against the Vietnam war were behind when she was born, and the promise of the seventies with civil rights struggles resolved and a fresh determination to change the world in full bloom. Her earliest memory was riding atop her father's shoulders in a protest, her best memory releasing helium balloons that said PEACE on the rubber faces from the cliff above the Golden Gate Bridge. At that moment, she'd felt as if she was on top of the world and it was waiting below for her like a golden apple. California had good memories, as well as the ones about tarantula-sized spiders and rats the size of raccoons.

By the time she'd finished her fried rice, she'd come to the realization that she was one of those women who'd never wanted children. A freak, by some standards, perhaps. And maybe one day she'd change her mind, but it didn't seem likely. But that might be because she didn't have all the right components necessary for a stable life for any children of her own. While going from commune to commune had been a unique, if not totally desirable, lifestyle for her as a child, it wasn't one she'd want for her own kids. And even if everything came together in just the right way, she still didn't see herself with a house full of rug rats. That was disturbing in a way, though she couldn't put her finger on the exact reason. Maybe she was defective. Or just selfish.

She was still pondering her shortcomings when the phone rang. Leaning over, she picked up the cordless. Before she could say "Hello," Morgan said, "Why aren't you answering your cell phone?"

"It's charging. And I'm tired of paying for new ones. I don't intend to use it except in an emergency."

"What constitutes an emergency for you—*not* getting locked in a basement with a body?"

"Bobby has a big mouth."

"Baroni's worried about you. He thinks you've gone over the edge."

"And what edge would that be?" This was getting irritating.

"Probably the one you just passed. What were you doing poking around the crime scene, Harley?"

"When did it become your business?"

That stopped him. She could almost hear his wheels turning. He might be super-sexy, but he didn't own her. Borrowed her for a while, maybe, but there was no signed lease. She was free to do as she pleased. And somehow, that was irritating, too.

"So," he said more cautiously, "it's not my business. That doesn't mean I want to see you get hurt."

Damn. Good answer. It was really confusing, and she wished Cami hadn't even brought up all that stuff about being alone and biological clocks and crap. She sighed.

"Thanks. I think."

"You're welcome. I think."

There was a moment of awkward silence before he said, "I'm on duty later tonight, but if you're not busy tomorrow night, maybe we can do something."

"Like what?"

"I'm sure we'll find something we agree on. Dinner, a movie . . . "

"A real date? Haven't had one of those in a while. It sounds intriguing."

Morgan laughed and she felt better. This was really stupid, feeling so suddenly awkward all because of some damn biological clock and Cami's Chicken Little warnings. Next time she saw Cami, she'd give her a wedgie she wouldn't forget for a while.

"Funny, Harley," Morgan said. "So be thinking of a place you want to eat—not Taco Bell—and what movie you want to see. As long as it's not some chick flick, I don't care."

"You sure? I think the Orpheum is showing *Casablanca*. That has excitement, danger, guns, all the things guys like."

"Right. Not enough to outweigh the other stuff."

"Ah, the love element. Yeah, that is boring. Good thing for you there's a new Jackie Chan movie out then, huh."

"Now you're talking."

When they hung up, Harley reflected that even though Jackie Chan was one of her favorites, it was irritating that Morgan disliked "the other stuff." This was crazy. She really was going to smack Cami when she saw her again. It wasn't that she wanted to be in love, because she'd tried that once and it hadn't worked out well at all, and she had no intention of being dumb enough to go looking in all the wrong places again, but now she felt defective. Like there was something seriously wrong in her life. Besides the fact her family was inherently insane and she had nothing better to do than stumble over corpses lately, it was a kind of wrong that was more personal.

Great. Just great. When had she become the kind of woman to sit and worry about her love life, or lack of one? She couldn't let Cami's anxieties become hers. She had to shake this stuff quickly or she'd end up living in an apartment crammed with cats, dogs, and assorted other creatures, a neighborhood legend, the "crazy cat lady" or something. Maybe Cami was on her way to that distinction, but she didn't intend to fall into that trap. Oh no.

She called Morgan back, and when he answered, she said, "How about a house call, officer?"

"This doesn't involve Taco Bell, does it?"

"No. I've already eaten. But I have . . . *needs*."

"I'm on my way."

The line went dead and Harley smiled. Oh yeah. He had just the right antidote for any woman's ticking biological clock.

"Talk dirty to me."

Harley pried open one eye and peered at Mike where he lay sprawled out on the other side of her bed. Ropy muscles glistened in the dim light of one of her perfumed candles—an attempt at romance—and his chest still rose and fell a little quicker than normal. She smiled.

"I don't think you can handle any more right now."

"I'll rise to the occasion."

"I thought you were on duty tonight?"

He groaned. "You sure do know how to ruin a moment."

"It's a talent. Women in my family are famous for it." She leaned over and ran a finger over his washboard abs. Luscious. Yep. He was just the thing to put her world back into the right kind of perspective. She'd have to remember that the next time she made the mistake of listening to Cami.

"Speaking of women in your family . . . " He turned over on his side and caught her wandering hand, smiling when she made a disappointed sound. "I'm not on the case, but I've heard that the evidence is stacking up against your aunt. You might suggest she get an attorney."

"I thought you told me to butt out."

"Yeah, well . . . this is a little different. Offering advice to a relative isn't the same thing as going around finding bodies and getting locked in basements."

"Optimist."

He sighed. "I used to think you were the normal one in your family."

"And now?"

"I'm not so sure. You're more normal than your parents, but that's not saying so much."

"You should meet Yogi's side of the family."

"I'd rather not."

"Very wise of you. They make Diva's side look boring. I have cousins who'd give the guys in that movie *Deliverance* a run for their money."

"Remind me to thank my parents for being from Pennsylvania."

"Don't let Grandmother Eaton know you're a Yankee."

"Harley, the Civil War is over."

"Hoo hoo, a lot you know. It's only over for Yankees. The Eaton side of the family has never forgiven nor forgotten. And you don't even want to know what the Davidson side does for fun down there in Mississippi."

"It doesn't involve white sheets, does it?"

"Of course not. They're not racists, just rednecks. Actually, I like them much better than I do the Eatons, who like to think they're aristocratic when they're really just snobs. Except for Granddad. I don't know how he turned out so nice, but he did. He's what my grandmother refers to as *a true Southern gentleman*. Of course, the Eatons used to be bootleggers, you know."

"You're scaring me."

"I'm just trying to enlighten you as to the kind of people in my background. So don't expect too much from Aunt Darcy. She's a product of her environment."

"And Diva?"

"Is unique. There's no one else like her. Except maybe Nana McMullen. She's my great-grandmother on Diva's side. She was born just before the roaring twenties and prohibition, then went through the Depression, and she has lots of stories she likes to tell, usually just to annoy the hell out of Grandmother Eaton. It's fun to watch. Proof that no matter how old you get, you can still torment your family."

"Nana sounds scary."

"Not *Nah-nah.* Nana. Like the last two syllables of banana. And she is scary."

"Remind me to skip your family reunions."

"Are you kidding? That's the only time it's enjoyable being in this family. Of course, a certain amount of drinking is essential if you want to get through the festivities without decking anyone. Or to ease the pain when you get decked by a drunken second cousin."

Morgan scooted closer and threw his leg across her, pinning her to the mattress while his hand did some delicious exploring. Harley didn't even consider resistance. He'd be the one to have to explain why he was late for work, not her. All she had to do was enjoy.

So she did.

Nine

Tootsie looked up with a surprised expression when she got to the Tour Tyme offices at the same time he did.

"Baby, I didn't expect to see you until at least ten."

"It was too nice a morning to sleep in. I had a relaxing night."

"I can tell. Morgan, I presume?"

She smiled. "The man really does curl my toes."

"Too bad he doesn't do the same thing for your hair."

"Sometimes you can be such an old maid. So what's on the agenda today?"

"Mud Island, Beale Street, and AutoZone Park with a group of businessmen from Tokyo, or Victorian Village and the Dixon Gallery with some ladies from Iowa."

"Tough choice. Iowa gets me, despite the lure of Japanese businessmen who won't know a word I'm saying."

"They probably speak better English than you and I do," Tootsie said, and Harley figured he was probably right.

Tootsie started up the computer and did all the little organizational chores that were his habit while Harley fired up the coffee pot, one of those industrial size ones that was idiot-proof. When she took Tootsie a cup of coffee, black, no cream or sugar, he handed her a printout.

"What's this?"

"All the info I could find on Cheríe Saucier and the Plotz family. Still working on all the Harry Gordons. Number forty-six has a rap sheet, so . . . Good God. What'd you do to this coffee?"

"Nothing special. Why?"

"It's strong enough to wake the dead. That's probably a handy advantage for you lately, but we seem to be corpse-free in here today. How many coffee packets did you use?"

"One." Harley checked the coffee filter, and found two packets. "Sorry. They must have stuck together."

"Here. I'll make the coffee. You just read. The number four van is being washed, so you'll have to leave a little early to pick up Iowa at their hotel. Names and times are on the schedule."

Harley scanned the printout. Interesting. Anna Plotz Merritt had moved to Atoka, but her sister Frieda had stayed in St. Louis to work, then Cincinnati, then disappeared from the radar screen a couple of years after. No record of her marriage, death, or career choices. So that left a wide-open area when it came to possibilities.

"My bet's on Frieda using her dead sister's identity," Tootsie said, sitting back down at the computer with a fresh cup of coffee.

"It's a distinct possibility. Which leads me to wonder why she'd feel it necessary to do that. There's no criminal record for Frieda. Why should she pretend to be someone else?"

"Maybe she needs to be someone else because of a divorce, credit fraud, or just because she doesn't like her name."

"Yeah, but to take her dead sister's name? That's too creepy, even for the Cheríe Saucier that I met. Of course, she may be psychotic. And she may be a killer. Harry's dead, and so is Julio. We don't know why, and until we figure that out, we won't know where to look for the killer."

"You make me nervous when you use *we* while talking to me, baby."

"Just general reference. Don't worry. I have no intention of dragging you into this except as my research assistant. Okay—research supervisor. You're a genius when it comes to this kind of thing, as you well know."

"It doesn't take a genius to do a little on-line tracking, just someone who knows where to look. I just ask the question. *Ask Jeeves* and *Google* do all the work."

Surprised, Harley said, "You're kidding—so I could find out all this stuff just by going on Google?"

"Darling, not even on your best day. It was a joke. I use a special database that requires an access fee."

"Oh." She grimaced. "I'll pay any fees."

"Don't worry about it." He waggled his brows mysteriously and whispered, "Steve uses it a lot more than I do."

"Ah, the imaginary Steve. One day you'll have to stop blaming all your crimes on him, you know."

"Maybe. So come to my show tonight. It's a special revue. I'll be dressed as Madonna."

"I have a date with Morgan."

"He'll love it."

"I don't think so. He doesn't seem that open to new things."

"Then now is the time to find that out, don't you think?"

Tootsie was right. No point in wasting time on a man who might have prejudices that she wouldn't understand and wouldn't like. Best to find out early on if he was a keeper or a time-waster. She nodded.

"What time do you go on?"

"Ten. At Numbers. You know where that is, don't you?"

"Cooper-Young area, isn't it? And no, I don't know where it is."

He gave her directions, and Harley said she'd be there, with or without Mike Morgan. It was going to be an interesting evening.

The ladies from Iowa were middle-aged and slightly reserved, but really seemed to like the nineteenth century houses at Victorian Village. They'd done Graceland the day before with Charlsie, and were still talking about the seventies styles Elvis had loved, and the shops where they'd obviously spent a lot of tourist dollars on CDs and Elvis memorabilia. One of them had an Elvis wristwatch that played *Hound Dog* on every hour, but other than that, Harley had no gripes about them.

When the Fontaine House tour guide got to the part of her spiel about the resident ghost in the upstairs bedroom, Harley wondered if Aunt Darcy's husband was related to the old family who'd once owned the house. Then she wondered if Paul Fontaine had any connections to his wife's design shop. Maybe she was leaving out a logical suspect. So far, she'd suspected Darcy, Madelyn, and Amanda of at the very least not telling all they should, and at the worst, having had a hand in Harry Gordon's murder. If Paul Fontaine, Aunt Darcy's indulgent but often absent husband, thought Darcy was having an affair with Harry, that'd be a good reason for him to kill Harry. Not that there was a dearth of people who'd seemed to want Harry dead. He hadn't been the most popular guy in Memphis. And she still didn't know all she should about Harry. She really wasn't that good at this detective stuff. But then, she hadn't been that good at corporate banking, and even her tour guide skills were less than they should be. She had to be good at something. Everybody had a talent. What was hers?

While the Iowans were still touring the house, Harley went outside and dug in her brown leather backpack for her cell phone. She turned it on and dialed Tootsie.

When he answered, she said, "I've got an idea. No, not that. Don't be obscene. Since there are a lot more Harry Gordons than there should be, try narrowing the search to Frieda Plotz in St. Louis or Cincinnati, or both. If Frieda doesn't show up, try Cheríe Saucier. You may have to go back a few years. There's got to be a connection between her and Harry before they got to Memphis. Oh, and while you're at it, if there's anything you can find out about Paul Fontaine's financial interests in his wife's shop, that'd be very helpful. Yes, I know I'll owe you big time. Twenty percent of my pay and the purple cocktail dress you've been trying to talk me into giving you. It's my last, so this is a huge sacrifice. It's strapless, so buy your own bra."

She hung up and turned off her phone, then stuck it back into her backpack. She'd check her messages later, after she got the ladies out of the gift shop and while they were touring the Dixon Art Gallery and gardens. There'd be plenty of time then to sit on a bench in the shade and enjoy the weather and catch up on personal messages.

By the time she tactfully removed the ladies from the gift shop and herded them to the van, it was lunchtime. Lunch was a brief stop at the Dixie Café where the ladies tried fried green tomatoes with catfish and hushpuppies. Harley attempted to convince one of them that the whole catfish wouldn't be as good as the filet, but she insisted. When the waiter brought out the entire catfish, tail and fins intact, Harley was prepared. Quickly leaning across the table, she promptly chopped off the tail and filleted the fish with an efficiency she hadn't known she possessed, and explained, "Just think of this as Southern lobster."

The horror on the woman's face disappeared, and she gave a shaky laugh. "Well, I hope it tastes better than it looks."

Harley smiled. "I assure you it does. Have a hushpuppy. They're really good, too."

She understood. Her first encounter with fried catfish had been less than wonderful. Some said it was an acquired taste, but she thought it had more to do with an inherited tolerance for cornmeal and lard. Diva had never considered those part of the basic food groups, and Harley's early childhood had done nothing to prepare her for Southern delicacies. Dulse and bamboo shoots were familiar, but not nearly as tasty as fried cornbread.

After eating her fill of hushpuppies, slaw, and drinking a half-gallon of sweet tea, Harley ushered her group back out to the van for the next stop on their tour. A wind blew popcorn clouds across the bright blue sky, and heat soaked into pavement and asphalt that was made even hotter by car engines and exhaust.

Dixon Gallery on Park Avenue was a sprawling building tastefully flanked by beautiful gardens, donated by an old Memphis family and kept up by the city. Rotating exhibits from Fabergé eggs to Monet paintings inhabited the spacious gallery, and outside in the gardens, the seasonal plantings kept an entire staff of gardeners busy full-time. Harley sat on a concrete bench in the shade just off the circular rose planters. Greenhouses held exotic plants, and a fountain in the distance hosted water plants.

Squinting against the bright light and fighting the rare urge for a cigarette, Harley dialed Tootsie. "Find out anything?" she asked when he answered, interrupting his spiel.

"You're a pest."

"I know. You keep telling me that. One day you're going to hurt my feelings."

"I say it with love."

She smiled. "I know that."

"Well, you called at just the right time. It seems that the most likely of our Harry Gordons has a rather interesting history. Back in the eighties, he worked as a rare coin dealer, before there was a big dust-up about him switching valuable coins for worthless pieces. Then after a brief stint in a Missouri prison he pops up again in another town and career."

"Did that happen to be St. Louis, perhaps?"

"Don't you catch on quick."

"That must be where he met Cheríe or Frieda or whoever she is. My bet's on Frieda. How close am I if I say that Harry got into the antique business after prison?"

"Right on the money. In Cincinnati. He went to work for a dealer who imported pieces from Europe, Africa, all kinds of exotic places. And that's when Cheríe Saucier pops up for the first time since she died. Damn. That sounds funny, doesn't it?"

"Hilarious. Okay, so now we know they probably knew each other in St. Louis, and when he got out of the joint, she followed him to Cincinnati. So how'd he end up in Memphis?"

"There were some complaints in Ohio from people who claimed they'd purchased pieces that were copies instead of genuine. This time ole Harry got five years in an Ohio prison, but he got out early, time off for good behavior. That's when he went to work for your aunt eighteen months ago. And Cheríe went to work for him, best as I can tell. Privacy laws keep a lot of good info secret."

"Unless you're the IRS."

"Did I ever mention that I once worked for the IRS?"

"Tootsie, you're amazing."

"I've heard that. As for Paul Fontaine, he has no financial involvement with Designer's Den that I can find. Now I have to get back to work before Mr. Penney gets nosy. Later, baby."

Smiling, Harley punched in the code to retrieve her messages. Morgan had called. He was at the hideout but would call her again later. The hideout. Sheesh. Undercover cops really did get too full of themselves on occasion. Bobby was right about that.

Carefully putting her cell phone back in the leather case inside her backpack, Harley sat for a moment on the bench and thought about all the seemingly unrelated pieces that were slowly fitting into some kind of pattern—Harry, Cheríe, antiques, stolen coins, art objects and smuggling. Same kind of business, just a different location and delivery method. It still didn't look good for Aunt Darcy.

A breeze picked up, washing the air with the sweet scent of roses, and she looked toward the circular rose beds laid out like a giant wheel. A few Dixon workers labored, and visitors strolled idly in the sunlight. A nice day. She'd go check on her group in a moment, see if they were enjoying themselves or ready to move on. One of them had mentioned the new panda exhibit at the zoo, and Harley was hoping they'd decided against it. It wasn't unusual for a group to change destinations since Memphis Tour Tyme liked to emphasize that they were the flexible tour service instead of holding clients to rigid schedules. Sometimes, since tour agencies had sections of Memphis they divided up, one of the other branches of Tour Tyme took over but kept the same driver. She wanted to get this over with for the day. If she got out early enough, maybe she'd have time to track down Anna Plotz Merritt. It wasn't far to Atoka, if she could remember the best way to get there.

As she was contemplating her route, one of the ladies strolling along the paths stopped to talk to a man digging a hole in one of the rose beds. She wore a huge floppy hat, a sundress that looked like a Vera Wang, and sandals that looked like Payless. Harley frowned. There was something very familiar—wait. Of all the people to see here.

She stood up and sauntered toward the rose beds. Neither of them seemed to notice her, but conversed in tones too low for Harley to hear what they said, even when she got right up on them, close enough to touch the expensive folds of the sundress.

"Well hello, Miss Saucier. Fancy meeting you here."

Cheríe Saucier whirled around, obviously startled, and her eyes went wide, then thinned to narrow slits. "Yes," she said tightly, "what an unpleasant surprise. I hear your aunt's about to be arrested for murdering Harry. Shouldn't you be with your family?"

"Well, one must work to pay the bills, you know. Not everyone prefers stealing to honest labor."

Cheríe sucked in a sharp breath between her teeth, then managed a prissy smile. "Tell that to Darcy Fontaine. Of course, she's a thief *and* a murderer, so I doubt she'd listen. She's more the kind to, say, leave bodies in cellars."

"I knew it was you who locked us in. Too bad we got out, isn't it?"

Cheríe smirked. "I don't know what you're talking about. But then, neither do you. You've just got a lot of questions without answers."

Harley glanced toward the workman, who kept his head down, doggedly digging a hole for a potted rose bush like he didn't want to get involved.

"I have a few questions I'd like to ask you," she said instead of rising to the bait, "but I'd rather do that in private. Unless, of course, you prefer talking to the police."

"Fine." Cheríe barely glanced at the workman leaning on the shovel, his head down to show the crown of his straw hat. "You can lead the way, since I had to ask directions to the gallery entrance."

"Strange, finding you here, of all places. You don't seem the type to enjoy a bit of culture. I'm curious why you're here. Mind sharing that with me?"

"I believe the entrance is this way," Cheríe said. "You have about forty-five feet to ask your questions."

There wasn't a chance to argue as Cheríe started off along the bricked path that led up to the house. After a brief hesitation, Harley followed. She got this really strange feeling, like there was something weird going on, but when she glanced behind her, she didn't see anything out of the ordinary. Just the visitors still ambling along, and the rose bush still waiting by the half-dug hole to be planted.

She caught up with Cheríe near the house. "Look, you can either answer my questions or I'll pass along what I know to the police and you can talk to them. It's up to you."

Halting, Cheríe turned to glare at her, mouth all set in a straight line like she'd just bitten into a sour apple. "What do you want to know?"

"How long you knew Harry, if you met him in St. Louis or knew him before that, and how well you know Frieda Plotz."

For a long moment, Cheríe Saucier just looked at her. The brim of her hat dipped over her forehead, shadowing her expression, but Harley could still see that she was startled at hearing the name Plotz. *Good.*

Apparently, Cheríe had a quick recovery time. She shrugged impatiently.

"I became acquainted with Harry Gordon around five years ago. In St. Louis. I've never met the other person you mentioned."

"Right. You do know I'll find out the truth eventually, don't you? And worse—the police probably already know everything. If I can find it out, I assure you that they're much more efficient than I am at that kind of thing."

It seemed best not to mention Tootsie, or the fact his roommate was a cop and probably unaware of the methods Tootsie used to get information. It was better that way.

"That doesn't concern me," Cheríe said, though Harley was willing to bet it not only concerned her, but scared the hell out of her. "I have nothing to hide. Unlike your aunt. Did you know she was overheard threatening Harry? One of her employees heard her scream at him that she'd see him dead and in hell before she let him ruin her business."

"You know, I find it very odd that you're the only person I've heard say that. Why hasn't this supposed *employee* said anything to the police? It'd seem like pretty important information. If it wasn't coming from just you."

Spite glittered in Cheríe's eyes. "Oh, don't worry. I told the police all about it. Just ask her. She'll tell you the same thing she told me, and I'm sure she's told the cops by now, too."

I'll be glad to," Harley said, growing uneasy since it didn't seem like Cheríe was lying about it. "What's her name?"

"Find that out yourself. I have no intention of doing your work for you. Though what you think you're doing is beyond me, since all you seem to have managed is to make yourself look like an idiot and piss off the cops."

Unfortunately, that was far too close to the truth.

"Now stay away from me," Cherie said abruptly. A gust of wind caught at the brim of her hat and she put up a hand to hold it on her head.

Harley lifted a brow. "Wow, some biceps you've got there, Miss Saucier. You look pretty strong. Strong enough to, say, lift a dead man and hang him off some elk horns."

"Come near me again, I'll swear out a complaint for harassment," Cherie hissed, sounding so much like a cobra that Harley wouldn't have been surprised to see a forked tongue flick out and fangs dripping with venom. Ouch. Must have hit her where it hurt. She smiled.

"You think this is harassment? Just wait. If I'm going to pay a fine, I'd rather it be after I get what I want. I already know you're not who you claim to be, and that you're neck-deep in a nest of vipers. You don't have to go down with them. If you know who killed Harry, tell me. Or better yet—tell the police."

For a moment, something flickered in Cherie's eyes, and Harley could have sworn it was grief. Then the moment passed, and the woman gave her a look of loathing. "Go to hell."

"Thanks for the invite, but I'm having too much fun here."

Cherie turned around and began walking fast, away from Harley and toward the gallery. When Harley followed, Cherie broke into a run and pushed past exiting visitors to go in the back way. Just as Harley got there, a gallery employee pulled the door closed.

"Go around to the front, please," he said, shaking his head when Harley tried to open the door anyway.

"But I'm with someone. She just went in—a flowery dress and big hat?"

Still shaking his head, the man turned with his back to the French door, and Harley gave up and ran around the side to go in the front way. There were only two exits or entrances that she could recall, so maybe she'd catch Cherie coming out the front way.

There was no sign of her. By the time Harley got inside, she had no idea where in the maze of walls, hung with paintings and flanked by glass cases, Cherie could have disappeared. Not that she'd get any more information out of her, but if she could unnerve her enough, maybe she'd make a mistake of some kind. It had been Harley's experience that rattled people tended to commit unexpected follies.

Like herself, for instance.

Unexpectedly, Cherie Saucier rounded a corner and ran into her, looking as startled as a deer caught in the headlights. Before Harley could react, Cheríe did.

The hushed quiet of the gallery shattered as Cheríe yelped, then gave Harley a shove that sent her stumbling backward into a glass case set against the wall. Barely staying upright, Harley seized on the first object at hand and flung it at Cheríe's head. Cheríe ducked. Pottery smashed into a dozen pieces, flying through the air, and someone screamed. Not Cheríe. She ran, but one of the employees rushed Harley like a Dallas Cowboys linebacker, tackling her around the waist and taking her down to the floor.

Trying to wiggle free to go after Cheríe, Harley quickly realized that the two hundred pound woman had her in a death grip. She went limp, but that only gave the employee a greater incentive to squeeze the air from Harley's lungs. Right before she got to the passing out stage, the weight miraculously lifted, and Harley sat up coughing and sputtering.

"Dammit, you nearly killed me," she got out, but by then the employee had backup, and Harley was hustled off to the office to make explanations while the police were summoned. Not one of her finest moments.

Fortunately, one of the Iowa women had seen Cheríe assault Harley, or it could have been much worse. As it was, Memphis Tour Tyme had to make good on the broken Edwardian vase and promise not to send Harley back to the art gallery. Mr. Penney was most unhappy with her.

"Your personal problems are overlapping onto company time," he said, and his usually dour expression went even more grim than normal. "Perhaps you need a leave of absence to sort out your family affairs."

"Uh, unpaid?"

The look he gave her indicated affirmative, and Harley escaped Penney's office as soon as possible. Tootsie shook his head when she leaned over his reception desk.

"Baby, you're lucky you still have a job. He wanted to fire you. Fortunately, I convinced him that wouldn't be in his best interests."

"Just what kind of hold do you have over the ogre? There must be something. He's not the understanding type. He's one of those ultraconservatives that borders on fanatical."

"Don't look a gift horse in the mouth, baby."

"I never have understood that cliché."

"It has something to do with telling a horse's age. Or being smart enough to shut up while you still have a job."

"Ah. That last I understand quite well. Thanks, Tootsie. Well, I'm going to look at this as a positive opportunity."

"Oh please, God, don't tell me."

"Yep. Now I have more time to focus on who killed Harry. If Cherie is to be believed—and since she's already told the police about it, it's pretty hard to unring that bell—there's a witness who overheard Darcy threaten to kill Harry. If there is a witness, and this witness did tell the cops Aunt Darcy threatened Harry, then I want to find out who it is and what they heard. It's certain Bobby won't tell me anything, even if I went temporarily insane and asked him."

"Any hope of talking you out of this?"

"Not much. The sooner the police have the real killer in custody, the sooner Aunt Darcy pays me the five thousand she'll owe me, and the sooner I can come back to work. After a short vacation, maybe. Alaska might be nice this time of year. I've heard those cruises can be very relaxing."

"Darling, I'm sure you'd manage to change all that."

"I'm beginning to think that's my talent. I've been wondering about it. Everyone has a talent, y'know? Maybe mine is snooping."

Tootsie lifted a brow and pursed his lips. "That's not a talent, honey. It's more on the level of snoring. Not quite annoying enough to get you killed, but close."

"Okay, we'll refer to it as my new habit then. Did you find the address of the sister in Atoka, by chance?"

"By Internet, not by chance. Darling, think about it before you carry that fine little ass of yours all the way out to the wilds of Atoka. Two people have been killed. I'm not at all sure you should do any more snooping."

"You're probably right. Now, about that address . . . "

Tootsie gave it to her, though not without a lot of eye rolling, pouting, and warnings that she should let the police handle it and not risk getting into any trouble.

"Don't worry," she said, "I'll be careful. Just don't mention any of this to Morgan tonight, okay? No point in worrying him."

"Um hm. You two just make it in time for my performance tonight. Let me meet this man of yours so I can see for myself if he's good enough for you. You'd think he'd be keeping you home at nights instead of letting you run the streets and sleep with corpses."

Harley shuddered at the memory. "Stop complaining. All night in the dark with a corpse and a crying Cami taught me a few things."

"Let's hope it's the right things. I'm not seeing much improvement yet."

"You'll see. I'm much more cautious."

He sighed. "Somehow, I don't find that as comforting as I once would have. Lately, your survival skills have been stretched to the limit."

"Don't *worry*," Harley said again, "I have no intention of getting into any trouble."

And she meant that. She really did.

Ten

Morgan surprised Harley. When he showed up at her apartment looking delicious in a dark blue knit shirt and tight black jeans that hid none of his best attributes, she half-expected him to refuse to go to Tootsie's show at Numbers.

Instead, he shrugged. "Sure. No problem, if you'd rather go there than a movie."

"Uh, you *do* know these are guys dressed up as women, don't you?"

He grinned, and she loved the way it deepened the sexy groove on one side of his mouth. "Yeah, I know. We had the place under surveillance one time. No, I won't tell you why. That was a few years ago. Everything came out all right."

"You're a man of constant surprises," Harley said. "Is there anything else I should know about you?"

"If you mean, do I like to play dress up in fishnet hose and women's underwear, no. But that doesn't mean I have a problem with guys who do. As long as they stay on their side of the fence, if you know what I mean."

Harley smiled. One more mark on the plus side of her mental checklist. As a boyfriend, he had real possibilities. Not that she was looking. No, the best thing to do was just float along and see how things worked out. To hell with her biological clock or Cami's warnings. They were two different people.

"Then I'm sure we'll have a good time," she said, "because I understand most of those guys are really good at fence-sitting."

Morgan gave her a skeptical look, but didn't balk, so she figured he was doing all right.

After Wally burgers at Morgan's favorite dive, a hamburger joint on Poplar that served cheeseburgers named after the first owner, cold beer, and hot grease, they went out the back door to reach Morgan's car. It was jammed between an old van and a Jaguar. Wally's had an eclectic clientele. Cool night air washed over Harley's arms and the back of her neck, and crickets in the weeds behind a tall wooden fence that had seen better days almost drowned out the sounds of traffic. Red, blue, yellow and green lights along Poplar flashed off and on, advertising liquor stores, restaurants, dollar stores, and a major pharmacy. The ripe smell of fried onions had permeated Harley's clothes, and she rolled down the car window to air out.

"You didn't eat much," Mike said, and she shrugged.

"I'm not that into cheeseburgers as big as truck tires. One of those could feed a family of four for a week. Besides, you ate my leftovers so nothing went to waste."

"You sure you're not a vegetarian? I never see you eat burgers."

"If you're referring to half a cow between two buns, no, you'll never see me eat that much meat. No wonder that's your favorite place to go. Talk about a value meal."

"We could have gone somewhere classier. Somewhere you usually go."

"Like Sekisui? Somehow, I didn't figure you as a sushi kind of guy."

He laughed and changed the subject. "So how do you like my ride?"

"Nice. One of your undercover cars?"

"Nope. Not anymore. I bought this at the police auction a while back."

Harley nodded approval. It was an older model Corvette, a red convertible that had either been extremely well kept, or completely remodeled. Maybe the last, because this one had a built-in CD player in the dash.

"Is that Meatloaf?" she said when a familiar song played, and then sang along to *Paradise by the Dashboard Lights*. That song always put her in a good mood.

"It reminds me of my foolish youth," she said when Morgan asked if she wanted to hear it again. "I lost my virginity to that song. In the back seat of a car, with the dashboard lights—such a romantic glow. Ah, those were the days."

"Half the teenagers in the eighties lost their virginity during that song," Morgan said with a laugh. "The power of suggestion."

"Oh please. As if any of us needed a suggestion. All we needed was the right person and fifteen minutes alone."

"That long? Most teenage boys have the staying power of a gnat."

"Yeah, but I think Bobby had been practicing alone in his room at night."

"Bobby . . . *Baroni?*"

Oops. She caught his surprised glance at her and managed a careless shrug. "That's the one. It was a long time ago. We both realized pretty quickly we function much better as friends."

For a minute he didn't say anything. Harley wondered if it bothered him, but even if she'd wanted to, there was no way to undo what she'd said. After a moment of silence, she figured he'd had time to get over the shock and said, "I'm not usually the kiss and tell type. I just kinda forgot for a minute that you know him."

"Don't worry. Your secret's safe with me."

His grin let her know he wasn't that bothered. Another mark on the plus side. Damn. If the past was any indication, right around now she'd find out his divorce wasn't final yet or his mother wanted him home by midnight to massage her feet. She hated waiting for the other shoe to drop. The suspense could get unbearable.

"Has it occurred to you," she said to change the subject, "that Harry Gordon's car wasn't at the shop when he was murdered? How did he get there? And who has it now? Dead men don't usually drive."

"Probably the murderer. Or it's been ditched somewhere, sold to a chop shop and is in ten different counties by now. The police haven't found it yet. But they will."

"If it was the murderer, that lets Aunt Darcy off the hook, wouldn't you think? She can't drive two cars at once."

"And she can't account for all her time, either. She could have come back for it. Taken a taxi out there. Gotten someone to pick it up. Gave it to a crack dealer."

"Now you're bordering on the ridiculous, but I get your point." Obviously, the police had already investigated all those possibilities. There had to be another explanation. One that she liked a lot better. One that didn't make it so plausible Aunt Darcy could have murdered Harry.

Harley settled back against the car seat and tried not to think about it. The night was gorgeous, not to mention the man sitting beside her. The top was down on the car, the smell of magnolia blossoms was heady, and Diva had said everything would turn out all right in the end. Right or not, Harley was going to go with that promise for the evening.

Numbers was full of gorgeous women who weren't. Lucky for her that her self-esteem was pretty healthy, Harley thought, or she'd feel extremely intimidated by these *ladies* who'd been born with a Y chromosome. How could men look as damn good as women? It didn't seem fair somehow.

"Hey baby," a familiar voice said right behind her, and Harley turned, then jumped back when confronted by what looked very much like Madonna in her Viking queen costume. Silky blond hair that fell around bare shoulders framed a carefully made-up face, complete with the tiny mole at the corner of red lips. He wore black leather, fishnet hose, and carried a short whip, and the bra had huge brass brads along the straps, band, and the tips of very pointed cups.

"Good God, Tootsie, those things are dangerous. You could poke someone's eyes out."

He laughed and wiggled the sharply-pointed bra cups. "Like 'em?"

"They'd make great oil funnels. You look very Goth. Is that *cleavage*?"

"Of course, dahling," Tootsie said with a laugh. "A little bit of false advertising never hurts. So, is this the hot boyfriend?"

He was looking behind her, surveying Morgan through long false eyelashes that did nothing to hide his obvious assessment.

"Oh. Yeah. Mike Morgan, this is Tootsie Rowell, Madonna's evil twin sister."

"No, I'm Madonna's *better* twin sister." Tootsie shook hands with Morgan, and it was odd seeing him look like a woman and act like a man as he made eye contact and offered a firm hand grip. He seemed to size Morgan up, but Morgan was doing the same. Harley tried not to roll her eyes. Even men in bras had that male territorial thing going on, it seemed.

"Okay, now that the introductions are over," she said in a chirpy voice meant to convey reassurance to both men, "show us where you want us to sit."

Their version of arm wrestling ended, and Tootsie smiled. "Very nice." He looked back at Harley. "There's been a wardrobe malfunction—don't get excited, it's nothing like Janet Jackson's—so instead of wearing my black velvet evening gown and long white gloves, I've dressed as the Viking queen. It just seems so very appropriate anyway, don't you think?"

He seated them at a table in front and ordered them a complimentary beer. Then with a promise to return after the show, he disappeared into the back. Harley watched him go, admiring how good he looked in spike heels and the black leather bikini studded with brass buttons.

"Nice guy," Morgan commented, then frowned and said, "Or nice girl. Which does he prefer?"

"He's not sensitive about it. He's come to terms with his lifestyle and doesn't really care what everyone else thinks. He's very well-adjusted."

"That's good to know. Not many in his position are so lucky."

This was totally weird. A conversation about the lifestyle of a cross-dresser and gay adult in current society was not something she'd ever envisioned having with a man like Morgan. Or anyone else. Thankfully, the show started and four black guys dressed as the Supremes in soft rainbow shades of chiffon came on-stage and did a great job with *My Baby Love*, then segued into *Where Did Our Love Go* before relinquishing the stage to Tootsie-Madonna.

With his blond wig, Viking queen costume, and alto vocals, Tootsie was a hit, as he'd promised. Just like in Madonna's video, some well-built young men in tight black leather pants hefted Tootsie onto their shoulders and carried him around while he belted out *Material Girl.*

Harley sighed. "He's got great legs. And he might be wearing the wrong costume for that song, but he's much prettier than Madonna."

Morgan just grinned.

After the show and Tootsie's standing ovation, he came to sit down at the table in front, still in drag. "You were great," Harley said. "And I mean that sincerely. You're fantastic."

"I don't have Madonna's range, but I do all right." Tootsie lifted a beer. "Here's to all our friendships, may they endure everything that life throws at us."

They clinked beer bottles together and Harley said, "*Sláinte.*"

"Did you just say something naughty?" Tootsie asked with a lift of his carefully plucked eyebrow.

"No, it's Gaelic for 'to your health.'. My great-grandmother taught it to me years ago. She likes to take a wee nip now and then of what she refers to as her beverage, but I happen to know it's a quart bottle of beer. PBR. Warm. Hidden between the washer and dryer in her laundry room."

"PBR?"

"Pabst Blue Ribbon."

Morgan looked amazed. "Do they still make that?"

"They do."

Laughing, he clinked his half-full beer against her second one. "Then slaw—what?"

"Slawn-cha m'hor, cor-deh," she enunciated, "or great health, friends."

"*Sleinte cairde!*" they all said in unison, and Harley smiled happily. The evening was going along much better than she'd dared hope. Warmed by friendship and two Coronas, she felt almost giddy.

It was bound to go downhill.

A little past midnight, when the club had thinned out some and even those unemployed were considering going home, Harley made one last trip to the bathroom before they left. The lights had gone out in the long hallway. It was pretty dim except for the glow from the bar and an exit sign, but she had already made a few trips and figured she could find it even in the dark.

One glance in the mottled bathroom mirror was enough to convince her that four beers were past her limit; she looked like something out of Fright Night, with her hair in wispy spikes on one side, limp on the other. And she had what she referred to as Christmas Eyes, green orbs surrounded by bloodshot red. Yep. Time to call it a night.

Just as she was getting her jeans pulled back up and tucking the ends of her tee shirt into the waistband, the bathroom light went out. "Hey! I'm still in here!"

Man, these guys closed early. Most bars stayed open until two, the cutoff time for serving alcohol. Muttering to herself, she fumbled with the latch on the stall door, then eased out and felt her way along the tiled wall. She bumped into the sink and ricocheted off the opposite wall, swearing loudly as she careened toward the door. She felt like a pool ball. That thought made her giggle.

"Six-ball in the corner pocket," she sang out as she wrenched open the bathroom door, and ran right into a solid wall of muscle. Before she had time to apologize, a smelly bag was yanked over her head and her arms were pinned in a viselike grip as she was dragged a few feet down the hallway and out into the alley. She knew that last only because she felt a warm breeze on her bare arms and heard the noisy rattle of the central air unit that cooled the club. There was something else, too—a car motor close by. It sounded like it had bad gas, the pistons knocking loudly.

Whoever had her meant to put her in that car, and she was just as determined not to go as he was to force her into it. It was a fierce struggle. Somehow, Harley got her legs up, bent, and one foot braced on each side of the open door, resisting his efforts to wedge her inside. Breathing hard, he swore at her in an unfamiliar language that didn't need an interpreter to understand, then grabbed at her legs. To do that, he had to release one of her arms. She made instant use of that flaw in his plan, and blindly grabbed for a handful of his clothes to pull him off-balance.

Fortunately, she'd grabbed a handful of his anatomy that effected her immediate release. He made a high-pitched sound like a loose fan belt and dropped her, and she gave a hard twist of her wrist just for good measure. His family jewels were probably missing a few stones by now, she figured as she crawled away and stumbled to her feet, ripping the bag from her head to yell for help.

That was when someone smacked her on the side of the head and she saw stars explode in front of her eyes. A veritable meteor shower of them. She hit the ground in the alley hard, felt her palms scrape on asphalt, and heard bells ringing and drums thumping loudly.

Music? How lovely . . . Unable to move, she just lay there staring up at the stars rotating in the sky like pinwheels.

Then someone bent over her, squeezing her cheeks together and peering into her eyes. "Hey, are you all right? Talk to me, honey. Focus . . . that's right, both eyes looking in the same direction at once, now."

A face slowly came into focus. She blinked. Diana Ross? "Why'd you break up the Supremes?"

Diana laughed and said to someone else nearby, "She's coming around. She's just not making much sense yet."

"Trust me, she doesn't make much sense when she *hasn't* been hit in the head," a familiar voice said. "I've never met anyone who can't even go to the bathroom without getting into some kind of trouble."

That would be Morgan, Harley thought hazily. *He sounds upset.*

While Diana Ross helped her sit up, Tootsie came back from the mouth of the alley. He was breathing hard like he'd been running. "I couldn't catch him. She okay?"

"Except for being hit in the head, she's just fine. Maybe it knocked some sense into her, though that's not likely." Morgan knelt in front of her, examining her head.

Sounding sympathetic, Tootsie said, "I can't believe someone tried to kidnap her. That's never happened here before."

"It was only a matter of time with her running loose. Look at her. She'll have a huge lump on the side of her head. She's lucky that's all she got."

"Don't talk about me like I'm not here," Harley said crossly. "I can still hear, y'know."

If Morgan hadn't looked so worried, she might have been really mad at him, but the look he gave her said a lot more than his words. "Can you get up?"

She nodded. "Yeah. I think."

But she was so wobbly he had to grab her before she hit the pavement again. He slid an arm around her back and held her against his side, while Diana Ross fluttered around with his hands outstretched saying, "She looks like she's going to pass out."

"I've got her. She won't fall."

That was the good thing about Morgan. She could depend on him to hold her up when things got really shaky.

"Until I'm ready to drop her on her ass, that is," Morgan added, and Harley revised her opinion to reflect that he could certainly be unpredictable.

Once back inside, with a Coke in one hand and a bag of ice held to her now throbbing head, Harley eyed Morgan warily when he pulled up a chair right in front of her and sat down.

"So what happened, Harley?"

"I don't know. I went to the bathroom and the lights went out. When I came out, this guy was there with a bag that he pulled over my head. Then he dragged me outside and tried to get me into his car. I, uh, managed to get hold of his goods and he let go of me. I didn't get far before I got hit in the head with something. And the next thing I know, Diana Ross is telling me to focus."

Morgan just looked at her for a moment, and then he grinned. It was unexpected and a relief. "You grabbed his crotch?"

"Well, I didn't mean to. It just happened. Not that I'm sorry."

"Did you get a good look at him?"

She started to shake her head, then winced at the stabbing pain and thought better of it. "No. But he spoke a foreign language."

"Did you recognize it?"

"Spanish, I think. Maybe Italian. I'm not really up on that kind of thing."

"How about his car? Did you get a good look at his car?"

"No. It was dark. Blue, maybe. Or green. Maybe black. Well, it all happened so fast and all I could think about was getting away—but the motor was noisy, like it was missing, or had bad gas. A kind of *ka-chink ka-chink* sound, like rocks rattling around."

"That only applies to three-quarters of the cars in Memphis."

"I know. Sorry."

"That's okay. It was probably the car that I made earlier."

She looked at him quizzically. "Uh, what does that mean?"

"Earlier, I thought we were being followed. I made—identified—someone behind us."

"Tonight?"

"Yep. Dark blue Pontiac, older model, bashed-in left front fender, vanity plate in the front that said *Hombre* in purple glitter."

"And you didn't think it worth mentioning to me?"

"You gotta be kidding. All I needed was you playing detective tonight. Besides, I thought it'd work out better if I called it in and had him checked out."

"Apparently, it didn't. Did you get his plates?"

"Expired plates registered in Ohio."

She perked up. "Cincinnati, maybe?"

His eyes narrowed slightly. "Maybe. Why?"

"Oh, no reason. No reason at all."

If only her head didn't hurt so badly, she could think this through. It was a wonder her brains weren't scrambled, having been knocked around three times in only a few weeks. There was definitely something to be said for wearing helmets. From that thought, she leaped to the related connection with motorcycle helmets, to the motorcycle in her parents' garage, to having been followed. Of course. If she was being followed, they'd expect her to take her car. And she knew just the thing to throw them off.

That was the reason she had Morgan drop her off at her parents' house that night, instead of taking her home where she knew she'd be more comfortable and happier. It was a price she was willing to pay to find out what she could about Cheríe Saucier. She just knew Cheríe was behind this latest assault. Now it was personal. The bitch had cost her.

"Are you sure you're all right?" Mike asked again when she had his car door open in front of her parents' bungalow-style house on Douglass. "I can take you to the Minor Med for an x-ray if you're feeling bad."

"No, I'm fine. Or will be once I've had a good night's sleep.

Honest. I'd just feel better if I didn't stay alone at my apartment tonight. Besides, you have to be at work early and I've been neglecting Diva and Yogi lately. I promised I'd spend some time with them, and this seems like as good a time as any."

All of that was true, except for her motivation. And he didn't need to know that. No point in worrying him unduly. He obviously tended to fret about things.

"I don't know why," he said slowly, "but I have an uneasy feeling about this."

"Don't. I'm fine. I'll be fine. Nothing is going to happen to me here."

"My past experience leads me to believe otherwise."

"An anomaly. Murderers don't often show up at my parents' door, I promise. And King the Wonder Dog is here. He's a great burglar alarm and deterrent to crime."

"He's a one-dog demolition crew."

She smiled. "You know him so well."

"I'll call you in the morning to see how you're feeling."

"Not too early. I'll probably sleep in."

With Morgan watching, she stepped out of the car and closed the door, then went up the sidewalk to the front porch of the darkened house. Diva's wind chimes tinkled in a light breeze, and the air smelled of magnolia blossoms and wisteria, redolent with the suggestion of lemon and grape. As usual, the front door was unlocked, and King—contrary to her assertion he was a great burglar alarm—was nowhere to be found as she let herself into the house.

She found aspirin in the kitchen, and took two with a glass of water, then went upstairs to her old bedroom. It was much as it had been when she'd lived here, save for remnants of Diva's craft-making scattered on the dresser and on top of the bookshelves. Her brother Eric's room was across the hall, and her parents' room was at the end of the house. A big bathroom separated the bedrooms. The comfortable house was Yogi's childhood home and inheritance, safe and secure, a place Harley knew and loved. Not that she wanted to live with her parents. She just liked knowing that some things hadn't changed, as irritating as that might be at times.

As if conjured up by the word *irritating*, Eric poked his head in her bedroom door. "Hey, cool chick. Thought I heard somebody in here."

"You thought right." She eyed him. His hair was jet black this week, with a wide stripe of vivid purple down the middle. "Dude, you look like a psychedelic skunk," she said, and he grinned.

"Exactly the look I was going for. So why are you here in the middle of the night?"

"Homesick for Diva's cooking."

"Riiight. You'll have to come up with a better lie than that. I don't think even Diva likes her cooking."

"King seems to like it all right."

"King," Eric pointed out, "also likes to eat out of garbage cans. His taste buds can't be trusted."

Because that was so obviously true, Harley took the conversation in another direction. "I guess you've got class in the morning?"

"No, chick, it's summer. I'm out of class." He came in and perched on the edge of her bed. He wore a black *Slayer* tee shirt and baggy black pants with about a dozen silver zippers in the wide legs. "I'm teaching guitar to a few students for some extra cash."

"You've gotten a *job?*"

"Well, don't sound so surprised. I'm not a complete slug."

"Dude, I'm speechless."

He grinned and blinked his sleepy blue eyes. "Don't make promises you can't keep. So, I guess you'll be here for breakfast."

"Probably not. I've got a few things to do. Besides, I'm not sure I could stomach Diva's idea of breakfast. At least, not before noon."

"Do what me and Yogi do—eat enough to make her happy, then go to McDonald's for a sausage biscuit."

"I knew he'd been cheating. I found hamburger wrappers in his workshop a couple of weeks ago."

"Yeah, well, don't tell Diva. She thinks he's just eating bean sprouts."

"She probably knows better. It's not easy keeping secrets from her."

Eric shrugged. "Yeah, but she doesn't let on. It's like one of those secrets we all know but we all ignore, y'know?"

Because she did know, and because it was uncomfortably eerie that Diva far too often had the power of knowing what she was thinking, Harley decided to try to leave before her mother got up in the morning. It'd be so much easier than making explanations.

She'd have managed it, too, if King hadn't decided to belatedly do his burglar alarm duty and bark ferociously at her. He grabbed the hem of her old jeans she'd found in the closet and tugged like she'd come to steal the family heirlooms.

"Nice doggy," she whispered in an effort to get him to shut up, but despite gripping the frayed hem of her jeans in his teeth, he still managed to make such a ruckus that her father came out of his bedroom into the upstairs hallway.

"Harley," he said with a sleepy but pleased smile, "it's you."

"Yep, it's me. Hope I didn't wake you. It's early, almost the crack of nine."

Yogi nodded. His hair stood on end atop his head, his usual ponytail loose and touching his shoulders, his tee shirt and baggy boxer shorts a familiar sight. "That's all right. I should be up early anyway. Got a few things to finish up before the flea market this weekend. Then I have to go jogging."

"Jogging?" Harley stared at him. "You? Why are you going jogging?"

"King, stop that," Yogi said, and the dog finally released the leg of her jeans and sat down to stare adoringly up at her father. "Well, I've put on a little weight, and when I tried on my Elvis costume yesterday, I couldn't get it fastened across my stomach. Besides, King needs the exercise so he won't try to get out so often."

"I seem to recall saying that myself. Did you talk to the Border Collie Rescue group?"

Yogi nodded. "They said if he gets enough playtime, he's not as likely to try to roam."

Harley thought that was a bit optimistic of them, but anything that made Yogi feel better was certainly worth a try. She said, "That's nice, Yogi. Is it Elvis week already?"

"No, but I've only got two months to get ready. Want some breakfast?"

The good thing about her father was that he often took what she said at face value and didn't ask too many probing questions. So when she told him she'd decided to take her bike out for a spin in the nice weather, he just smiled and told her to have fun.

Diva, however, who got up and came downstairs to the kitchen before she could ease out the back door, fixed her with one of those riveting gazes that always made Harley feel like she knew all. "Be careful," she said. "Things are not what they seem."

"They rarely are. I don't suppose you have any specifics you'd like to share?"

Yawning, Diva shook her head. "You'll do what you feel you must anyway. It's your nature to be independent. It's one of your strengths."

That was nice, Harley thought, and smiled. It sounded much better to be independent than obstinate or stubborn, both of which had been applied to her far too frequently lately.

"Thanks, Diva. No, I don't want breakfast, I'm in a hurry. I'll be back later, and we can visit. I'll catch you up on everyone."

It was indicative of her mother's familial detachment that she didn't ask about her sister or parents, just commented vaguely that everything would turn out all right.

As Harley started for the door, Diva added, "Avoid geese, Harley. They nip."

Another obscure observation from the Sage of Douglass Street. "I will," Harley promised, and went out to the garage. Her bike was under a tarp and surrounded by paint cans, various PVC pipes, metal cabinets, ladders and old chairs, as well as car parts. A tricked-out Harley-Davidson Softail Deuce with over/under dual exhaust lurked beneath the tarp, and when she pulled off the heavy cover, she sighed with pleasure. There it was, gleaming with chrome, gold and black and all hers. Twin 88 cams made it purr like a kitten or roar like a lion.

She took her helmet off the buddy bar and fired up the bike, fastening the straps under her chin while it idled. Yogi met her in the driveway.

"Give me a quick ride? It won't take long."

Eying him, she nodded. "Jogging to McDonald's?"

"Don't tell your mother."

"Are you kidding? And lose any leverage I might have for the future?"

Yogi grinned and straddled the bike behind her. McDonald's wasn't far, and by the time they'd cruised through the drive-out window and back down Highland to Douglass, he'd finished his sausage biscuits. How he ate with a forty-mile an hour wind in his face, she had no idea, but he managed just fine.

"You've got sausage grease on your mouth," she said when she dropped him off at the end of the driveway, and he did a quick, guilty pass of his hand over his lips. "Diva probably knows anyway," she added, and he shrugged.

"As long as I don't give her proof, she's happy."

"I never thought my father would have to hide a love affair with a hamburger."

"Cheeseburger and sausage biscuits." Yogi grinned when she shook her head and gave the bike gas. Really, dealing with family peculiarities could be interesting and amusing.

Next stop was the design shop. It'd reopened for the employees to tidy up this morning. The only obvious evidence of the murder was a shred of yellow crime tape that had come loose and been blown into the top of a tree where it fluttered like a banner. Several cars were parked in front. She recognized none of them. A *Closed* sign still hung on the door, but she went in anyway.

A thin woman wearing a brown pantsuit with a coral scarf draped around the neck met her three steps into the showroom. Her brown hair had been pulled back into a tight bun on the nape of her neck, and she had a look on her face like she'd just stepped in dog poop.

"I'm sorry dear. We're closed . . . for inventory. May I help you?"

"It's possible." Harley smiled, aware that her jeans and tee shirt marked her as a customer unable to afford so much as a pillow from Designer's Den. "My aunt is Darcy Fontaine."

"Oh?" She sounded slightly incredulous.

"Yes. I'd like to ask a few questions of the employees."

"I'm afraid that's not possible. They're all rather busy."

"Too busy to keep dear Aunt Darcy out of prison?"

Miss Dog Poop hesitated. With a little coaxing—and a show of ID in case she'd come to rob them—she was given limited access to the employees who'd shown up for work. Three had quit. Fortunately, by process of elimination that took a half hour, she finally found the designer that Cherie claimed had heard Darcy threaten Harry. In her early twenties, Linda Moore looked defiant but honest.

"Where did you hear her threaten to kill Harry?" Harley asked. "And when?"

"I didn't want to make any trouble for Mrs. Fontaine, but the police asked me if I'd heard anything odd between them and I had to say what I heard. I won't lie."

"I understand. Really I do. As long as it's the truth, it can only help." She hoped. Since it was out anyway, she might as well know exactly what had been said.

Linda hesitated, then said, "It was Thursday afternoon. I'd gone to get a pair of crystal candlesticks from the buffet in the Victorian Room. They were in the hallway just outside, before you get to the Edwardian Room. They got a bit loud, and I overheard them."

"What was said?"

"Mr. Gordon had come in with some kind of carved box in his hand. I didn't see it clearly myself, but Mrs. Fontaine stopped him. She said if he was endangering her business with that kind of thing, she'd see him dead. He laughed at her, and she said, 'I mean it, Harry. I'll kill you myself if I have to!' and he just laughed again and said, 'You don't have the guts to do it. Besides, you need me.' That's when I bumped into the case clock and they heard me." Flipping a lock of light hair from her eyes, she said, "That's it. That's all I heard."

Damning, in light of what had happened a few hours later. Was that why Darcy had been so rattled when she'd come out to the storage area Thursday afternoon? Had she seen Harry come in with more smuggled goods?

"Thank you, Miss Moore. I'm sure Aunt Darcy appreciates your help."

That lie should have made her nose grow a foot. It'd hardly be a help if Darcy ended up being charged with murder on the testimony of this witness. And that, unfortunately, seemed like a sure thing.

Before heading out to Atoka for a conversation with the Plotz sister, she cruised by her apartment building. Across the street, the park had its share of visitors, carloads of mommies and kiddies arriving at the zoo, bicyclists, and patrons visiting the Brooks Art Gallery. It wasn't too hard to blend in and still get a good look at the street running in front of her building, just to see if there were any cars staking out her car and apartment.

There was a dark blue Pontiac with a bashed-in front fender parked on Tucker as she'd thought there might be. Her stalker was so predictable, and obviously not too smart or he'd be in a different vehicle. She pulled over to one side under a tree, retrieved her cell phone—heavily padded by a leather case and wrapped in a thick scarf inside her backpack—and dialed Bobby. He answered on the second ring.

"Hi," she said cheerily, "I have a favor to ask."

"No."

"You haven't heard the favor yet."

"Whatever it is—no."

"Bobby, Bobby, you're being shortsighted. I may have Harry Gordon's murderer parked outside my apartment."

After a brief silence, Bobby said, "Then let him in. It'd solve so many of my problems."

"I know you don't mean that." When Bobby stopped laughing, she added, "He attacked me last night at Numbers. It occurred to me that he's probably the same guy who killed Harry, though I haven't yet figured out why. Anyway, I thought you might want to arrest him on some pretext, assault or illegal parking or whatever, while you connect him to the murder. I'm sure he's involved in it, and probably the guy who did it."

"Harley—"

"Ask Morgan about it. He was with me last night when I was attacked. He ran the guy's plates, and they're from Ohio and Harry Gordon was in Ohio before he came to work with Aunt Darcy."

"Harley—"

"The least you can do is talk to Morgan before you make an arrest."

"We already have a suspect in custody."

"You do?" She knew that she wasn't going to like what he said next, and she didn't.

"We brought in Darcy Fontaine this morning. Harry Gordon was killed with her gun, and so was Julio Melendez. Her prints are all over it, she had motive, and her alibi didn't hold up. I tried to call you, but you had your phone turned off."

"Oh. I thought Harry was killed by an elk horn."

"No, he was just hung on an elk horn. He was killed by a nine millimeter bullet. Just like the one that killed Julio Melendez."

Some investigator she was, Harley thought in disgust, she'd never even asked what killed Julio. Somehow, it hadn't seemed that important. Dead was dead.

"I didn't know Darcy even had a gun, Bobby. Are you sure it belonged to her?"

"Registered in her name, with her prints on it. It's a safe bet it's hers."

Aunt Darcy was just full of little surprises. Damn her. She could have at least mentioned the small fact she owned a gun that had turned out to be the murder weapon.

"So where'd you find the gun?"

"In Mrs. Fontaine's car."

A string of expletives danced in her head, but she restrained herself long enough to ask, "I suppose the case against her is pretty strong?"

"Strong enough that the DA is seeking an indictment. Sorry, Harley. I know she's your aunt, but it really looks like she's guilty."

"Bobby, Aunt Darcy may be a lot of things, but you know she's not a killer."

"That's not what the evidence says. And that's what we have to go by."

"Did you check out the other designers? The delivery guys? The office workers?"

"You know we did. They've all been ruled out. Except for Julio, and he was killed before Harry Gordon, according to the coroner."

She sighed. "Okay, will you at least check out this guy waiting outside my apartment? There's got to be a good reason he attacked me last night."

"Harley, I know any number of people who'd want to attack you. But I'll send out some uniforms anyway."

"Thanks."

"Stay inside until they've had a chance to check him out, okay? Don't do anything on your own. *Stay away from him*, Harley."

It seemed best not to tell him she was already outside. "I promise I won't try to talk to him."

"Or follow him or pelt him with eggs, or anything else."

"Bobby, you have such a vivid imagination. Or good memory. I seem to recall an incident in your childhood that involved a dozen eggs, a neighbor's house, and the police."

"Good-bye, Harley."

She smiled as she hung up. Sometimes it was so easy to fluster him.

Atoka was on the northeast side of Memphis, a small community that hadn't yet been swallowed up by the larger city, so it still had that country feel to it. The inevitable house trailers on one to ten acre lots were scattered about, with older homes on decreasing farmlands still in the majority. New subdivisions were springing up on bare lots of what had once been corn or cotton fields, big houses built so close together the residents could lean out their upstairs windows to exchange handshakes if they wanted. Suburban living at its finest.

Harley found Anna Plotz Merritt at the address Tootsie had given her, living in a mobile home on some wooded acres off the main highway. A dirt drive led off the narrow blacktop road, two deep ruts forming the approach to the trailer. *No Trespassing* signs were nailed to trees on each side of the drive. A steel cover stretched the length of the metal home, shading the door and windows. Broken lattice panels enclosed a small porch set on concrete, and a couple of lazy dogs slept in the shade. Neither dog bothered to acknowledge her arrival, other than the barest flicker of a tail. She switched off her bike, and silence descended as she propped it up on the kickstand.

Three steps led up to the deck and front door, and Harley navigated around half of a pair of old rubber boots, a naked doll baby with frizzy hair and blue ink tattoos, a few plastic blocks, a rugged Tonka truck covered in mud, and a huge stuffed duck squatting in a lawn chair. The latter had realistic looking feathers and seemed to be leaking. A strange hissing sound came from that direction.

Harley rapped twice on the aluminum storm door and heard someone yell out, "Wait a minute!"

She took a step back to be out of the way when the door opened. The leaking duck got louder. This time she looked more closely at it. It blinked a beady eye.

Startled, she took another step back just as the storm door opened and the duck launched at her in a furious flurry of feathers and hisses. Arms flailing, Harley missed the second step and slid down the rest of the way on her butt and elbows. The duck followed, landing atop her chest and nipping at her face. The beak was hard as wooden pliers, pinching her ear, stabbing her arms when she flung them up to protect herself. It *hurt.*

She'd never hit a duck before, but there was a first time for everything. Grabbing hold of whatever she could reach, Harley swung it at the feathered fury. The baby doll's head flew off, but so did the duck. A little shakily, Harley got to her feet.

Someone was laughing hysterically. It wasn't Harley. She looked up at the porch.

A brown haired, slender woman was bent over at the waist, her face knotted up with laughter. Actual tears slid down her cheeks.

"This is not funny," Harley said, but the woman she assumed to be Anna Plotz Merritt obviously didn't agree. She kept laughing. "I mean it," Harley said. "You should have some signs posted. Beware of Duck or something like that."

Shaking her head and wiping her wet face with the heel of her hand, the woman said, "It's not a duck. Gladys is a goose."

A goose. Of course. Diva had warned her. She really had to learn to interpret her mother's predictions better.

"No offense to Gladys," Harley muttered, "but who keeps geese on their front porch?"

"Geese are good watchdogs."

"Better than yours, anyway," Harley said with a glance at the still sleeping hounds. "Are you Anna?"

"Yes. And you are—?"

"Bruised, but my name is Harley."

Anna glanced past her to the chrome bike sitting between ruts. "Harley on a Harley, huh. Cute."

"Right. That's me. Cute. Mind if I ask you a few questions?"

"If you're selling something, forget it."

"It won't cost you anything but a little time." Harley tried her most innocent smile, but Anna apparently wasn't fooled.

"Oh no, anytime someone shows up at my door wanting nothing, it's always expensive. Usually it's a man, but if Gladys doesn't trust you, neither do I."

"Gladys is mistaken. I don't even eat meat. Much. Just a few questions, please. Then I'll leave." When Anna shook her head and reached for the storm door handle, Harley said, "It's about your sister Cheríe. She may be in trouble."

Anna paused and turned to look at her with narrowed eyes. "Cheríe is dead."

"I know, but her name isn't. Frieda's using it." While Anna looked like she might be thinking about that, Harley added, "And she might be in danger."

Maybe it was grudging, but Anna invited her inside where it was cooler. And goose-free. The trailer interior was surprisingly nice, with a huge plasma TV on one wall, state of the art sound equipment, expensive leather furniture, and what looked like new carpet. It was at odds with the very nature of the dwelling and general air of shabbiness, but maybe that was the point. Who'd ever think there was anything worth stealing in here?

"Nice," she said, and Anna nodded.

"When my husband died, he left an insurance policy."

"Your husband's death must have been recent."

"Yes. Are you here to talk about me or Frieda?"

"Well, in a way, both of you. I'm just wondering what you can tell me about your sister. It may have a bearing on what's happened."

"Look, I can tell you about what we did in third grade, but that's not going to be of much use to you now. I haven't kept up with her in the past few years. So how is Frieda in danger?"

"Someone killed her business partner, Harry Gordon, and if Frieda knows too much, she may be next." That was subtle, she thought, without accusing Frieda of killing Harry. "Do you know where Frieda might be staying? And why she'd be using her sister's name instead of her own?"

Anna looked distraught. "Harry . . . Harry Gordon's dead? Are you sure?"

"Yes. Don't you get the papers? Or watch the local news?"

"I . . . I've been out of town and unavailable. I just got back a few hours ago. No one's told me anything. When . . . how did it happen?"

"This past Thursday. He was shot." She tactfully left out the part about Harry hanging on an elk horn and how her aunt was a suspect in his murder, or that Frieda blamed Darcy. Some things were best left unsaid.

"No . . . no one called me." Anna stood up suddenly, wringing her hands. "I had no idea. And I haven't talked to my sister in a while. Months. Why would anyone kill Harry—her partner?"

"Well, the police seem to think it has something to do with his business dealings. And since your sister was in business with him, whoever killed him may want to kill her as well."

Anna had turned toward the window that looked out over empty fields and a wooded tract behind the trailer. She shook her head. "I don't know of anyone who'd want to kill either of them. I haven't been in contact with them lately."

Them? Harley frowned. "Did you know Harry Gordon well?"

"No. I never met Harry Gordon." She turned back to face Harley. "I only know of him through Frieda. She first met him in St. Louis."

"Did she work with him in Cincinnati, too?"

Anna hesitated, then nodded. "Yes. There was some kind of trouble with the owner of the antiques business not paying his taxes or whatever and he went to jail, so Frieda went to work for Harry."

"And she came to Memphis with him?"

"Is that a crime?"

"Not unless he violated the Mann Act and took a minor over state lines, and Frieda's well over eighteen, I presume. So who else was in business with them? Anyone named Julio?"

"Are you a cop?"

"Good lord, no."

"Then do you mind telling me why you're asking all these questions? I thought you were going to tell me why Frieda's in danger."

"Well, I'm trying to figure that out myself. See, two of the guys she worked with are dead and now no one can find her. I figure she's hiding because she knows they're after her, too."

"They who?"

"The smugglers. Harry's partners. Or I should say, former partners. That has to be who killed Harry and Julio. If Cheríe—Frieda—knows anything at all, they're looking for her."

Anna went pale, and her hands shook. "I don't know where she is. I haven't seen her."

"So you don't know the people who were working with them, or exactly what kinds of business dealings were involved?"

Anna waved one hand, her gaze moving past Harley toward the plasma TV on the wall. "I only know that they traveled a lot and brought back exotic antiques. Ivory, fur rugs, things like that. She used to give me things."

" Like that box on the table over there?"

Anna turned to look. A small white box about the size of a candy sampler sat on the kitchen table. Long, skinny dragons were carved on the top and sides, looping together.

"Yes," she said after a moment. "Frieda gave me that."

"Do you mind if I look at it? It's very pretty."

"Well . . . I suppose there's no harm." Rather grudgingly, Anna brought over the white box and held it out to Harley. "Be careful. It seems fragile."

Harley held it in both hands. It was quite pretty and surprisingly light. It looked much heavier. The bone was dense but porous. No machine had carved out these dragons and loops. It must be antique; she was no dealer and wouldn't know a new piece of ivory from an old one, but she could tell it was worth a lot of money. And it looked familiar, though she couldn't remember where she'd seen one like it before.

"Your sister is quite generous," she said, toying with the clasp of the locked box. "You two must be very close."

Anna held out her hand for the box. "Not really," she said rather coldly. "We don't see one another often enough for that."

As Harley handed it back to Anna, she said, "Don't you ever worry about anyone breaking in here, stealing things like this?"

Anna shrugged. "If anyone breaks in here, the last thing they'll be looking for is that box. I've got too much expensive electronic equipment for them to waste their time on that."

"Maybe so, but an alarm system might come in handy. Not that Gladys isn't formidable all by herself, but you never know what might happen."

"That's right," Anna said, "you just never know. Now, if you don't mind, I've still got to unpack. You know how it is when you've been away."

"Sure," Harley said. "Here's my business card if you hear from Frieda." She held out a Memphis Tour Tyme card with her name and number on it, and Anna took it grudgingly.

She wouldn't call, and no doubt the card would go into the trash the minute Harley got out of the driveway, but Harley suddenly remembered where she'd seen that ivory box. It had arrived the day she met Harry Gordon, and he'd taken it from her and gone into the shop with it. Now Frieda's sister had it, when Anna claimed she hadn't seen Frieda in months. Since Anna had been out of town, Frieda must have brought it here. Harry wouldn't have had time, not if he was busy stowing away priceless artifacts and being murdered, so Frieda had to have left it here. But when? Before or after Julio's and Harry's murders? And why bring it here at all? Of all the things smuggled in, why this one box carved with Celtic dragons? That small bone box just might hold a clue as to why Harry had been killed. And once they found out who had killed Harry, they'd find Julio's murderer as well.

Both men had been killed on the same day in the same place with the same weapon, so it had to be the same killer. And thieves fell out all the time. So Frieda Plotz a.k.a. Cheríe Saucier had just as much if not more motive to kill Harry than Darcy. Now all she had to do was convince Bobby of that.

Piece of cake.

Eleven

"No." Bobby looked unfriendly. His dark eyes narrowed to slits and his mouth set in a straight line that usually meant trouble for someone. Harley hoped it wasn't her.

Leaning over his desk, she tried again. "Come on, Bobby. At least investigate her. If I've come up with all this info on my own, just think what you could do."

"That's another thing. How the hell are you finding out this stuff so quickly? Is someone in my department feeding you info they shouldn't be?"

"Don't be silly. You're the only one I know in your department. Except for Officer Delisi, but I don't think he likes me very much. He's still holding a grudge since the King incident."

"*I'm* still holding a grudge since the King incident. Where are you getting your info?"

Harley smiled. "I'm not talking. I'm like a reporter. I can't divulge my sources."

"You're 'not talking' yourself right into jail time."

"But I'm not doing anything illegal. Don't be so grumpy. You're not at all cooperative these days. Trouble at home? Love life gone bad?"

"Shut up." Bobby leaned back in his chair and locked his hands behind his head. He had dark brown eyes that could be warm with humor or black with anger, and right now they were somewhere between those two shades. This conversation could go either way quickly.

"I think Cami's avoiding me," she said. "She hasn't answered any of my calls today."

"It's about time one of you showed some good sense."

"I kinda thought you might have something to do with that. Did you tell her to avoid me?"

"Since when has any woman ever paid attention to anything a man ever says? That'd be like expecting the Mississippi to run backward."

"It did once, you know," Harley said reflectively. "Back in the early 1800s when there was an earthquake—oh, never mind. I see that doesn't cheer you up."

"Harley—and I say this in friendship—go away. While you still can. Before I have to arrest you on obstruction or any other charge that applies. Go home. Lock your doors, stay inside and don't come out for any reason whatsoever."

"But what about my stalker?"

"Apparently he has better sense than you do. He's avoiding you."

"But he was outside my apartment today. I saw him. Did you talk to Morgan?"

"Twice. He confirmed you were assaulted. Doesn't that give you a hint that it'd be safer for you to stay home?"

"Where my stalker can get me? Please. He knows where I live. He followed us last night to the club and grabbed me in a public place. If he's ballsy enough to do that, just think what he'd do if he caught me by myself."

"Then stay with your parents."

"You think I'll be safer with *them?*"

Bobby grinned, and Harley felt a little better when he said, "Sorry. Temporary insanity. Diva would probably invite him in for herbal tea and a tarot reading."

"Maybe she could cleanse his aura while she's at it."

"Some things just don't change much. Okay. I see your point. But you've got to know it isn't safe for you to be taking risks. Look, you can stay at my apartment if you want."

"Is Angel still there?"

"No. Not as much."

Aha. Trouble on the home front. Well, Bobby never stayed with one woman for very long. It was bound to end like all the others, with everything short of a restraining order being filed and lots of verbal fireworks. That good, hot Italian blood made for high drama at times. Exciting and exhausting.

"Maybe I should go stay with Cami for a night or two," she said just to see what he'd say about Cami, but to her surprise he nodded.

"Yeah, that might be best. At least she'll listen to reason."

"Cami's easily swayed. I'm sure I can convince her to cooperate. Now look, I've given you all this good information about Cheríe Saucier and Harry Gordon, and you won't even follow up on it. Why won't you get a warrant to search Anna Plotz Merritt's house?"

"Dammit, Harley." Bobby had been leaning back in his chair, balanced on the two rear legs, and now he abruptly leaned forward so that the chair slammed down with a loud smack. "If you hadn't gone out there and meddled where you shouldn't, we just might have been able to get enough evidence together to justify a search warrant. You don't really think that box is still going to be there when we do get a warrant, do you? Not if it's important. No doubt, Anna Merritt is on the phone right now with her sister, and they're buying two airline tickets to Greece."

"Then you'd better hurry. That box is important. I don't know why or how, it just is."

Bobby stared at her. "When I wind up arresting you, take an insanity plea. No one will be able to prove otherwise."

"You can be so melodramatic. Look, I got the impression Anna didn't even know the box was there, so she doesn't know what she has, if she has anything. But obviously her sister thought that box was important enough to take it out there and leave it. I'll bet anything it ties in somehow."

"We may never know, now that you've warned her."

"I can see where that'd be a problem."

"Somehow, that's not as gratifying as it should be. Will you just stay out of this?"

"What about all the stuff Harry smuggled into the shop? Where is it now? Who bought it? And where's the money they had to make off it?" she asked.

Bobby scowled. "What, do you really think the MPD is stupid? And do you really think I intend to tell you anything? If you'd read the papers, you'd know there were artifacts found suspected of being stolen from museums in the UK as well as Mayan and Egyptian ruins. That's all I'm going to tell you and all you need to know."

"One more question. Was all of that found in Aunt Darcy's basement? Never mind. I see I'm right. So you're trying to clear her? I thought she'd been arrested."

"Let's just say she's in protective custody. Where you should be."

She stood up quickly. "No thanks. As I've said before, those orange jumpsuits aren't very flattering."

"It might be an improvement. What's that on your shirt?"

Harley looked down. Something brown and gooey was stuck to the front of the tee shirt she'd borrowed from Eric. She pulled out the shirttail to look at it, then realized what it was and said, "Dammit! Goose shit."

"What?"

She looked up at Bobby. "Be careful when you go to Atoka. There's a killer goose on the loose."

Something flickered in Bobby's eyes and she prudently left before he could act on it. There were times Bobby went pure cop on her and forgot all about their long friendship.

Cami was home when Harley arrived.

"Why aren't you answering your phone?" Harley asked when Cami opened the front door. "I've tried to call you all morning."

"I just got here. I do work, y'know."

"Oh yeah. I forget about that. You keep weird hours."

"Split shifts. Not so bad. I can come home and tend to my animals during the day, and still get home fairly early at night. What's up?"

"I need a clean shirt and I can't go home. Can I borrow one?"

"Sure. Do I want to know why you can't go home?"

Cami hopped over the baby gate she used to keep her dogs in the den, and Harley followed more slowly. "Not really. Did you get more cats?"

"No, just traded a few. Some of them got adopted this week."

Harley looked around the den as they passed through on the way to Cami's bedroom, where cats in various stages of serious sleeping were draped on the back of couches, chairs, and curled up in furry balls on the floor. None of them seemed to care about the dogs, and the dogs were smart enough not to push it.

"Which ones got adopted?" It wasn't that she really wanted to know. It was just idle conversation while she tried to think of a way to tell Cami that she needed to stay for a while because she was being stalked by a possible killer.

"Winky, Sprite, and Doodles. The calico, tabby, and tuxedo."

"I have no idea what you just said. Have you learned a foreign language?"

Cami grinned and tossed a clean tee shirt at her. "Yep. I speak Cat. Now why are you really here?"

"I always knew you were smart. I have goose shit on my shirt and need a clean one. Well, it's really Eric's tee shirt, but I still don't want to wear it."

"Should I ask how you got goose shit on your shirt?"

"It's a long story. I was trying to find out something about Cheríe Saucier. So I went to ask her sister. She has a goose on guard duty. Or maybe that's doody."

"Good lord, Harley. When did you become officially insane?" Cami ran a hand through her hair. It fell in silky soft strands into her eyes, making her look like a perplexed pixie.

"I'm not sure. Somewhere around puberty, I think."

Cami nodded in understanding. "So what are you doing now?"

"If you say yes, staying here tonight."

"I have to go back in to work at four-thirty, but I get off at eight-thirty. You can stay here with the creatures while I'm gone."

"Oh joy."

Cami grinned. "You survived last time."

"Only because I was numb."

"Come to the kitchen and you can tell me what you've been doing while I fix us some lunch."

While Cami did her microwave magic, Harley perched on a chair and gave her a recap of what she'd found out. Somehow, saying it aloud helped her put things in perspective, and just as she was telling Cami how Anna Plotz Merritt had seemed upset to hear about Harry's death, she had an epiphany.

"Damn!" she said, balling up her fist and smacking it into her other palm, "of course!"

Cami slid something from the microwave onto Harley's plate and gave it to her. "Of course what?"

"Harry Gordon was involved with Anna, too. Maybe that's why Cheríe killed him."

"I thought Cheríe was dead."

"She is. Frieda's using her sister's name."

"Why?"

"Maybe she doesn't like her name. Maybe she was named for a crazy old aunt or a brand of beer, and she thought Cheríe Saucier was sexier. People should watch what they name their kids. It can be demoralizing."

Cami arched a brow. "So says Harley Davidson."

"Exactly. I've considered changing my name. It was a decided detraction when I was in corporate banking, but it's been a bit of an asset since I've been a tour guide. No one ever forgets it. What is this?" She stared down at her plate. It had two preformed brown things on one side, and long, limp green sticks on the other.

"Mesquite grilled chicken breasts and asparagus. It's very good. And low carb."

Harley looked up at her. "You're still on a diet?"

"Yep. I've lost seven pounds already."

"Cami, you aren't fat."

"Not anymore."

Harley sighed. "Would it be rude to refuse a meal?"

"Nope. I'll heat it up for my dinner tonight. By this time next week, I should have lost at least ten pounds."

"That should come in handy if you ever want to get a job as a shadow. You're doing this for Bobby, aren't you?"

"I don't know what you're talking about. I put on some weight and I want to look good for the summer."

"Uh hunh. And it just happens that Bobby Baroni has been coming by to see you. Don't bother to deny it. You already confessed. And he said Angel isn't staying at his apartment much anymore. I'm assuming you're ignoring all my previous warnings about him, so I won't add any more you'll ignore. Just be careful. Bobby's track record isn't so good."

"I know that. And it's not like that with us. I just . . . enjoy his company without any kind of expectations."

"Cami, you have expectations from your cats. Which, by the way, are eying your dinner for tonight. I'll put it in the fridge."

She got up and covered the plate and stuck it on a shelf in the fridge, right beside a can of tuna and egg cat food covered with a cute green lid with a cat face on it. Maybe it wouldn't be so bad if Cami started seeing Bobby. He was the first man she'd shown a real interest in since her divorce, and the alternative might very well be a descent into the Crazy Cat Lady syndrome. That would be tragic.

After she'd made herself a peanut butter and jelly sandwich—using low carb bread that wasn't really too bad—she helped Cami clean up the kitchen and they went into the den. Several cats decorated the chairs, and having experience with their reluctance to be dislodged, Harley sat on the end of the couch.

"So why didn't you stay with Morgan?" Cami wanted to know, and Harley shrugged.

"I don't know. Probably because he's always on one of his secret undercover missions, and maybe because I don't want to get too close."

"Wait. He stays over at your apartment. You sleep with him. Can you *get* any closer?"

"Oh, you know what I mean, Cami. There's just something too personal about putting your tampons in a guy's bathroom. It seems . . . permanent."

"And that's bad?"

"No, it's just scary. What if we wake up one day and decide we've made a mistake?"

"Then you split up," Cami said, "and go on with your life. My life didn't end when Jace and I divorced."

"Not so you could tell, anyway." Harley looked around at all the cats and dogs strewn about the room like furry shoes. "But something happened to make you collect all these things."

"They're not *things*. They have emotions, and most of them know just what it feels like to be unloved and unwanted. Some of them have been abused, and all of them were scared. I knew just how they felt. They only want what we all want, love and security."

Harley looked at her a moment. Why had she never seen how deeply affected Cami had been by her divorce? Some friend she was, not to have noticed.

"You're right," she said. "Maybe we all go about it differently, but it's pretty universal to want to be loved, I'd say."

"And to feel safe."

"That too. Cami, are you sure you're all right? Because if you want to talk about Jace or anything, I'll be glad to listen. I can't give good advice since I'm obviously not that successful in the commitment part of a relationship, but I can nod in all the right places."

Cami grinned. "I'm fine. Really. It took a while for me to get past the divorce, but you were always there for me when I called. You were a great distraction. You didn't rehash all the drama and trauma and let me forget about it for a while. Don't think just because I've become involved in animal rescue that I'm in danger of ending up like Mrs. Trumble, crazy and spiteful."

"Don't forget dead."

"See? If she'd been nicer to animals, she might still be alive."

"That's not a recommendation, Cami. Think of the poor animals."

"We are horrible people, you know that? We shouldn't be so mean about Mrs. Trumble."

"That's one of the main differences between me and you, Cami. You think about things like that and I don't."

"You just like to think you don't. You're much nicer than you pretend to be. So, what are you going to do while I'm at work tonight?"

"Probably watch TV and catch up on phone calls. I've had this new cell phone for several days now, and it's still in good shape. Isn't that amazing?"

"I'm astonished. This must be a record for you."

"It's close."

While they'd been talking, one of the cats crept up beside the end of the couch and stared up at Harley, the end of its tail twitching back and forth. When she looked down at it, blue eyes looked back up at her. "Ah. Sam. Bitten any more guests lately?"

"He likes you," Cami said, and Harley shook her head.

"Forget it. I told you, I don't like cats. They don't like me. It's a mutual thing that works quite well."

"Uh hunh. Sam is pretty picky. He's been known to attack some people. It's made it hard to place him. He's very, um, energetic in his dislikes."

"You mean he bites."

"Oh yeah. He doesn't like children at all. I think whoever had him at first had small kids that tormented him pretty badly."

"I share his sentiment. Most little kids are selfish beasts. Come to think of it, most men are, too. I think they let their inner child out far too often."

"There are exceptions," Cami said, and Harley nodded.

"Thank God."

That led her to thoughts of Mike Morgan, and they talked about him for a while before Cami got up to do her litter box routine. Harley let the dogs out into the back yard, and stood for a moment on the large wooden deck under the shade of a huge weeping willow that draped over one half of the deck. Roses bloomed, and a wisteria, crawling over an arbor and along the fence, dangled soft clusters of flowers that smelled like grape. Very nice. Refreshing. It had a lush feel to it that she liked. Cami had done well.

"So you do all your own yard work?" she asked when Cami came out onto the deck to sit in one of the padded chairs under the willow.

"Not all of it. I pay someone to mow and edge, and I do the flower beds when I have time. Most of the stuff coming up is perennials that return every year. My yard guy should show up any time now. He's really good, comes by regularly to mow and I send him a check once a month. If he comes by today, just let him in the back yard. There's a lock on the inside gate you can undo."

"I think I can manage that. How will I know it's him?"

"Easy. He'll have a truck with a lawn mower and gardening tools in my driveway."

"I guess that would be a good clue."

"Harley, you won't go off on your own or anything, will you? You'll stay here?"

"You've been talking to Bobby."

"Well, he did call a couple of minutes ago. He's worried about you."

"I'm fine. I'll stay here. If only because I'm tired of getting whacked in the head and pooped on."

"These last few weeks have been—unusual. Even for you, Harley."

"I have to agree." She reflected for a moment, then said, "I blame it all on King. If he hadn't eaten half of Mrs. Trumble's car, none of this would have happened."

"And you wouldn't have met Morgan."

"The only bright spot."

"Or been in a position to try to help your aunt."

Harley, who had closed her eyes against the sunlight, opened one to peer at Cami. "Are you saying this is a good thing?"

"Well . . . I have to admit, you've somehow managed to help despite yourself. If it wasn't for you, maybe the police would never have found that other body."

"True. No one even remembered that old cellar was there. Except, obviously, whoever killed Harry and Julio." She thought for another moment, then said, "It all comes back to Cheríe Saucier. She worked with Harry. She knew that cellar was there. It had to be where they hid the stuff they were smuggling into the country. Homeland Security isn't checking all the cargo brought in on ships, so anything brought in like illegal ivory and endangered animal skins, or a few artifacts or any of that stuff would just be invoiced as merchandise. I'll bet there's a shipping manifest of some kind in Harry's home office."

"Harley—*no*."

"Don't worry. I'm sure the police have already searched. Wait a minute!" She sat up straight and smacked her forehead with her open palm. "Of course! It must be in that ivory box that Anna got from Cheríe. Or Frieda. Or whatever name she's using at the moment."

"Shipping manifests? Is it a big box?"

"Oh. No. It's a small box." Harley leaned back into the chair again. After a moment she said thoughtfully, "Though it's completely possible that the box has a key in it, to a safety deposit box, or a safe, something like that."

"So tell the police."

"I did. I told Bobby all I knew about the box. Maybe I should call back and tell him why I think it's important."

"Uh, I'm not sure that's such a good idea, Harley."

Already reaching for Cami's cordless phone, Harley shrugged. "All he can do is hang up on me."

After five minutes of listening to Bobby tell her to butt out of police business or he'd have her arrested for obstruction, interference, and God only knew how many other threats, Harley said, when he paused for breath, "I take it you're no longer interested in my assistance."

There was a long silence, then Bobby said tersely, "Give the phone to Cami."

She handed it over, sipped at her watered down sweet tea and stared glumly at one of the dogs lying in the shade. It was discouraging to be so unappreciated.

Cami mostly listened, said a few "Uh huhs," then hung up from Bobby and looked at Harley. "You okay, sweetie?"

"I'm fine. I should have known he wouldn't listen."

"It's not that he doesn't want to, it's just that . . . well . . . "

"I know. He's hampered by things like search warrants and proper police procedures. I'm not."

"Oh God. Please don't go anywhere. Bobby said he'd arrest you himself if you didn't stay out of this. I'm supposed to keep an eye on you."

"Don't worry, Cami. I'm not really up to it right now. I'll hang around here for a while."

"If only I could believe that."

"It's true. I'm not going off. In fact, I'll walk your dogs for you while you're at work."

"I have four dogs, Harley."

"Two at a time, then. Just show me where you keep their leashes. Isn't there a lake behind your house somewhere?"

"In the apartment complex down the block. There are also ducks and geese."

"Diva is so uncanny. She warned me about the goose, just like with the pug."

Cami nodded in understanding. "I remember her doing that kind of thing."

"If only she could be more specific, it'd certainly help. Of course, she likes to think she's helping with my mental and emotional growth when she tells me just enough to get me in trouble and not enough to help me avoid it."

While Cami got ready to return to work for her second shift, Harley chose the first two dogs she'd volunteered to walk. A fat beagle named Ranger and a frisky golden retriever mix named Baby barked excitedly when she waggled the leashes.

"Sure you can handle this?" Cami asked rather dubiously, and Harley shrugged.

"Of course. Nothing to it. Dog walking is not brain surgery."

"As long as you don't run into some guy walking his Doberman. Then it might require surgery."

"Ah, I'll get my pepper spray."

"Take the garage door opener with you. Here. And go out the back door so the other dogs don't try to get past you. They think they should all go at the same time. Oh, and watch for cats. They regularly try to get out."

"Jeez, Cami, do you have to go through this all the time?"

Cami just smiled. "So, want to put your car in the garage?"

"I'm on my bike, but yeah, maybe I should. Hold back the hounds."

Harley went outside while Cami hit the button to raise the garage door, then wheeled her bike inside. She parked it next to Cami's green Saturn. A fan in the middle of the garage ceiling kept it from getting too hot in there, and though there was lots of stuff stored alongside the walls, there was plenty of room. A long window let in daylight, and looked out on Cami's next door neighbor. Except for traffic, the neighborhood was fairly quiet.

It all seemed so safe.

Twelve

Dog walking was not her forte, Harley decided. Or Cami's dogs were particularly ill-trained. They wanted to go in opposite directions at the same time, had no concept of the words *heel*, or *stay*, or even *no*, and the elderly fat beagle had peed on her shoe instead of the bush he was aiming for. Her arm sockets ached from where they'd tried to do a two-minute mile and she'd tried to slow them down. She was in no mood to walk the other two, but there didn't seem to be much choice. They stood at the door waiting and wagging, with feral gleams in their eyes that vowed trouble if she reneged on her promise.

When she got back to the house, staggering from the drag on her arms by two energetic dogs that seemed determined to run instead of walk, the yard man was there. His pickup truck held a lawn mower and gardening tools, and he'd parked in front of the house. Harley managed a nod in his general direction as she stumbled toward the garage door and pushed the button on the opener. It whined upward and the dogs dashed inside toward the back door, dragging her with them. She barely got the door opened before they were both at the water bowls Cami kept filled. Harley headed for the fridge. A cold beer might undo some of the damage her bright idea of dog walking had done. Then she remembered that Cami kept the beer and wine in the old fifties GE refrigerator in the garage, and stepped into the garage to get one.

One of the two yard men stood in the driveway wearing a loose shirt and big straw hat that shaded his face from the sun. She gave him a wave and said she'd unlock the gate for him to mow the back yard. Sweat dampened her hair and shirt. It hadn't seemed that hot before she'd started, but maybe having to run the entire way back made a difference.

On her way back into the house, she hit the garage door button to close it against the west sun. It cranked noisily down as she went inside. After opening the gate for the yard men, she hit the couch with a sigh and her beer. The ceiling fan was on high, the wooden blinds were closed against the sun, and the remote was within reach on the glass-topped coffee table. *Heaven.*

Outside, the roar of the mower kept the cats glued to the wide kitchen window, but in the cool shade of the den, the dogs lay exhausted and too content to bother barking. She found an episode of People's Court that she hadn't seen, and settled on that.

She must have fallen asleep. The next thing she knew, Cami was home. Harley sat up in surprise, almost spilling the rest of her beer.

"Hey, what time is it?" she asked as she set her beer on the coffee table.

"Nearly nine. You look rested. Or is that exhausted?"

"Both, I think. Your dogs are manic. They dragged me to the lake and back, and one of them—the fat beagle—tried to tree a duck. It wasn't pretty. Even the squirrels were laughing."

Cami grinned. "Ranger's eyesight isn't what it used to be, but his sense of smell is still good. So, have you eaten yet?"

"Nope. After walking the dogs, I fell asleep. Didn't even wake up when the yard guy left, so you might want to check the gate and be sure it's locked."

"Is that a new pillow beside you?"

Harley looked down, and to her surprise, Sam the Siamese lay curled up next to her. He was purring, a steady vibration that she could feel as well as hear. When she moved, he opened a sleepy blue eye but didn't stir until she stood up. Then he stretched, yawning so wide she could see the back of his throat behind the pink tongue.

"He likes you," Cami said, and Harley shook her head.

"He just likes lying next to a warm body. Sometimes I feel the same."

"Whatever. One of these days you'll have to give in."

"That will be right after hell freezes over. I'm not a cat person."

Sam chose that moment to bump her free hand with his head, sliding under her fingers in an obvious demand to be petted. Reluctantly, she stroked his head a few times, then caught sight of Cami's smile and stopped.

"Frozen hell, right," Cami said when Harley walked past her on the way to the kitchen. "I feel the chill already," she called after her, but Harley managed to ignore that.

"Is there a Taco Bell near here?" she asked instead. "I'm feeling peckish, as Janet would say."

"Janet?"

"Grandmother Eaton's housekeeper. You know, Amanda and Madelyn know more than they've said so far. Cousin Maddie was there to see Harry, after all. She must have seen some little thing. Heard something odd. Maybe she didn't notice it at the time. It might have seemed unimportant. Or maybe she doesn't want to say who and what she saw there."

"You don't think she's involved, do you?"

"With Harry, yes, with the murder, no. She can be a vicious little ferret, but she's not a killer. I think enough time has passed, and with Aunt Darcy in jail, she might be more honest if I ask her a few questions."

"Harley—"

"Don't worry. I'm not going anywhere else. Just to talk to my dear cousins. I'll turn on my cell phone. Want to go with me?"

"No. And I don't want you to go, either. I told Bobby I'd keep you here." Harley cocked a brow at her, and Cami flushed. "Well, he told me to keep you here."

"Bobby means well, but he has control issues. It's all right, Cami. It won't take long. I shouldn't be gone more than an hour."

Cami looked at her a minute, then sighed. "Better take my car. It's started to rain."

"Thanks. Want anything from Taco Bell?"

"One of these days you're going to turn into a taco."

"Bean burrito with extra salsa and sour cream."

Cami rolled her eyes, an indication she didn't appreciate the fine dining at Taco Bell. How sad.

While Cami tended to her zoo, Harley went to freshen up, washing her face and trying to do something with her hair so it didn't look quite so unkempt. The beauty of her style was that it could go a day or two without brushing and no one could tell the difference but her. And Tootsie. But he was very attentive to things like that.

"Harley! Come help me!"

Cami's shout sent her running to the kitchen, where she found Cami by the open back door. "Good Lord, Cami, what's going on?"

"Two of the cats got out. Help me find them, Harley. They might come to you."

"Sure. Cats love me." Despite her sarcasm, Harley helped Cami search the garage for the missing cats. They found one behind the old refrigerator, and the other behind a ladder in the corner. After several scratches and a lot of cussing, the cats were safely inside and Harley went to pour hydrogen peroxide on her wounds. Cami, of course, had not been scratched. Typical.

"Well, that was fun," Harley said when she went back into the kitchen. "Now, if there's nothing else you can think of to keep me here, I'll just get going. Leave the door unlocked."

"Believe me, I'll still be up. Use the garage door opener. It's on the driver's side sun visor. I rarely lock the back door."

"That could be dangerous. When you talk to Bobby, tell him—"

"I won't lie for you. Not to Bobby."

"For heaven's sake, Cami, I wasn't going to ask you to lie, but even if I was, why is Bobby so different from anyone else I'd ask you to lie to for me?"

Cami's cheeks turned pink, and Harley sighed. She'd been so afraid of this. Despite all Cami's protests, she was much too attached to Bobby. Something would have to be done about that. Just as soon as she had time.

"Bobby's not different," Cami said defensively, "it's just that I'm not any good at lying to him. He always seems to know."

"No, he's just always been a good bluffer. Remember strip poker when we were fifteen?"

"I always thought he cheated."

"Well, he did, but even when he didn't, he could bluff us right out of our dainties. Just tell him to call me on my cell phone if he wants to talk to me, which I'm sure he will when he finds out I left the house."

"I'll just hope he doesn't call."

"Oh, he'll call. He won't be able to resist checking up on me."

Cami had opened the garage door, and she gave Harley the extra set of keys to her car. "Be careful," was all she said, but Harley knew what she meant and nodded.

"I will. This shouldn't take long. Madelyn was having an affair with Harry and I think it got too sticky. Maybe he threatened to tell Aunt Darcy or something. I don't know. But a face to face is necessary if I'm going to find out who, what, and when from either of them."

"I don't envy you."

"Neither do I."

That was true. Madelyn and Amanda could be formidable when they chose to be, both of them quite capable of retreating behind bitchy smoke screens.

Slinging her backpack into the passenger side of the car, Harley slid into the driver's seat and turned the ignition. Nice. And it was an automatic, another plus. Cami's car was relatively free of cat hair and dog hair, though a few stray strands were scattered over the front seats. The driver's window was down, and as she backed out of the garage, Harley hit the button to roll it back up.

A light rain fell, spattering on the car, and she hit the lights and windshield wipers as she pulled out onto the busy street. Five lanes of traffic ran in front of Cami's house, but it was fairly quiet this time of night. First, she decided, she'd go to Taco Bell, then eat on the way out to her aunt's house. Maybe a little onion and garlic in their faces would expedite answers.

That had to be it. She had to think outside the box, let go of all her theories and be open to new ones. Aunt Darcy hadn't killed Harry, and as far as anyone knew, had no reason to kill Julio. Of course, business partnerships went wrong all the time, and Julio hadn't seemed to be the kind of man to prefer argument to action. Harry really had the only obvious motive to kill him. That made sense, since the coroner said Julio died first. But if Julio hadn't killed Harry, then the most obvious suspects, at least the way the police seemed to be looking at it, were Aunt Darcy and Cheríe. If Harry had been killed by a woman, who put him on the elk horns? It took strength to do that. And rage. It just didn't fit. This wasn't a woman's kind of crime. Not even Cheríe Saucier with her hefty biceps could have lifted a man eight inches taller and at least seventy pounds heavier to hang him on a door.

Damn. She'd been thinking so hard she'd turned the wrong way, she realized, and swung down a street that led through the neighborhood to go back the right way. About the time she reached the main road, her cell phone rang. She reached over to fumble in her backpack for it. It'd be Bobby, of course.

"Do not answer that," a rough voice said from the back seat before she could reach her phone, and she let out a startled yelp. When something hard nudged the back of her head and he added, "Shut up!" she clamped her lips tightly shut.

Never argue with a man with a gun, she decided as her cell phone quit ringing.

"Go the way I tell you to," her stowaway said next, and she realized he had a thick accent. Her stalker?

This couldn't be good. She peered into the rear-view mirror, but he nudged her again with the gun barrel and told her to keep driving.

"How'd you get in here?" she asked after a moment, hoping to keep him diverted while she inched a hand toward her cell phone.

"Both hands on the wheel, *chica*. Pull into that driveway. There."

"The apartments?"

"*Sí*."

The apartments, the lake . . . after being dragged down this road and across the grass earlier by dogs, she knew she wasn't too far from Cami's house. All she had to do was catch this guy by surprise, abandon the car, and run through the trees to get to safety. Lights were on in apartments ringing the lake, but dark shadows hugged the buildings and stretched to the shore. Trees crowned a slight rise to her left, then sloped sharply downward to more apartments and backed up to the cove right behind Cami's street. Dogs barked, sounding muffled by the misty rain and low fog. The Saturn's windshield wipers slapped rapidly back and forth at about the same tempo as her heart rate.

Using the gun as a prod, he pointed her toward a curve of the lake where cars usually parked to watch the ducks and geese. She put the car in park, wipers still going back and forth, occasionally making a screeching sound when the rain slowed. The engine idled, and she tried to see if anyone was out walking their dogs in the rain. Not a soul, just a few dark shapes by tall reeds that were probably nesting ducks. Where was an attack goose when she really needed one?

Silence stretched, and for a moment she thought the guy in back had fallen out. She glanced up in the rear-view mirror again and caught a glimpse of dark eyes behind a dark ski mask rimmed in red. To her surprise, the guy climbed over the seats and plopped down on the passenger side, dumping her backpack onto the floorboard. It was dark where they sat, but even with the knit ski mask that covered his head and face there was something vaguely familiar about him. That was puzzling. If it was her stalker, she hadn't caught even a glimpse of his face the night he'd attacked her.

"Okay, just who the hell are you?" she demanded in what she hoped was a firm, authoritative tone. "You've been following me and I want to know why."

"José. I must talk to you. You are the only person who can help me."

That was a surprise. "I didn't think help was what you had in mind."

"Well it is."

He said *is* like *ees*. Harley shrugged. Maybe she could negotiate here. Maybe he was more desperate than murderous.

"Why'd you hit me in the head the other night?" she asked, planning to distract him long enough that she could open her car door and escape.

"I did not hit you. After you ran, you hit the edge of the open Exit door."

"Oh. You sure about that?"

"*Sí.* I saw you. Perhaps I should have tried another way to talk to you."

"Ya *think?* So what do you want with me?"

"You must tell the *la policia* . . . they have arrested the wrong person. She did not kill Harry Gordon."

"Then who did? You?"

She was glad she didn't understand Spanish when he swore, then said, "No, it was not me! I was there after the store closed, waiting for my brother Julio."

"Inside the store?"

"No, no, I helped them unload heavy crates, then went to the store. When I came back, I waited across the street like always. Sometimes I meet him there, but this day, he never came out. Only the blue car was left finally, so I went inside. I saw Harry Gordon, and I knew at once he was dead, so I ran to go back to my car. Then I heard someone calling for him, so I hid in a big chest. I was afraid they would see me and think I had killed him."

José paused, and Harley heard him take a deep, raspy breath. After a moment, he said in a hoarse voice, "Two women came while I hid there, both with hair the color of yours. One, she came first and left fast, then the other came in a big white car and I thought she would never leave. When she did, I heard you come in the front door and ran fast to get out before the police came next."

Harley thought about that a moment. He'd been there when she came in, and maybe he'd been the one to bang the door. But it'd been her aunt's car she'd seen driving away. "Tell me," she said, "did you hear any gunshots? A fight?"

The ski mask-covered head indicated negative.

"So why haven't you told this to the police? Oh wait—are you here illegally?"

"*Sí*, but it is not just that. My brother, he is dead because of what he knew. Maybe I am next."

"How much did Julio know about the smuggling? Is that why he was killed?"

His eyes glistened behind the ski mask as he nodded. "*Sí*, it has to be. He knew too much."

That was unnerving. It looked like open season for smugglers, which wasn't so bad, but she didn't want to end up mistaken for one.

"So how'd you find me?" she asked. "How did you know where I'd be tonight?"

"I saw you. Today, earlier. And I saw you when you came to the gardens."

"What gardens—wait. You're the guy who was digging holes for rose bushes. And you came to cut the grass, too. I knew you seemed familiar. Just how well do you know Cheríe? You looked like you knew her pretty well. What were you two arguing about?"

"I have something she wants. And she thinks maybe I killed Harry."

"Did you?"

"No! That is why I come to you. Perhaps you can help me. I have bad experience with the American police. If they catch me, they'll take me to jail."

"If you and your brother were in on the smuggling, that's probably where you need to be. It might even be safer for you if you know too much."

"*Ay*, do not be stupid." José shoved the gun barrel into her ribs, and in the shadows he sounded so fierce she shuddered when he said, "I want to find who killed Julio, so will do what I must to stay out of jail."

"Okay, okay, just get that damn thing out of my ribs," she protested, her heart slamming against her ribs even harder than the gun barrel. "No jail. Gotcha. So how do you expect me to help you?"

"I know something that may help you find out who killed my brother."

It was tempting. Very tempting. But making deals with a gun-toting man in a ski mask would be the height of stupidity. She shrugged. "That's not my job. The police handle that kind of thing."

"That day at the gardens when you fell into the glass case, someone said you were in the paper. They said you found the killer of your neighbor."

"Well yes, but that was more or less by accident. Although I did do pretty well for an amateur, if I say so myself."

"Then you will do well for me." He jabbed her with the gun again and she let out a yelp of pain that apparently startled him. He jerked back, smacking his head against the window.

Harley grabbed for her door handle at the same time as he grabbed for her. She let out a yell and yanked her arm free, still fumbling for the door handle with her other hand. It all went so quickly she was never sure afterward exactly how it happened, but suddenly José started screaming really loud and swinging his arms. Growling and hissing, he went into some kind of odd, hysterical fit, slapping at his knit-covered head in the dark.

Shocked, she hesitated, peering at him in the shadows while rain beat on the car and fogged up the windows, wondering if he needed medical help. Somehow, she got the interior lights on, and was startled to see a furry thing atop his head. It seemed to be alive.

Reaching out, she plucked the gun from José's hand quite easily. Excellent. It was much better having the upper hand. And the gun.

José used both hands to pry off the cap and furry thing on his head. Harley altered her first guess that it was a raccoon as she recognized it, right before he flung it into the back seat.

"Hey, don't hurt him!" she protested.

Holding a hand to his face and ear, José gave her a wild look and got his door open. He nearly fell out, then stumbled off into the rainy darkness around the lake. José's still open door kept the interior light on. Harley turned to look in the back seat.

"Sam, what are you doing in the car?"

Sam didn't have much to say, just crouched there on the seat with his ears flat and blue eyes narrowed into wicked looking slits.

She grinned. "Good boy. You're not so bad for a cat."

When he shook his claws free of the knit cap and started to lick himself, she decided it was time to take him home.

Thirteen

"There he is!" Cami reached for Sam at once, the frantic look in her eyes giving way to relief. "I didn't miss him until I got out the food bowls. He's always first when he hears the can opener."

"Give him extra tonight. He saved my butt. I'll tell you about it later, but if Bobby calls, I can tell him I don't have to worry about my stalker anymore."

Cami's eyes got wide. "Did you run over him?"

"Good God. No, I didn't run over him. You're scary. Is your yard man's name José?"

"No, but he has helpers sometimes. Why?"

"I think my stalker mowed your yard today."

"Oh, I'm sure Mr. MacDonald would never hire a stalker to help him. He has his position as full time groundskeeper at the Dixon gardens to think about."

That explained it. Well, there was an old saying about nothing in life being a coincidence, and this sure qualified.

"I'll be back. I really need to talk to my cousins. José—my stalker—says he saw both of them at the shop after it closed the day Harry was killed."

"*Both* of them?"

"Yep. Don't tell that to Bobby, though. I want to be sure José's not just lying."

He wasn't. Harley knew it was true the moment Madelyn and Amanda exchanged quick glances and started to deny it at the same time. She put up a hand to stop them.

"Never mind. You're both lying. Why?"

Madelyn answered first, a little too quickly. "I'm not lying! I was there just like I said. Just me and Harry."

"Right." Harley turned to Amanda. "I've talked to a witness that you obviously didn't see. Now's the time for the truth, before I tell the police."

Amanda bit her bottom lip and glanced at Madelyn, then shook her head. "No," she said in a soft whisper, "I wasn't there."

"Okay, here's the way I see it. Madelyn was having an affair with Harry, and you went to talk her out of it. Harry got angry, there was a struggle of some kind, and one of you had the gun from Aunt Darcy's car—"

"*No!*" they both said at the same time.

"Then try the truth for a change. Remember, the truth shall set you free. Hopefully."

Amanda sucked in a deep, quivery breath while her sister glared at Harley. It didn't faze her. Harley stood firm. If she knew the truth, maybe she—or a damn good lawyer—could figure out a way to make it sound less damning.

"He was already dead when I got there," Madelyn said after a moment. "It was horrible. I was supposed to meet him at his house, but when he didn't show up . . . I . . . I went by the shop."

"I said the truth, Maddie dearest. You weren't supposed to meet Harry. He was at the shop to meet someone else. Who was it?" She just knew she'd say it'd been Aunt Darcy. It was the only rational explanation for her refusal to tell the truth.

"*I* know," Amanda said unexpectedly, and her round chin came up defiantly. "No need to go on, Madelyn. It was me. He was supposed to meet *me*. Don't look so surprised, Harley. I may not be a great beauty, but Harry never cared about that. He cared about me." Huge tears welled in her eyes. "It didn't matter to him that I'm fat, or that I'm not the smart one. He liked me for who I am. No one's ever done that before. Except Madelyn." She turned to her sister. "I know you were trying to protect me, but it's all right. I loved Harry and he loved me. I didn't kill him. I'd never have hurt him."

Harley just stared at her cousins for a moment, and knew they were telling the truth. It was too weird not to be true. Damn. There went the theory about Aunt Darcy and Harry that had been building up at the back of her mind. Well, she was nothing if not resilient.

"What about you, Maddie? You were there, too. Did you kill Harry for messing around with Mandy?"

"Why would I kill Harry? I told Amanda he wasn't good for her, but I certainly didn't feel strongly enough about it to kill him. Or kill Juan, or whatever his name was. The Mexican guy that did all the unloading."

Madelyn turned to her sister and said softly, "I'm sorry. Really I am. I know you cared for him a lot. I just wanted to protect you."

Looking at Harley, Amanda said, "Neither of us killed him. I swear it."

She wanted to believe them. And really, she thought they must be telling the truth. It was a bit of a stretch to think either of them would hang Harry on a hook after shooting him. Unless it was Julio who'd done that. But he'd died first. So back to square one.

Putting her hands on her hips, she decided a little payback for their lying was justified. "I just hope the police buy your stories, because neither of you have alibis that'll stand up."

That should give them something to think about.

When she was retelling the story to Cami while digging through her Taco Bell sack to see if she'd missed anything, Cami asked, "But if Amanda was there, too, why didn't José see her car?"

"I pointed out that flaw in their stories when they were tripping all over themselves trying to convince me they were telling the truth. Apparently, she parked in the next lot over, an empty parking lot for an accounting company. He probably never looked in that direction."

"Do you believe them?"

Finding a few stray nachos in the bottom of the sack, Harley stuck one in her mouth. "Yep. It's too stupid not to be true. Mandy is having an affair with Harry, and Maddie decides to confront both of them, but she gets there after Harry is already dead and Amanda has long gone. She thinks Amanda killed him, Amanda thinks Madelyn killed him—I never knew they could be so damn noble."

"Then that means that Cheríe Saucier may have killed Harry because she was jealous of Amanda. Maybe she really wanted your cousin to get the blame for it."

"So who killed Julio? The coroner said he was killed before Harry. My bet is that Harry did it."

Cami put a hand to her head. "I've got a headache from thinking about all this. How do you cope?"

"Aspirin. Or beer. Either helps. So, how's our stowaway? Has he recovered yet?"

"Sam? He's fine. Hiding somewhere, but he always does that."

"I feel like doing the same. I can't believe it's only ten-thirty. If it's okay with you, I'll stay here tonight anyway. My stalker won't bother me anymore, I don't think. He just wanted me to tell the cops he didn't kill Harry. Which reminds me—have you heard from Bobby?"

"Twice. He said you didn't answer your cell phone."

Harley checked it and found the battery had run down. She plugged it in to charge. There were two messages from Bobby—both rather tacky reminders that she'd promised to stay out of trouble—and three from Morgan, who was still at the hideout but would call again later. The last message was from Diva, one of her melodramatic prophecies.

"Harley, watch out for the dead man."

"What is it," Cami asked when Harley shook her head and sighed. "Bad news?"

"No. One of Diva's prophecies again. I'm to watch out for the dead man."

"Ah, a ghost is your stalker."

"He definitely seemed very alive to me. Which reminds me, his gun is in your car. Under the front seat. Bobby needs to run it for identification, I guess."

"It's not the gun that killed Harry and the other guy, is it?"

Harley shook her head. "No. That was Aunt Darcy's gun. You know, I really should ask her why she even has a gun."

"Maybe she was afraid of Harry Gordon. Or—" Cami stopped, but Harley finished her sentence for her.

"Or maybe she meant to shoot him."

It looked like evidence was stacking up against Darcy.

Harley slept later than she meant to the next morning. When she woke, she wasn't all that surprised to find Sam curled up in a furry comma on her pillow. He was purring, a soothing noise that she found oddly relaxing.

"Don't get used to this," she said, but he only purred louder. "I know what you and Cami are up to, and it won't work. I don't like cats. I have scratches to prove cats don't like me."

Sam opened one eye, blinked slowly, then stretched out a paw and tapped her lightly on the nose. Whatever he meant by that, it satisfied him, and he went back to sleep. She lay there for a while longer, letting her mind go from possibility to possibility.

Madelyn and Amanda had arrived after Harry was dead. Aunt Darcy hadn't been there at all. Cheríe had shown up—very conveniently—after the police arrived. That left either the sister in

Atoka, or Julio's brother. But that didn't make much sense, either. If José killed Harry for killing Julio, he wouldn't still be looking for his brother's killer.

It kept coming back to Cheríe Saucier. She was the only one who had motive as well as opportunity. Jealousy over Harry, as unlikely as that seemed after having met him, had to be the motive. According to Bobby, her alibi was rock-solid, but that didn't mean she wasn't a good suspect. After all, Aunt Darcy had been with her mystery man, and she was still a suspect.

Maybe the smugglers were ticked off about not getting their money. Did Harry owe them for the stuff brought in? Or did he pay up-front? It was unlikely any smuggler would risk getting stiffed by shipping stolen artifacts without being paid first, but then the recipient wouldn't pay first without guarantee of getting the goods. Harry's out-of-town trips and visits overseas were shopping expeditions for a lot more than Portuguese armoires. He smuggled out the stuff in cheap furniture, shipped it to himself to the shop, then arrived back in Memphis in time to pick it up and get it to its final destination. But what about the money? There had to be a lot of money involved. He'd have to have bank accounts the IRS couldn't trace.

She really needed to call Bobby again, but she had hung up on him last night when he yelled at her. Really. He could get so excited. Like it was her fault José had hidden in Cami's car. After thinking for a moment, she decided to try Morgan instead. He just might have info he could be coaxed to share.

"Can you talk?" she asked when he answered, and after a short pause he said yeah, but he sounded a little grumpy.

"Where have you been, Harley? I left messages for you."

"I know. It was one of those nights. I'll tell you about it later. Listen, I know you're not on this case, that you're off somewhere playing bad guy, but sometimes you hear things. They've arrested my aunt for Harry Gordon's murder."

"She hasn't been formally charged yet."

"But she's in custody?"

"For now. They won't be able to hold her much longer without formally charging her."

"So Bobby was telling the truth? She's just in protective custody?"

"You'll have to ask him that. Harley, what are you up to now? And don't bother telling me you aren't up to anything. I know you better than that."

She was thinking fast. If it was true that Darcy was just in protective custody, then the police thought she was in danger from the real killer. That was good. And bad. The real killer was still loose, and Darcy hadn't exactly made herself low profile. Somehow, she didn't think it was José. And she knew for a certainty it wasn't Madelyn or Amanda, and nine-tenths sure it wasn't Aunt Darcy. Except for Cheríe, she'd about run out of suspects.

"Harley, are you still there, or are you just thinking of a way to get information out of me without being blunt?"

"You know me so well. Yes. That's exactly what I'm doing. Will blunt work?"

Mike said something nasty, then made a huffing sound. "It might. Depends on what you want to know. You get one question."

"Who do the police think killed Harry and Julio if they don't think Aunt Darcy did it?"

"Again, you'll have to ask Baroni that question."

"Bobby just yells at me lately. He can be very testy. Okay, I have another question—"

"Sorry. Only one question allowed."

"But you didn't answer it!"

"Yes, I did. You just didn't like the answer."

"This is an unattractive side of your personality, you know."

He laughed. "You're assuming I have a two-sided personality."

"Maybe I'm wrong. Okay, gotta go now."

"Wait—Harley, I know better than to ask you to promise not to do anything but stay home where you're safe, but do us all a favor and let the police handle this. They're better at it than you."

"That's true. But I have certain advantages they don't."

"I'm scared to ask."

"I don't need pesky things like search warrants."

"Harley, that's called breaking and entering."

"Not if you're invited inside."

Morgan made a strange noise, and before he could ask what she had in mind, she said a quick good-bye and hung up. She had things to do. Places to go. People to see.

After a shower and change of clothes, she left a note for Cami telling her that she'd be back later and that she'd borrowed some of her clothes, then revved up her bike and coasted down the driveway. It was a sunny day, washed clean by rain the night before, one of those nice late spring days Memphis boasted of in travel brochures.

The trip to Atoka didn't seem as long this time. And she had her Mace ready in case she ran into Gladys again, though she rather hoped she didn't have to pepper spray a goose. It didn't seem very fair, somehow.

There was an extra car in the driveway when she arrived. Harley slowed before she ended up blundering into a situation she wouldn't like. It was a blue Mustang with Missouri plates, new and shiny. It didn't seem likely that it'd be José, so she parked her bike on the strip between the ruts where it wasn't as muddy, and hung her helmet off the handlebars. Mace and phone at the ready, she approached the mobile home. Like last time, the dogs didn't bark and hardly raised their heads to acknowledge her arrival, and fortunately, there was no sign of a goose lurking on the porch.

Voices came from inside, a little loud at times, and she paused before interrupting.

"You know where she is," a man snarled, sounding menacing, "and you better tell me!"

"I swear I don't," came the reply, and Harley recognized Anna Merritt's voice. "She never tells me where she's staying. I haven't even heard from her lately. I swear it!"

When it seemed like he was going to get even more threatening, Harley rapped loudly on the door. A distraction might help, and, after all, she had her Mace handy. After a moment, Anna appeared in the doorway. She looked a little relieved to see Harley.

"It's you again," she said, but didn't sound too unfriendly. "What do you want?"

"I have a few things to talk over with you. Mind if I come in?"

"Well . . . " Anna glanced over her shoulder. "I have company right now, but maybe you can come back later."

"No, I really need to talk to you now. It won't take long. I can just sit out here on the porch until you're free, if you prefer."

"That's all right." Anna unlocked the storm door and swung it open. "Come in."

Harley gave her small Mace canister a good shake just in case, and kept it in her palm as she went inside. A rather large man stood in the center of the living room. His head nearly touched the wooden beam that ran the length of the ceiling. He had gray hair, blue eyes, and an unpleasant expression.

"Hello," she chirped, eying him as closely as he was watching her, "how are you?" Not that she really wanted to know. It was just something to say while she tried to gauge the tension level.

Ignoring her, he turned to Anna. "I'll be back later."

"Oh, don't let me run you off," Harley said. "I just came by to chat for a few minutes. Are you the brother, Bernard Plotz?"

It wasn't that she thought he was, just a shot in the dark, but after a brief hesitation, he said, "Yes. Bernie."

"Aha," Harley couldn't resist saying, "the Plotz thickens."

He scowled. "And you are—?"

"Intruding on a family reunion, I see. Maybe I should just run along."

There was something definitely odd going on here. Anna looked tense, Bernie looked mad, and the hair on the back of Harley's neck tightened. She didn't need to get in the middle of a family fight, that was for sure.

Before she could edge back to the door, Bernie moved to block her. "What are you really doing here?"

"Well, that's between me and Anna."

"And now me." He towered over her, suddenly seeming much too large and menacing.

Harley thought fast, then blurted, "I wanted to tell Anna that I'm supposed to meet her—your—sister in a little while. At the shop."

"You heard from Frieda?"

"Well . . . kinda. I, um, bumped into her by accident. She seemed kinda scared and said to meet her today, so that's where I'm headed. Just wanted to let Anna know she must be all right." Harley edged the Mace lower in her palm, finger on the nozzle just in case. This guy didn't look at all friendly. But to her relief, he pushed past her and out the door without another word. After a moment, she heard a car door slam and gravel grind as he took off down the driveway.

Harley looked at Anna, who sagged onto a chair arm and put her hands on her knees. "I don't believe Frieda told you anything," she said, and Harley shrugged.

"Well, she did push me into a glass case. Rather strong upper body. Does she work out?"

Anna didn't say anything, just looked at her, and Harley smiled. "They're both involved in the smuggling, aren't they?" When she shook her head, Harley said, "Yes they are, and you're probably just as mixed up in it as your sister. You know all about everything."

Anna stood up. "No. But if I did, I wouldn't tell you. It's time for you to go."

"All right, but one more thing—have you looked in the ivory box that Frieda gave you?"

"Why?"

"Because it probably contains what your brother wants. He's looking for Frieda, right? I don't think it's for a family reunion. He's one of the smugglers. Maybe a courier. He has to want the list of stuff, to find out where it went, or where the money is, or something like that. He didn't act at all like the kind of guy who's looking for his sister out of brotherly love."

Anna gave a short bark of laughter. "Well, you're wrong there. Look, I don't know what to tell you, just what *not* to tell you. Please go. If he realizes you lied, he's liable to come back, and I don't think you'd like what he'd do next."

"Aren't you afraid for your sister?"

"She has better sense than to hang around the shop where . . . Harry was killed. I doubt she's even in Memphis any longer."

"Unless she has a reason to be here—like lots of money?"

Anna pressed her lips tightly together, and Harley recognized that she'd said all she was going to say. After an awkward moment, she told Anna to call if she changed her mind and gave her another card that'd probably be thrown away. She eased out the door, half-expecting to be attacked from some angle.

Thankfully, there was no sign of Gladys the goose. Their one encounter had left a lasting impression, and she was in no hurry for a repeat.

As soon as she got out on the main highway, Harley pulled over into the parking lot of an old country store and gas station. She unfastened her helmet and hung it from the handlebars, and still straddling the bike, called Bobby.

He didn't sound very pleased to hear from her. "All I asked was that you stay home and out of harm's way, Harley, and you can't even do that. What's the matter with you?"

"Do you want this information or not? It's important, but suit yourself."

Bobby said something tacky, then said, "Okay, tell me the information that you think's so important."

"I shouldn't since you're being so hateful, but I thought you might want to know that one of the smugglers is on his way to the design shop at this very moment. He thinks he's going to meet Cheríe Saucier there. He's very insistent on speaking with her. I'm sure it has something to do with the smuggled goods and money. Oh, and he—"

"Harley, whatever you do, do *not* follow him. Do you hear me? Stay away from your aunt's shop. That guy's dangerous. I'll have to radio a unit to make sure no one there gets hurt."

A little irritated, she said, "It's not open today. The insurance company has to come in and do their inspection before they can even make repairs."

"Did you stop to think what might happen if Cheríe really is there?"

She hadn't, of course. "Don't worry," she said. "I'd put my money on Cheríe. She's got the upper body strength of a Lowland gorilla."

"Harley, dammit—!"

"Oh, she won't show back up there. It'd be stupid. Besides, Bernie's her brother, and he's just after Cheríe because she has something he wants."

"Harley—"

"I don't know why you think I'm stupid. Maybe I get a little too enthusiastic at times, but I know better than to follow a killer. Past activities not counting. Do you think he's the one who killed Harry Gordon and Julio?"

"Harley—"

"After all I've done for you today, sending him where you can find him, you can at least let me know what happens. You have my aunt in protective custody, and—"

"Not anymore. Her parents' lawyer sprung her a couple of hours ago."

That wasn't really good news. Not with some deranged smuggler desperate to find where the goods and/or money had been hidden. *Damn*, she thought.

"Look, Bobby, I know I've told you this before, but I really think that ivory chest is important. Harry had it, and now Anna has it, and—"

"Go home, Harley. Let us handle this. Believe it or not, we've already got a pretty good idea of who he is and what to do. Just *go home*."

"Does Aunt Darcy know this guy is on the loose?"

"Where are you, Harley? I'll send a unit to escort you safely home."

"Aren't you sweet. I'll be just fine. You'd better hurry, or you'll miss Bernie. He's most likely already at the shop."

She hung up before he could say anything else, and dialed her aunt's house. Amanda answered.

"Mandy, whatever you do, don't let anyone into the house."

"Harley? Is that you? You have some nerve, calling here after all the trouble you've caused us. If it wasn't for you poking your nose where it doesn't belong, everything would be a lot better."

"You're right. Look, listen to me. It's vital that you do *not* let anyone into the house that you don't know, and I don't care who he says he is. Do you understand? There's a killer on the loose and you could be his next target."

"I'm tired of your tricks, Harley. Don't call here again." Amanda hung up.

"Damn," said Harley, and tried the number again. This time, the answering machine picked up. They had Caller ID, of course. It could be a real nuisance.

There was no answer on Darcy's cell phone either, and she left a message just in case she decided to go by the shop. Surely, after just getting out of jail, that wouldn't be her first stop, but there was no telling what she was liable to do. It had seemed like such a good idea to send Bernie off on a wild goose chase, but in retrospect, maybe it hadn't been so smart. Like most of her good ideas lately, they too often turned out to be really bad.

Harley called Grandmother Eaton on the off-chance that Darcy had stopped by on her way home, but Janet answered and said her grandparents were out for the day.

"Did they say where they were going?" Harley asked.

"To an art show and wine tasting, I believe."

"An art show? Are you sure that's where they are?"

"That's what they said. Shall I give them a message, Miss Harley?"

An art show—no doubt, that was Grandmother Eaton's polite term for bailing their youngest daughter out of jail. "No, just ask them to call me when they get back, please."

For several minutes she sat in the shade of a huge pecan tree that draped over part of the gravel parking lot, considering her options. Bobby was right. She should go home and stay out of it. Being stupid and getting in the way would only make things worse.

She put on her helmet and started the bike with a push of her thumb. The smooth throb of the engine was always satisfying. Riding her bike, she always felt powerful, as if nothing could harm her. Except, of course, for the Memphis drivers that never seemed to watch for motorcycles or the daring and foolish pedestrians crossing the street.

She meant to go home where it'd be safe and she wouldn't cause any more problems. She really did. But somehow, she found herself headed out east to the Fontaine residence instead. It'd only take a minute to warn her aunt and pigheaded cousins to stay in their house, then she'd go home.

That was the plan, all right.

Fourteen

"Look, Harley, I told you—"

"Amanda, this is important." Ignoring her efforts to block the doorway, Harley stepped into the entrance hall. "Where's Aunt Darcy?"

"None of your business. Haven't you done enough damage?"

"You don't blame *me* for her arrest, do you?"

"If not for you, most of this wouldn't have happened."

Harley stared at her. "You can't believe that. Aunt Darcy asked me to help her find out if Harry was smuggling in illegal imports, but neither of us expected him to get murdered."

Angry tears welled in Amanda's eyes. "Harry wouldn't be dead if you hadn't started your meddling. I just know it."

"So this is about Harry, not your mother, then." Harley tilted her head to one side, eyes narrowed a bit. "You're not that selfish, are you?"

"Of course not!"

"Good. I was hoping you weren't making this about you instead of Aunt Darcy. Now where is she? I came here to warn her that the guy who killed Harry might come after her. That was what I was trying to tell you on the phone, but you wouldn't listen."

Amanda's eyes had gotten larger. "She's not here."

Harley got an ache in the pit of her stomach. "Tell me she's not at the shop."

"She said there was something there she needed. Oh God, Harley, do you think—?"

Instead of answering, Harley pulled out her cell phone and dialed Bobby. He didn't answer and she left a message. Damn. He was never there when she needed him most. Maybe he was already at the shop. She hoped. She tried Darcy's cell phone again, but no answer. *Damn.*

When she dialed Morgan, he picked up on the second ring. "Yeah."

"Hey, I need you."

"If this is a booty call, I'm a little busy right now, but I'll be glad to come by later."

"How thoughtful, but I have a different kind of problem. I can't reach Bobby and I think my aunt's in trouble."

Morgan quickly became all business. She gave him a brief summary of her suspicions, and he told her to stay where she was, and he'd make sure Baroni got a unit to the shop.

"You'll stay there, right, Harley?"

"Wild horses couldn't drag me away, I promise."

She was shivering by now, more with anticipation than actual fear. When she looked at her cousin, Amanda was bug-eyed and huddled in misery on the edge of a bench in the hall.

"Where's Madelyn?" Harley asked.

"Playing tennis with Trey."

"Good lord. I've never known her to actually exercise before. She must really like him."

"I guess. Harley, what's going on?"

"Get Madelyn in here and I'll tell you what I know, which isn't much."

She waited in the kitchen. Aunt Darcy's pretty, pickled-wood cabinets had taken expert finishers weeks to achieve a subtle blend of weathered streaks to match the tiles on the walls and white-oak floors. A bay window with stained glass panes reflecting rainbows of light looked out on fountains and gardens beyond French doors. Everything gleamed bright and shiny and expensive, and she thought of Diva's kitchen with its cluttered counters and dreamcatchers and how much more welcoming it seemed. Money definitely wasn't everything.

Just as she was deciding that Darcy Fontaine must have unrecognized talents, Amanda burst back into the kitchen with Madelyn in tow.

"Where's Trey?" Harley asked.

"He, uh, went home." Madelyn looked out of breath, hair disheveled, lips slightly swollen and eyes still a bit glazed. Harley smiled.

"Must have been some tennis game."

Madelyn lifted a brow. "It was."

"Well, we could stand here all day and discuss your love match—pun intended—but I'd rather make sure that you two understand what I'm trying to tell you. Harry's killer is still on the loose and I have info that he might end up here. Where's Uncle Paul?"

They exchanged a look, but finally Amanda said, "Mama and Daddy are separated. It's only a trial separation, but he's . . . he's not living here anymore."

"Oh. I'm sorry. That's got to be hard on all of you." There didn't seem to be anything else to say about that so she moved on. "Make sure all the doors and windows are locked. And keep trying to get Darcy on her cell phone."

"Where are you going?" Madelyn sounded panicked. "You're not going to leave us here alone, are you?"

"I sent the police to the shop, so if Aunt Darcy's there, she'll be just fine. I'll check the pool house and lock it. Turn on your alarm when I go out, and—"

"Don't you dare leave us, Harley Jean Davidson! You started this mess, and you'd better stay right here with us until we're safe."

Madelyn looked downright vicious. Her thin nose quivered, her lips were drawn back over her perfect white teeth, and she looked as if she really might bite at any moment. A definite improvement from her usual haughty expression.

"Well, since you asked so nicely, I suppose I could wait until Aunt Darcy arrives. We can pass all that free time catching up on the past few years."

That last suggestion was met with a less than enthusiastic response, so Harley ended up going around checking all the doors and windows with her cousins bunched behind her like two scared mice. Safety in numbers seemed to be their watchword for the day.

Just as she was ready to suggest they find a more constructive way to wait, the sound of a car arriving in the circular driveway broke the tension.

"It's Mama," Amanda said from the front window, and Madelyn rushed to open the door as her sister added, "Oh, and she has someone with her."

The hair on the back of Harley's neck stood up, and she started toward the entrance hall with her Mace and cell phone handy. "*Wait*," she said, but it was too late. Madelyn had opened the door for her mother and the man Harley knew as Bernie.

Darcy looked catatonic. There was no expression at all on her face, and Harley realized it was the look of an animal caught in a trap—numb futility. Bernie, however, was quite animated.

"You said it's here, so you better get it," he said to Darcy in a distinctly unpleasant tone. "Now move!" He jabbed her in the back with the barrel of a gun, while Madelyn and Amanda squealed as he slammed the front door closed.

About the time Harley decided it'd be more prudent for her not to be noticed, he saw her.

"*You*—biker chick—get your ass over here."

Palming her Mace, Harley thumbed what she hoped was the speed dial for 911 on her cell phone as she reluctantly walked toward them. Holding her hands behind her back, she edged close enough to satisfy him, but hopefully just out of reach.

"How nice to see you again, *Bernie*. No need for guns. We're all cooperating. Aren't we, Aunt Darcy, Maddie, Mandy? Fontaines are always co—"

"Shut up. Get over here with the other two. Now!"

He didn't look at all agreeable. She edged closer. His free hand lashed out to grab her by the arm, and her cell phone flew from her hand to land on the floor. It went in several different directions at once. Reacting, she sprayed the Mace at him, jerking free at the same time. The spray caught him on the side of his face and back of his head, not exactly as effective as she'd have liked. Still, it was enough to make him let go of her but not the gun. Instead, he slapped a hand to his eyes and hollered words Harley had never heard before.

Shaking his head, he turned his gun in her direction and said a few words she *had* heard before. Blinking as his eyes got all teary, he gave her a watery glare. "Think you're smart, don't you? Give me that spray or I'll put a bullet in you."

That seemed like a fair trade. She promptly handed it over. Aunt Darcy and her cousins huddled together as if for protection, cowering against the wall. They looked at her as if she could do something, but she'd temporarily run out of ideas. The cell phone and Mace had been her only weapons. Now she had to depend on her wits, so that meant she was in big trouble.

"Girls, I'm sorry," Aunt Darcy was saying. "I didn't know what else to do but bring him here. He kept telling me I have something he wants—"

"Don't talk to each other," Bernie snapped, wiping at his red face.

"Want me to get a cold cloth for your face?" Harley offered. "You're getting all red."

"Shut up."

"I don't mind. Really, I don't. It won't take but a minute to go to the kitchen and—"

"Shut up! All of you get in the kitchen. Now!"

He herded them into the kitchen, and keeping the gun on them, rummaged through a few drawers, dumping contents on the floor as he searched. He came up with a ball of thick twine and tossed it at Harley.

"Okay, biker chick. Tie them up tight. I'll check, so better make sure you do it right or they'll wish you had."

The inference he made with the waggle of the gun set her right to work. Aunt Darcy had come out of her daze, but was shivering with terror.

"Is he going to kill us?" she whimpered.

"I hope not. Sorry I have to do this, but—"

"Stop talking," Bernie snarled. "Just do what I told you to do."

Harley finished in silence, tying them as loosely as she dared, but still tight enough that it would take them a while to work free. If they were left alone to do so. Bernie had to be after something that he thought Frieda had hidden. It couldn't be the smuggled goods, which he had to know the police had seized by now. What would be so important he'd take all these risks? So important he'd kill to get it? It could only be one thing.

As she stood up slowly, she said, "Are you looking for invoices or a ledger?"

Bernie narrowed his reddened eyes at her. "Yeah. You know where it is?"

"I'm pretty sure I do."

"Pretty sure ain't good enough."

"But it's a lot better than looking in all the wrong places like you're doing. Darcy doesn't have anything. She didn't even know exactly what Harry was up to with all those illegal imports. It was just by accident that she found anything. But I know where it's hidden."

He looked at her for a minute as if trying to decide if she was lying. She put on her most truthful expression and hoped for the best. After a moment, he gave an abrupt nod. "Okay, tell me where it is."

She took a deep breath. "I'll have to show you. You're obviously in a hurry and can't waste much time. But you can't hurt my aunt and cousins. That's the deal."

He brought up his pistol. Light from the windows gleamed dully on the barrel. Harley had a moment of panic that left her lightheaded. He had no reason to take her anywhere. All he had to do was shoot one of her cousins or her aunt, and she'd tell him anything he wanted to know. She hoped he didn't think of that, or wasn't willing to risk a shot being heard by neighbors. After all, this was a quiet neighborhood and a gunshot was liable to be noticed.

"All right," he said. "A hostage isn't a bad idea. Hand me that string. I'll tie you up so you don't get any ideas. Then you're going to show me where the ledger is."

This wasn't quite what she'd had in mind, but at least she'd get him away from here and her cousins. Aunt Darcy looked up at her with wide eyes, her lips quivering.

"Harley—don't."

"It'll be all right. Really it will. He'll get what he wants, and then he'll leave us alone." It was hard to sound calm when her heart was pumping like crazy and her knees were wobbly. And she just hoped she was right.

Bernie seemed to have a plan. And he apparently had figured out that the cops would be at the shop, because when she suggested they go there first, he said he wasn't falling for that shit.

"Get me, little girl? You better not be stalling me. You'll regret it if you do."

"Okay. Whatever you say. I just thought it might have been moved or something, but it's still where I last saw it, I'm sure."

"And where was that?"

"Atoka."

Bernie swore again, harshly. "I knew that bitch was holding out on me."

"Well, I don't think she knows what she has. Maybe Cheríe gave it to her but didn't tell her what it was or why it's important."

"Frieda gave her the ledger?"

"It's hidden inside something." And if it wasn't, she was in deep doody. "Mind me asking why it's so important?"

"Don't get too nosy. If I tell you, I'll have to kill you." He laughed like it was a joke, but Harley didn't find it amusing. He'd already killed at least one person, she was sure, and maybe two. She had no desire to add another notch to his pistol.

"That's okay," she said, "I'm not that curious." The string he'd tied around her wrists had been pulled tight enough to cut off her circulation, and she twisted her hands to ease the strain. It gave a little, and she caught her breath. He hadn't knotted it good. She didn't dare look down at her wrists clasped in front of her. To put him off-guard, she chattered about her parents, her bike, her job, and anything she thought would distract him while she worked her hands loose, until finally he slammed his open hand against the steering wheel and yelled at her.

"You're a damn nuisance, you know that? Just shut the hell up or I'll shoot you and look for the damn ledger myself!"

"Sorry. Just trying to pass the time. You don't have to get so excited."

It seemed to take forever to get to Atoka, even in Aunt Darcy's sleek Lexus. Bernie had made her aunt trade cars, and she wondered if he'd left his at the shop. And if Bobby or Morgan were already there staking it out, or if they'd gone to Darcy's house to check on them. It'd be a huge comfort to know someone was already looking for her.

When they pulled onto the rutted driveway, two cars were parked near the mobile home. Harley had a flare of hope. Were the police already here?

Bernie braked abruptly at the end of the driveway. "This better not be a setup."

"One of the cars is Anna's. I don't know the other one. Anyway, how would it be a setup if I didn't know you were going to take me hostage, and I've been with you this whole time?"

Logic wasn't his strong point, it seemed. He growled at her, "If you've tipped off the cops you'll regret it."

"Regret is my middle name, believe me, but you broke my cell phone so I obviously had no way to call anyone."

Despite her denials, Harley hoped like hell the cops were there. She didn't see any good way out of this if they weren't.

Just her luck. It wasn't the cops. She knew that immediately when the storm door swung open and Cheríe Saucier stepped out onto the porch. Bernie said something under his breath and roared down the driveway, slamming the car into park and hurling himself out the door, gun in hand.

"Frieda! Damn you, bet you didn't expect to see *me* any time soon!"

Cheríe had come to a complete stop and stared at Bernie like he was a ghost. For a minute she didn't say anything, just stood there with her mouth open and eyes wide. Harley saw something like terror in her eyes and knew it was time to make her move.

Bernie had left the car running, keys still in the ignition, and she scooted across the seat and behind the wheel. Her wrists were still bound, though a lot looser, and she managed to put the car into gear and grab the wheel as it lurched forward. She stomped on the gas pedal. Aunt Darcy's nice, shiny Lexus had a lot of power. It shot toward the parked car at the edge of the trailer and crashed into it, crumpling fenders with a terrible shrieking sound. Damn. Not at all the direction she'd meant to go. Steam rose from under the hood with a loud hissing noise.

A little disoriented by the collision, and breathless from the air bag that mushroomed out like a chalky marshmallow, Harley fought her way free just as Bernie reached in the still open door to grab her.

"Stupid bitch, what are you trying to do, kill me?"

"Turnabout seems fair play," she muttered as he hauled her out of the car and threw her to the ground. Landing on her back, she glanced over at the porch just in time to see Cheríe make a mad dash toward her car. She had the ivory box in her hands.

"She's getting away with the ledger," Harley said when it looked like Bernie intended to shoot her, and he whirled around.

"Damn you, Frieda, you better stop!" To make his point, he fired at her. The bullet pinged off something metal and both Frieda and Anna shrieked.

Frieda took off across the field, clutching the box to her chest, and Bernie ran after her. It was obvious he hadn't been prepared for a foot chase, as his panting and swearing got louder. He paused, fired a shot that went wild, and then took off after Frieda again.

"Do something!" Anna shouted, and Harley realized she was looking at her.

She blinked. "Do what? He's got a gun. Call the police."

"They'll never get here in time. Can't you do something before he kills her?"

"He's not that good a shot. Besides, he's *your* brother, you go after him."

"Oh for heaven's sake, he's not my brother! Just stop him, please!"

Harley got to her feet and found that the string around her wrists had almost come off. She tugged her right hand free. "I hope you're dialing nine-one-one," she said as she started across the field, "and tell them to *hurry!*"

She had no idea how she was supposed to stop Bernie from killing

Frieda. If he really wasn't her brother, then he wouldn't hesitate to shoot her. What did he have to lose now?

A line of thin trees fenced in the field on one side, and Harley saw Frieda disappear into them, with Bernie not too far behind. He was gaining on her, and all it'd take was one bullet to bring her down. Harley paused to pick up a broken branch from the ground, just so she'd have a weapon of sorts. Maybe she could come up behind him and whack him in the head with it before he knew she was there. And maybe he'd hear her behind him and turn around and shoot her, the more logical part of her brain protested.

Why should she even care if he killed Frieda anyway? She was just as unpleasant, no matter what name she went by, and part of the same smuggling operation. Of course, she didn't really want to see her dead, but was it worth risking her own life?

All those thoughts whirled around her head as her Nikes dug into ground still soggy from the last rain. Her chest ached and she dragged in air that smelled of damp ground and wildflowers just beginning to bloom. Arms pumping, she closed the distance between her and Bernie. He was just ahead of her, reaching the line of trees, when a white flash rose up out of the ground at his feet.

Stumbling, he let out a startled yell and fell sideways. Harley saw his gun fly through the air. She changed directions and dove onto the pistol while Bernie beat at the feathered fury attacking him with bill and huge wings. By the time she got to her feet with the gun in hand, Gladys had Bernie bleeding.

Harley panted, "I never thought I'd be glad to see you, Gladys. Hold it there, Bernie—I have the gun now, and I know how to shoot."

That wasn't really a lie. She did have the gun and she figured she could pull the trigger if she had to, not that she'd tell him that, of course.

"Shoot the damn thing!" Bernie yelled, but Harley had no intention of doing anything like that. The goose backed off a bit, watching both of them with wings outspread. It made a hissing noise that sounded ominous. Harley glimpsed a fuzzy bit of gray fluff peeking out from some kind of nest on the ground behind Gladys. Ah, so that was what she was protecting. Babies.

Keeping a wary eye on Gladys, as she didn't quite trust the goose not to go for her, too, she edged around and motioned with the pistol. "Get up slowly and she might not peck you to death."

The goose hissed louder, lunged at Bernie and nipped him on the leg, then retreated back to guard her nest. Bernie cussed some more. Harley smiled. Anna was right. Geese had the element of surprise that made them better than an attack dog. Who'd have ever thought Mother Goose could inflict so much damage?

Bernie stumbled to his feet and held his hands in the air when Harley advised him to, glaring at her as he said, "You let Frieda get away, damn you!"

"I wasn't the one chasing her, you were. Now go back to the trailer. Walk slowly and keep your distance. Anna called the police and they should be here any minute."

He laughed. "Not unless *you* called 'em. You don't think she'd call 'em, do you?"

Harley hesitated. She hadn't thought of that. Of course Anna wouldn't call the police, not when her sister was involved in the smuggling. That meant she was on her own with Bernie—if he really was Bernie. She thought about what Anna had said earlier.

"You know, Anna said the strangest thing. She said you aren't her brother."

"Did she? Well, I guess she'd know her own brother, wouldn't she."

Harley frowned. "I'm confused."

"Right. Look, give me that gun." He took a step closer to her and held out his hand. "Give it to me and I won't shoot you."

"Do I look that stupid? Don't answer. Just keep your distance or you'll find out what it feels like to wear a bullet as a nose ring."

She hoped he didn't see the fear in her eyes, or notice the way her hands shook and the barrel of the pistol wavered, but he watched her closely.

"You won't do it. You can't. It's harder than you think to shoot a person if you haven't ever shot anyone before."

"Well, I guess you'd know all about that, wouldn't you. You shot Harry."

He grinned. "Right. Harry Gordon is dead. I'm still here, though. And I'm telling you to give me that gun before you get hurt."

"Don't push your luck. You might get surprised." She motioned with the pistol. "Head back to the trailer. We'll wait on the police there."

"Sure you want to do that? I don't think Anna or Frieda are too fond of cops. They might not want you to call them."

"The person with the gun makes the rules. Now walk!"

To her relief, he slowly turned around, hands still in the air, and started walking toward the mobile home. As they got close, Harley saw Anna and Frieda get into the only car that still ran and take off down the driveway. Bernie started cussing again. She felt like doing the same.

The least they could have done was hang around and make sure she was okay, since she'd saved Frieda's life. But apparently, there was little gratitude for her efforts. "No honor among thieves, I see," she muttered. "That's the thanks I get."

"Told you," Bernie said, and she felt like smacking him with the pistol. "Frieda's a cold-hearted bitch. I oughta know. This isn't the first time she's left me holding the bag."

"Save your true confessions for the police. I'm sure they'd love to hear what you've got to say."

By now they'd reached the edge of the trailer, and before she realized what he intended, he broke into a sprint and went around the corner, disappearing from sight. Damn! She came to a halt. Now what did she do?

"Hey, you can't outrun a bullet," she called after a minute, but Bernie didn't answer. He was probably waiting around the corner with a big stick, so she went the other way, back around the rear of the trailer to come up from the other end. Her heart thudded so hard against her ribs it hurt, and her stomach muscles got tight. Breathing wasn't an option. She didn't see Bernie. He could be anywhere.

This kind of thing looked so different on TV. If she was at home watching this from her chair, she'd be shouting *Look behind you, stupid!* or *He's under the porch!* It was a lot more fun when she wasn't the one in danger.

Every hair on her head and arms had to be standing straight on end. She developed a twitch in her left eye. For what seemed like forever, she stood there uncertainly, not wanting to go backward, and not daring to go forward. Lord, what a time to have to go to the bathroom. She sucked in a deep breath and took a big step toward the porch. The dogs were gone from under it, not that they'd have barked anyway.

A tingling sensation ran down her spine, and for some reason she recalled Diva saying, "Watch out for the dead man."

She turned, and just as Bernie rushed her, she leaped out of the way so he only brushed against her. It was just enough to send the pistol spinning out of her hand and across the concrete patio. They both dove for it at the same time.

Fifteen

"Let go!" Bernie snarled, holding Harley by the arm and shaking it to make her lose her grip on the gun.

Flat on her stomach with his knee in her back, she held on to it for dear life. Then he hit her on the side of her head. Her ears rang, everything went blurry, and pure rage gave her a surge of energy neither of them expected.

Gritting her teeth, she pushed up from the concrete so quick and hard he lost his balance and went sideways. Before he could get up she kicked him, not caring where, just slamming her size sevens into him wherever she could. What came out of her mouth sounded like gibberish even to her own ears, and she was vaguely aware of Bernie going into the fetal position with arms covering his head and his knees drawn up to his chest.

Then he snaked out an arm and grabbed her ankle and gave a jerk. She went backward to land on her rear in a jarring thud that made her bite her tongue. Bernie went for the gun she still held in her hand, and she fought desperately to hold on to it.

Adrenaline was no match for size and strength, to her dismay. Bernie wrenched the gun from her hand and stood over her, panting for breath.

"Sure you want to shoot me?" she managed to get out. "Someone's bound to hear the shot and call the cops."

"Not in the country. People out here are used to hearing gunshots."

"Right. But you're going to need a hostage." It was a desperate ploy, and it worked. He thought about it for a moment, then gestured with the gun.

"Get up. No more tricks or I'll shoot you."

Harley didn't doubt that he meant it. He had a feral gleam in his eyes that more than said he'd even enjoy it. If she let him get her away from here, she was doomed. She had to stall, to keep him here long enough for help to arrive, but how did she do that?

She got up slowly. "What are you going to do now?"

"Just get in Anna's car. And shut up."

Anna's car was sandwiched between Aunt Darcy's and the trailer. It was a beat-up old Ford that the crash hadn't done much damage to, none that could be seen, anyway. It looked the same to Harley as it always had, while her aunt's Lexus had a crumpled front fender and the hood had buckled. They just didn't make cars like they used to, she supposed as she limped toward the Ford.

"I have to go to the bathroom," she said, and when Bernie swore at her, added, "Believe me, you'd much rather I do that here than in the car."

"If this is another one of your tricks—"

"Spastic colon. It happens when I get nervous. I'm surprised I haven't already made a mess. It won't take long, I swear."

After a moment, he grabbed her by the arm and dragged her toward the steps leading into the trailer. "I'm gonna stand right outside the door, so don't get smart."

"If I was smart, I wouldn't be here in the first place."

That was all too true, Harley thought as she went up the steps and into the trailer. It was a mess. Clothes were scattered around and lamps overturned, drawers open and stuff all on the floor. Bernie walked her down the narrow hall to the bathroom, and after checking it out, he gave her a push inside.

"Hurry up before I decide you're too much trouble as a hostage."

Hurrying was the farthest thing from her mind, but she didn't share that with him. Best to just delay as long as she could and hope like hell Bobby had gone to Darcy's house looking for them. He'd put two and two together. She just prayed it'd be soon enough.

The bathroom was small and wood-paneled, with a tub, vanity sink, toilet, and washer and dryer. A small window was over the appliances, but one look was enough to tell her she'd never be able to fit through it. And even if she would, she'd have to take it apart before she could, as it had those glass louvers like many older mobile homes.

She flipped up the toilet lid so Bernie would think she was using it, and quietly opened the vanity doors. The usual necessities were there, toilet paper, shampoo and conditioner, and all the other things women required for basic hygiene and feminine improvement. Anna had seemed like the old-fashioned kind of girl, and just as Harley thought she wouldn't have one, she found it in a drawer: a steel nail file. She slid it inside her tee shirt at the waist, then made some more noise for Bernie's benefit. A little more searching turned up a purse size can of hair spray that she tucked into her waistband close to the nail file. Bug spray would have been better, but she'd have to go with what she could find.

Bernie rapped on the door. "Better hurry it up or I'm coming in there."

"All right, just another minute. I think I'm almost done." She flushed a couple of times just to stall a bit longer. After spraying deodorizer, then washing her hands so long the top layer of skin probably went down the drain, she dried her hands and opened the door.

Bernie looked at her suspiciously. "You're up to something."

"Right. Anna stored her grenades in the bathroom. I've got three in my pocket."

"Smartass."

"Well, as my mama always says, better to be a smartass than a dumbass."

"Yeah, if your mama could only see you now, huh."

"Point taken. Mind if I get a drink of water? My throat's dry after all that running around in the field."

He gave her a shove ahead of him into the living room. "Get your ass in the car. If you try anything else, you're dead."

He didn't sound at all tolerant about more delay, so Harley walked toward the front door as slowly as she dared. Once she got in that car with him, there'd be no finding her in time. She went down the steps one at a time, past the general debris and toward the car.

"Hey," she said, suddenly struck by a memory, "weren't you driving a blue Mustang last time I saw you?"

"What's it to you?"

"Nothing. I just notice cars sometimes." Not often enough, apparently, or she'd have remembered that Harry Gordon's blue Mustang was still missing. What an idiot she was!

Bernie put her in the car and tied her hands in front of her with a strip of cloth, this time making sure it was tight enough that she couldn't wiggle free. Then he took some tools to the steering column to hot-wire the car, as Anna hadn't been thoughtful enough to leave the keys.

"Jack of all trades, I see," Harley muttered, hoping against hope he wouldn't succeed. It started right up. She leaned her head against the window and sighed. She should have listened to Bobby. And Morgan. And Cami. And . . . well, the list went on. They'd tried to tell her. Why did she always think she could do things she obviously wasn't equipped to do? She hadn't fit into the world of corporate banking. She wasn't really a good tour guide, forgetting her spiel half the time, and the rest of the time, annoying the clients as much as they annoyed her. Maybe she should try something else. Limo driver, perhaps. That couldn't be too bad. No spiel to remember, nothing to do but ferry drunks around town while they went to big, important parties while she waited in the limo with a Coke and listening to the radio. Yeah, that wouldn't be bad. And she wouldn't run into a lot of dead people with a job like that. All she had to do was get out of this mess, and she'd give up any attempts to help anyone else. Ever again. She'd leave it to the police next time, if there ever was a next time. If she survived this time.

Staring out the window, Harley caught a glimpse of movement in the side mirror on the car. She blinked. There was someone behind Darcy's car. Surely she wasn't imagining things. It had looked like a man hiding back there . . . could it be? But if the cops had arrived, they'd show up with sirens wailing and flashing lights. And they'd send more than one guy.

While she was trying to decide if help had arrived or she was in even bigger trouble, Bernie got out of the car. He bent down to say, "I'm going to move that car out of my way, but I'm watching you, so if you even look like you want to get out and run, I'll shoot you. Understand, Blondie?"

"Perfectly. I'm fine right here."

As soon as he straightened up, she fumbled with the waist of her jeans and pulled out the hair spray and nail file. She tucked them both between her legs and hoped he wouldn't notice.

When a loud yell erupted behind her she looked in the side mirror to see Bernie go flying backward. Swiveling her head, she saw out the back window another man leap on top of him, and for a moment she didn't recognize him. Not until she heard a loud voice cursing in Spanish did she realize who it had to be—José. And he'd provided her with the perfect chance to get the hell out of there.

Grabbing her weapons just in case, she managed to get the car door open and took off for the road. If Bernie came after her, she might stand a chance if she got out into traffic where people could see her, she reasoned, and hoped that José kept him busy long enough for her to make it.

Behind her, gunshots rang out, followed by more yelling. She didn't want to think about what might be happening to José, and kept running. As soon as she could get to a phone, she'd call the cops. More gunfire, and this time, she felt something hot whiz past her head. She dove to the ground, heart pounding so loud she couldn't hear anything but the blood rushing to her head. Now she really had to go to the bathroom, and wished she'd thought of that earlier.

She couldn't lie there forever, and after a few seconds passed, she pushed to her feet. The nail file was lost in the grass somewhere, so she grabbed the hair spray and took off again. She ran clumsily with her hands still tied in front of her, fear pressing down and her heart in her throat. The line of trees along the property line lay just ahead of her, if she could only make it past them. A few more yards and she'd be on the road out of sight.

Just as she reached the trees an arm snaked out to grab her. She screamed and pressed the nozzle on the hair spray, twisting toward her attacker and aiming upward for eyes and face. It didn't do much to get her free, but she did recognize the low, irritated voice.

"Ow! Dammit, Harley!"

She almost collapsed with relief. "Morgan? Where the hell have you been!"

Wiping at his eyes and blinking, he muttered, "Glad to see you too, babe. What'd you hit me with?"

"Hair spray. Listen, the guy who killed Harry is here and he's fighting with José. We need to help him."

"*We*, hell. Stay here."

"No, don't go out there, you'll get shot!" She grabbed him when he pushed her behind the trees and started around her. The look he gave her should have turned her to stone. The timbre of his voice was inflexible.

"Stay *down*. My car's over there. Get in it and stay there. Don't do anything else stupid. Backup's on the way."

"Mike, wait until they get here." He wasn't listening. He'd go out there and get himself killed, and it'd be her fault. Her throat knotted and she couldn't say anything, could only watch while he unclipped something on his boot. Then she noticed the gun in his hand, heavy, lethal.

He gave her an impatient glance. "Dammit, *go*, Harley. I need to get in position while they're busy fighting."

This was a side of him she hadn't seen. He looked almost feral, a glitter in his eyes that bordered on ferocious. His expression had gone sharp, intent. Like a wolf. He wore a Kevlar vest over his black tee shirt, an empty holster strapped to his thigh, the butt of a small pistol sticking out from his boot top, and with the pistol in his hand, he looked like he could handle almost anything, including a rampaging rhino. She swallowed her panic.

"Sure. I'm going," she said, then crouched down behind a tree to watch as he ran in a cautious, bent-over lope police used when confronting an armed criminal. He took cover behind a bush for a second, then ran toward the opposite side of Darcy's car from where Bernie and José were still fighting for the gun. José was obviously a better match for Bernie than she'd been, but she had no idea which one of them had the pistol.

Morgan briefly positioned himself behind the car, watching them struggle. Harley knew she was supposed to go to his car, but she couldn't. It was like watching a train wreck about to happen, all her muscles tensed and air locked in her lungs, paralyzed with some kind of dread fascination.

So far, neither José nor Bernie had noticed him, they were each so intent on getting the gun from the other. Harley couldn't tell who had it, just saw a blur of fists and feet. Air locked in her lungs until she got lightheaded. Damn, there was nothing she could do. She'd only be a distraction if she tried.

Then Morgan stood up and shouted, "Police! Put down the weapon!"

José shouted something in Spanish and Morgan shouted back. Bernie grabbed for the gun in José's hand and wrenched it free, then whirled around.

"Drop the weapon!" Mike shouted, his arm braced atop the trunk of Aunt Darcy's car and his revolver steady. For a moment, there was no sound, just the face-off between the two men.

Then everything seemed to happen in slow motion. Bernie's pistol spat orange flame, Morgan fired back, and Harley watched in horror.

Sixteen

"Noooo!" The scream erupted from her throat despite her intention to keep silent. Harley leaped to her feet. She didn't know what she meant to do, only that she had to help Morgan, who had hit the ground and rolled.

Then she saw him take aim again from his prone position, heard the sharp report of his pistol, and Bernie jerked backward as if hit with a two by four. He flopped around for a moment like a fish, then lay still. José stood up and looked down at him, then over at Morgan.

"He's still breathing."

"Hands in the air," Morgan ordered, slowly getting up with his pistol still aimed and ready. "Now lock your hands behind your neck and get down on your knees."

José did as he was told, and Mike approached cautiously. He leaned over and took the gun from Bernie's hand and stuck it in his waistband. Then he looked toward Harley where she'd stopped halfway up the rutted driveway. His mouth twitched.

"You never listen to me. Go to my car and call for an ambulance."

When she got back, Bernie was sitting up with his hands cuffed behind him and José sat close by, cuffed as well and glaring at him. She looked from them to Morgan.

"So what's up?"

"Flesh wound. He'll be fine. Wanna tell me what's going on here, Harley?"

"I'd love to, but I have no idea. Bernie said he's Anna and Frieda's brother, but Anna said he's not. None of them get along very well, it seems, as he tried to kill Frieda after calling her a few unkind names. José is Julio's brother and I have no idea why he's here or how he found us, but I'm ever so grateful." She paused to take a deep breath. "Anna and Frieda left with a box that has invoices or a ledger full of names. Or maybe bank account numbers. Anyway, it's important and Bernie here is willing to kill to get it. So how did you know where I was?"

Mike grinned. "You called me. When we got cut off, I called Bobby. He was at your aunt's house by that time, and told me where you and your friend here must have gone."

"*I* called you?"

"Yep. I heard something about Bernie, guns, and your cousins, then him tell you to shut up, and figured you hadn't stayed where you'd promised to stay."

"Yes, I did. It wasn't my idea to leave. Talk to Bernie about that." A little indignant, she added, "And I was trying to call nine-one-one anyway, not you."

"See? Even by accident you know who to call."

About that time sirens wailed an approach, and several police cruisers screamed into the rutted driveway with an ambulance close behind. It was over.

Abruptly, Harley plopped down on the ground and put her face in her palms. She started shaking and couldn't seem to stop, even when Morgan handed over the prisoners to be read their rights and put into the car and the ambulance, and then came to kneel down beside her.

"Hey," he said gently, "it's okay. You did good."

She peeked at him between her fingers, and her voice came out all quivery. "I know."

Morgan laughed and said, "That's what I like most about you—your modesty."

"And all this time I've been thinking it was just my body."

He leaned closer to rest his forehead against hers. "I'll be glad to prove my appreciation of that part of your assets later."

Harley sighed. "I'm going to hold you to that promise."

"As long as you hold me tight, babe."

Bobby arrived before the ambulance left, and he ignored Harley for a few minutes before he walked over to where she sat on the trailer steps in the shade. "I'm not going to say what's first on my mind. You can thank me later. Now, just tell me what happened, from when you arrived at your aunt's to the present."

"It's nice to see you again, too, Bobby, and yes, I know you're glad to see me alive and relatively unharmed."

"Right, good to see you, glad you're okay, now tell me what happened. While it's still fresh in your mind. Don't leave anything out."

When Harley got to the part where Bernie had been attacked by the goose, Bobby began to laugh. He didn't stop even when she told him to shut up or she wasn't going to say another word, and after a moment, he just shook his head.

"Only you, Harley. You're a trouble magnet, but it's always something screwy. No jury will ever believe this."

"Then just call Gladys in as a witness. But you better have her in a net first."

Bobby sat down on the step beside her and looked at her. "You know, I should charge you with something. Obstruction or whatever would get you off the streets. You've become a menace to society."

"Fine talk from a man who used to think it was funny to put salt in his mother's sugar bowl, and a garter snake in his aunt's underwear drawer."

"I was ten, and my mother should never have told you all those stories."

"She was just trying to warn me, and anyway, you're still a legend in our neighborhood."

"One more reason I moved as soon as I could. None of which has any bearing on the fact that I'm really concerned about you lately. First, all that business with Yogi and the dog and all those jewelry thieves. Now you've gotten mixed up in two more murders and almost been killed yourself. Don't you have any sense of self-preservation at all?"

"Of course I do. I was only trying to help Aunt Darcy. She's family, you know."

"Uh hunh. Not to mention she offered you money."

"Well, that, too."

"How much would it take to make you stop?"

"Too late. It's all over now. Isn't it?"

Bobby just looked at her for a moment. "Maybe this one is, but unless you're moving out of town, there's always tomorrow."

"How Scarlett O'Hara of you. So when do I find out all the details?"

"You know I can't discuss an ongoing case." Bobby paused, looked at her, and then dragged a hand over his jaw with a rasping sound. It looked as if he hadn't shaved in a day or two. "Guess I could think out loud, though, since we're old friends and all. As long as I get a promise you'll remember this is only conjecture. Nothing's proven until the DA makes a case."

Harley put out her right hand, little finger curled. "Pinky promise."

Grinning, Bobby linked his finger through hers and they solemnly shook on it. "Okay," he said, "just keep this to yourself."

"Not even Cami? Never mind, just tell me why Bernie killed Harry, and probably Julio."

"You've got it backward. Harry killed Bernie and Julio."

Harley stared at him. "Wait. Harry's dead. I saw him, remember? Unless . . . you mean Bernie is really Harry?"

"Yep. After serving time in Ohio, he was extradited to Missouri for old charges, and he just got out of jail there a month ago. The way I figure it, he tracked down Bernie and Frieda, who had changed their names. Bernie took on Harry's identity, and Frieda took on her dead sister's name. It would have caught up to them eventually, but apparently Julio got greedy and wanted a bigger piece of the pie, and Bernie and Frieda didn't want to share. Bernie shot Julio and hid his body, and then the real Harry showed up. Since he started the whole operation and went to jail for it, I imagine he demanded either all the profits or merchandise, or he was so mad at taking the rap in Ohio alone he killed Bernie. Either way, it looks like he killed Bernie, after Bernie had already killed Julio."

"But . . . the gun. They were both shot with Aunt Darcy's gun."

"Bernie took it from your aunt's desk, killed Julio, and still had it when Harry showed up. Harry probably wore gloves when he shot Bernie, and then stuck the pistol in the nearest car, which happened to be your aunt's. Your cousin Madelyn told me she showed up, saw that Harry was dead, then saw her sister leaving from the parking lot next door and thought the worst. She took off when you showed up. Meanwhile, the real Harry must have been going crazy with all the activity in a shop that was supposed to be closed. He didn't have time to look for ledgers or bank account numbers, so he took Bernie's car, the blue Mustang you saw, switched plates and ditched it when it got too hot. From what I can figure out, José here thought it was this Harry who killed his brother."

A little dazed, Harley shook her head. "How'd you find out all this stuff?"

Bobby grinned. "Easy. When fingerprints proved Harry Gordon wasn't Harry Gordon, it all came together pretty quick. We just had to find Harry and Frieda."

"Well, I did that for you. Shouldn't I get some kind of reward?"

He stood up. "In the first place, they found you, not the other way around, and second, there was no reward offered, and thirdly, you were more of a hindrance than a help."

"Bummer."

"Look at it this way, you're still alive and you'll get paid by your aunt."

She perked up. "That's true."

"Now, do us all a favor and go home. You can show up at the precinct tomorrow to give an official statement."

"But what are you going to do about Anna and Frieda? They got away."

"We'll find them. We've got the make and plates on the car Frieda's driving, and we've put out an APB. They'll get picked up before long. Just don't try to help, dammit. Okay?"

"No worry. I think I'm done for the day. Or year. I've had enough excitement to last me a long time."

"Good. If only I could believe that."

Harley smiled. Sometimes Bobby could be so untrusting.

She had Morgan take her to her aunt's house for her bike, and found to her surprise, that Darcy hadn't retreated to her usual form of medication but was quite sober and alert. And grateful.

"I'll never forget how you went with that murderer just to save us, Harley," she said with a tear in her eye. "It was so heroic. You're the bravest person I know!"

"Well, maybe not the bravest. I was pretty scared," she said modestly, and heard Morgan cough to cover up a snort of laughter. She ignored him, and let Darcy lavish praise on her for a few more minutes before she said she had to go.

"Wait—here, sugar," Darcy said, and handed her a check. "It's what I owe you, with a bit more for all your trouble."

Harley's eyes bugged out and she got a little lightheaded. "Aunt Darcy, this says ten thousand dollars."

"You're worth every penny. Besides, I can afford it. If not for . . . everything . . . maybe Paul and I wouldn't have realized how much we mean to each other. He's moving back in, and things are going to be all right again. I told you I was with a man the night Harry was killed, remember? It was my divorce lawyer. Madelyn took me to my Junior League meeting, but I called a taxi and went to meet an attorney, then went back to the meeting in time for her to pick me up. When I found out you'd seen my car at the shop when Harry was killed, well, I thought . . . I just didn't know what to think. I couldn't tell the truth without incriminating my daughter." She paused and took a deep breath. "It was all such a mess, but Detective Baroni, he really was nice about all of it. When he finally convinced me that telling the truth would be best for not just me but all of us, that we were in danger as long as I didn't, I believed him but I was still so afraid."

Darcy looked over at her husband, who stood quietly nearby. Her expression softened. "Then Paul came to talk to me. He convinced me I needed to tell everything I knew."

Uncle Paul smiled. He never said much. Maybe living in a household of three talkative females had drained his conversational skills. Not especially tall, but very distinguished looking with gray at his temples and an expensive suit that shouted "money" much louder than anything he could have said, he just nodded at his wife.

"So I finally told all that to the police," Darcy said, "and now . . . now I don't want a divorce. And I've agreed to go to . . . to AA. Paul's been very supportive. I owe you so much, sugar."

Well, a hero, *and* a therapist. She was really getting good, even if by accident. There were times everything just seemed to go right.

As Morgan walked her out to her bike to follow her home, his cell phone rang. He got it on the second ring, said a few terse words, then hung up and looked at Harley.

"I promised Bobby I'd see you home, but that was the hideout. We've got some things going down and they need me. If I leave you, do you promise not to get into any more trouble?

"Believe me, I've had all the trouble I can handle. I'm ready to go home and soak in the tub for a few days, maybe even play with my rubber ducky and plastic boat."

He grinned. "I'll join you later if I can."

"Hurry back, sailor. When this ship goes down, it'd be nice if you were there."

"You scare me."

She just smiled. Morgan left in his car—actually, a car that belonged to the MPD—and she fired up her bike and put on her helmet. If she was lucky and the traffic wasn't bad, she could be home in fifteen minutes.

As usual, her luck remained bad. An accident on Poplar tied up traffic for miles, so she took the interstate and got off at the Nonconnah exit. Might as well run by to tell Cami what had happened.

After all, she was involved in this too. Then she'd take another route home and bypass the wreck that'd probably take hours to clear away.

Cami was surprised to see her. "Hey, Harley, I didn't really expect you back today."

"Wait'll you hear this—Harry Gordon is alive."

"What?"

"Yeah, I just had to see your face when I told you that."

It didn't take too long to tell her most of the story, and she finished by saying, "As soon as they catch Frieda and Anna, they'll be able to find out all the stuff that was smuggled in and who bought it. It ought to be interesting to see just who in Memphis knowingly bought illegal artifacts and goods, don't you think?"

"Frightening, too. Heads will probably roll. No wonder everybody wants that ledger. It's almost as valuable as the illegal goods if you're a criminal who doesn't mind a little blackmail."

"I imagine Darcy will lose a few clients over this. But she's agreed to go to AA. Oh, she and Uncle Paul are getting back together."

Cami blinked. "I didn't know they were apart."

"Neither did I. Apparently there was some kind of reconciliation brought on by Aunt Darcy being in danger. Romantic, huh? Oh, and she paid me, too."

Cami looked underwhelmed until Harley whipped out the check and showed it to her. Then she let out a squeal. "Ten thousand dollars! My God, Harley, what are you going to do with it?"

"Pay some debts, buy a new cell phone if it doesn't take too much of it, and save the rest."

"That's so responsible of you."

"I know. Lord. Now I sound like Grandmother Eaton. Maybe I should take a cruise with some of it. Ever been to the Bahamas?"

"No, but I've been to Acapulco. My honeymoon with Jace. In retrospect, that was the best part of our marriage. It went downhill from there."

Harley nodded sympathetically. She was just about to offer condolences when the doorbell rang and the dogs started barking so loudly Cami wouldn't have heard her anyway.

"Put them out in the back while I get the door, would you?" Cami yelled as she headed to the door, and Harley opened the French door leading to the deck and back yard and then stood back as all the dogs tried to get through it at the same time. Maybe all dogs were alike. They were remarkably similar to King. Loud, obnoxious, but fortunately for them, cute enough that the rest didn't really matter as much as it should.

When she heard Cami give a startled cry, she turned to see two women push their way in the front door. She recognized them immediately: Anna and Frieda. And they didn't look very friendly.

"What are you doing here?" she demanded as she started toward them, then saw the pistol in Frieda's hand. "Not that you aren't welcome, of course."

"José said he left something with you. I want it."

Harley blinked. "I don't know what you're talking about. He didn't leave anything with me but his gun, and the police have that."

"Yes, he did. I talked to him earlier. José had something that belonged to me and he said he'd trade it to me if I gave him information on where he could find Harry. He said you have it."

"Well, José lied. Is that how you found me here?"

Frieda looked smug. "I made a deal with him, and I'll make one with you—give it to me and I won't kill both of you. If you don't, I'll start with your little friend here."

Cami looked pale but defiant. "If Harley says she doesn't have it, she doesn't. She's not dumb enough to risk our lives for whatever it is you think she has."

"Guess we'll find out then, won't we?" Frieda aimed the pistol, some kind of revolver, and slowly pulled back the hammer with her thumb.

Harley's heart beat so loud it drowned out everything else, but Cami let out a shriek that could peel wallpaper. It even startled Frieda. She jerked, and the shot went into the ceiling.

Seizing the moment, Harley rushed toward her, but Anna got in the way. She grabbed at Harley's arms and tried to stop her, and just as Harley broke free, Frieda let out a scream. It took only a few seconds to recognize what had happened.

Frightened by the loud noise, Sam had attacked Frieda just like he had José in the car, and still clung to her leg. It looked like he'd dug in with all claws, holding on to her pants and leg as Frieda frantically tried to pull him off without losing skin. Cami leaped forward to protect the cat from the wild blows aimed at his head, and Harley grabbed for the pistol.

After a brief tussle, Frieda was outmatched even with Anna trying fiercely to intervene, and Harley had the gun in her hands. She aimed it at both sisters.

"Better put your hands up or this thing might go off by accident."

Cami finally got Sam detached from Frieda and immediately dropped him when he lashed out at her, too. The cat took off with tail high in the air while Harley kept her eyes on Frieda and Anna.

"Cami, call the cops. I think they'll be really interested in catching up with these two. I hear they've been looking for them."

It seemed to take forever for them to get there, but in reality it was only about five minutes before a cruiser pulled up outside with siren going and lights flashing. Not long after those officers arrived, Bobby showed up. When he saw Harley he just shook his head.

"Hi, Bobby. Fancy meeting you here," she said, and the look he gave her was grim.

"This is beyond even your powers of idiocy. Why didn't you go home like I told you? I thought Morgan made sure you went home."

"He got a call from the hideout, then there was an accident on Poplar, and well, I thought I'd just come by here for a few minutes. Good thing, or Cami would have been in real trouble."

Cami, still pale and shivering, nodded. "That's true. That guy who tried to kidnap Harley last time told those women she has something they want. We don't know what it is, though."

"I do," Bobby said. "And I got the same story from him just a short time ago. When he's excited his English isn't that good, so it took me a while to understand what he was saying. José lied and told them he gave you something he'd gotten from his brother in exchange for them telling him where to find Harry. He claims he didn't mean to cause you any trouble. He never thought they'd find you. I was on my way to your house, Harley, when I got the call to come here."

"So here we are all together again. Funny, how we keep meeting like this, isn't it?"

Bobby didn't answer. He just gave her a look and turned to Cami. "You all right?"

She nodded. "Just a few scratches from Sam."

"Sam?"

"A cat." Cami glanced at Harley and grinned. "He's Harley's cat."

"Harley has a cat?"

Before Cami could reply, Harley said, "No, Harley does *not* have a cat. Harley doesn't like cats. Cats don't like Harley. And why am I talking about myself in the third person? I think I'm having a breakdown. That must be it. Stress can do that, I've heard. I need help. A vacation. A cruise to the Bahamas."

She closed her eyes and thought about a ship alone on the ocean with water all around, riding the waves toward sand and sun . . . palm trees, piña coladas, margaritas, lots of sleep and no interruptions . . . a dark-haired man with blue eyes and a killer bod . . . sweaty sheets . . . oh yeah.

"Don't fall asleep in the middle of a crime scene, Harley," Bobby said, jerking her from her pleasant fantasy. "You and Cami go in the kitchen for now."

Harley glanced over at Anna and Frieda, handcuffed now and being led out the door to the waiting patrol cars. "So what is it they think José gave me?"

"The rest of the bank account numbers. Bernie was too smart to keep everything in one place. He hid stuff at the shop, in his home office, and a few other places. Apparently Julio got hold of some account numbers and told Bernie he'd given them to his brother for safekeeping while he negotiated a bigger piece of the take. Bernie objected, and that's when he killed Julio with your aunt's gun. So Cherie, or Frieda, only had part of what she needed to withdraw money from some offshore bank accounts."

"So did you find the missing bank account numbers?"

Bobby shook his head. "We'll find them eventually. I hope."

"And names of clients? Did you already find those?"

"Found those first. There are going to be some mighty unhappy people when this gets out, as it will soon enough."

Harley nodded. "Keep my name out of it, or I'll have to leave town for a while."

"Don't worry. Most of the buyers are in St. Louis and Cincinnati."

"My head's beginning to hurt," Harley said. "I feel a vacation coming on."

"I thought all you did was vacation. Don't you ever work?" Bobby asked, rather unkindly, she thought.

"It's time I leave," she said with as much dignity as she could manage.

Bobby looked at her innocently. "Was it something I said?"

Harley said something rude that made Cami laugh and Bobby scowl, then made her way around police still in the den digging the bullet out of the ceiling and freaking out the cats, and went home. There was a hot bath ahead of her, and if she was lucky—a hotter man.

Seventeen

This time, Harley's luck was good. The hot bath with a piña colada candle burning and a nice margarita in her hand was only the prelude to sweaty sheets and the dark-haired guy with the killer bod. Some things were worth waiting for, Harley mused sleepily when she woke the next morning. Life could be just fine.

When her phone rang, she started not to answer it, then thought better of that and reached for the cordless on her bedside table before it woke Morgan. She mumbled a hello, and Diva said in a cheerful tone, "The universe has blessed you."

"I know. Can we discuss that later? I'm a little sleepy right now."

"Tell Bruno his aura needs cleansing."

"Mike Morgan. Bruno was just his alias while he was working on a case, remember?"

"Of course I do, Harley, but when he's undercover, he has to play a part. Did you catch the dead man?"

It was too early to try to follow Diva's mercurial switches in conversation, but she did her best. "He caught me, but it turned out okay. Now he's in police custody. Aunt Darcy is off the hook."

"Tell the police to check out the armoire in her shop. You know the one. There's some kind of papers or numbers taped to the bottom of a drawer."

Harley perked up. "I had a feeling there was something I should do about that armoire. I just never got around to it."

"You have more of a gift than you think, Harley. Perhaps you should open your mind to it and embrace it instead of resisting it."

"It's not a gift. It's a curse. You never know enough to really help me, just enough to get me confused." Silence greeted that comment, and she sighed. "All right, I know—I need to learn how to listen."

"That would help."

Maternal guilt was much more powerful than any psychic ability. Harley ended the conversation by promising to visit later in the day.

Yogi was in training for his annual Elvis contest in August. Maybe she could arrange to be out of town that month. It was always a source of great embarrassment to her to see him stuffed into an Elvis jumpsuit and gold necklaces.

"I'm doomed," she muttered to the ceiling, and Mike rolled over to look at her.

"Why?"

"My parents."

He nibbled on her right ear lobe. "They aren't that bad."

"You've met them, right?"

For a moment he paused in the nibbling, then shrugged. "Well, at least they're interesting. It could be worse."

"Right. I could be living with them again."

"They can't be too bad. Look how good you turned out."

She smiled. "You're only saying that because it's true."

"Modesty is such a turn-on." His lips began to work down her throat.

She sighed. "Thank God. I was beginning to think you'd never get down to business."

Morgan always knew just the thing to take her mind off whatever she was thinking about. There was just something about a blue-eyed man with dark hair and great pecs and abs . . .

After a visit with her parents—during which Yogi coerced her into going jogging with him and Diva insisted upon cleansing her aura—Harley headed for Cami's house. She needed a bit of sanity before calling Tootsie to have him put her back on the schedule next week.

"It would have been nice," Harley said to Cami, "if Bobby had told me that the dead man wasn't Harry Gordon, instead of keeping that information to himself. It might have saved us both a lot of trouble."

"You know police can't compromise their cases by giving out that kind of information. And look at it this way—you got a big reward for your efforts. Still taking that cruise?"

"I decided to save the money. For emergencies. Taxes get a lot of it anyway, so what's left goes into savings."

"I'm impressed. That's very responsible of you, Harley."

"Right. How depressing. Pass me the bag of Reese's."

Halfway through the bag, Cami said, "Angel moved back in with

Bobby."

Harley looked at her. "You all right?"

"Of course. I told you, we're just friends. Well, all right—I guess I was beginning to like him a little too much. Maybe this is best."

"Don't worry. Angel won't stay long. They never do. I told you, Bobby has a history of temporary relationships. One of them will file a restraining order on the other soon, then it'll all be over and if you really want him, you can be there to sweep up the pieces."

"I'm not sure I want to be the janitor in his life, thank you. And I'm not unhappy, really I'm not. It hadn't gotten to the point where I cared too much yet. At least I'll still have him as a friend."

"Yeah, Bobby can be a good friend. Even if he has been rather upset with me lately."

Cami laughed. "I know. You should have heard him."

"Oh no, what I did hear was enough for me. One of these days I'm going to learn to speak Italian so I can understand what he says when he's really mad. Or maybe I won't."

"That'd probably be best," Cami said with a grin. "What he says in English is bad enough at times."

"Do you know if he found what Cheríe and Harry were looking for in that armoire? He basically told me to butt out when I called him this morning to tell him what Diva said, but I know he'll check it out."

"When he called to say he wouldn't be making our cookout tonight because of Angel, he said they'd had another development at the design shop, so I imagine so. He sounded very happy about it."

"The missing offshore bank account numbers, no doubt. Sometimes Diva is uncanny."

Cami looked thoughtful. "Maybe I need to have her read my palm or cards again. She said life changes with every decision we make or don't make."

"That's truer than I'd like to think about. So what'd you do with the dogs you took from Anna Merritt's place?"

"Fostered them out. One of our rescue members has a farm in Fisherville. She took the goose and her goslings, too."

"Lucky her. Gladys bites. And poops indiscriminately." As Harley unpeeled the wrapper around another peanut butter cup, she felt a gentle tap on her shoulder and looked around. A pair of blue eyes looked back at her, slitted a little, and whiskers in a triangular face twitched.

"He loves you," Cami said, and Harley had to admit it seemed to be true.

"What can I say? I'm devastating to the male gender."

"Take him, Harley. Sam has never liked anyone else but me before. You're his only choice."

"I don't want a cat. I don't like cats."

"He likes you."

"Which only proves that he's mentally unstable. Cats never like me, and I return the sentiment."

"He saved our lives, Harley."

Damn. "And I appreciate it, though I'm not fully convinced he didn't do that for reasons that had nothing to do with me."

"Cats are different from dogs. They choose who to like. Dogs are indiscriminate. They like anyone who'll feed them."

"Cami—"

"Besides, maybe he's some reincarnated soul mate from a former life. Diva says King has that kind of connection to Yogi."

"Diva says a lot of strange things. And besides, King is most likely the reincarnation of a crime boss, not Yogi's lost love."

"Even John Gotti had to have love in his life. Look at Sam. He loves you, Harley."

"I'm not taking him. I don't want to clean litter boxes. I don't want the responsibility of a pet. No. I'm not taking him."

Cami just smiled. Sam rubbed against Harley's shoulder, looked up with slitted blue eyes and made a purring sound. She shook her head.

"It'd never work. I like living alone."

She thought about that when she got home and pulled her Toyota up under the shade of the oak tree in the back. Sarah Simon's car was in its parking slot, but the Spragues' was vacant. Peace and serenity settled around the brick house, welcome and comforting. She must be crazy.

When she opened the car door, she saw Sarah peek out her window. Maybe being alone too much could lead to insanity. Not the good kind, like artists, writers, and actors, but the kind where she'd sit at the window and gibber, or stay locked in her apartment, afraid to come out. Just great. She'd have to go and apologize for almost running over her, if she could get Sarah to come to the door. Later would be soon enough. Now she had things to do.

Harley opened the back door of her Toyota and reached inside for the day's shopping. It was heavier than she'd thought, and she staggered a little under the weight of the plastic bag. A bell jingled and cans clanked. She set the sack on the pebbled ground, then leaned back into the car to grasp the handle of a soft-sided carrier. As she pulled it toward her, slitted blue eyes stared at her through the mesh holes and a loud purr rattled the sides. She smiled.

At least cats didn't bark.

Not yet the end . . .

Harely's Next Adventure

SUSPICIOUS MIMES
The Blue Suede Memphis Mysteries
Book Three
Excerpt

"Elvis lives." Harley Jean Davidson didn't really mean that, but what else could she say when her father was looking so expectant, waiting for her to comment nicely? "I'm sure he'd be pleased if he could see you dressed up like him," she added.

Yogi grinned and twirled so that his jeweled white cape flashed in a glitter of green, red, and blue stones her mother had carefully sewn into what looked like eight yards of satin. Sunlight coming through the front window gleamed off the stones, almost blinding her. *Good Lord.*

"This year, I've had to turn down gigs. I've been practicing." Yogi struck another pose, this time with one leg behind him, the other bent at the knee in a half-crouch, his arm flung out in front like he was trying to hail a taxi.

Harley barely kept from rolling her eyes. She dreaded Elvis Week. It came every year in August, the momentum building up to a climactic frenzy of Elvis-related activities downtown and at Graceland. Perhaps she wouldn't dread it so badly if Yogi hadn't made a habit of tugging on a white jumpsuit and impersonating The King, whom he still admired more than twenty years after Elvis's death. It'd been greatly humiliating when she was younger and more concerned with the opinion of her peers. Now it registered a lesser blip on her radar screen.

Over the years, she'd learned there were far worse humiliations her parents could generate than an unnatural attachment to a long-dead celebrity.

When she looked over at Diva, her mother said to Yogi,

"This is the year you'll be famous."

Strong accolade, considering Diva's uncannily accurate predictions. She might miss some of the details, but lately she'd been right more times than not. That should please Yogi.

"Of course," her mother added, "it won't be quite as you expect, but your name will be linked with Elvis's in a spectacular way."

That was a little unsettling. In light of the past few months of unwanted publicity, Harley would have preferred anything but spectacular. "Our family has been in the news quite enough, thank you verra much," she said, her accent on the last phrase a really bad imitation of Elvis. It made Yogi smile, as it always did.

"This is the year I'll win first prize," he said jubilantly.

"Always a runner-up, but now I think I have a real shot at it. Preston Hughes dropped out."

Preston Hughes was Yogi's archrival in the Elvis impersonator contests. His rendition of *Love Me Tender* brought down the house every time. The judges loved him.

While Yogi could imitate Elvis fairly well, he didn't have the vocal range Hughes did.

"I'll do what I can to be there," Harley said, "but August is our busiest month, you know. All those tourists wanting to do Graceland means we have every van full. It's still July, and I did eight runs yesterday in twelve hours. I'd take a load out there, drop them off, go back for another one, bring another group back, take another one. I don't know how Tootsie kept it all straight, who went where, and when, but he did. He's amazing."

Diva smiled. "The candlelight vigil this year will be interesting. Perhaps you should skip it, Harley."

Harley looked at her. "I'd love to, but that's our busiest night. All drivers are needed. Mr. Penney would fire me if I missed it. And I'm on shaky ground as it is after all that's happened."

"I know. But I have a feeling that you should miss it anyway."

"I wish you hadn't said that. I'm already committed. Tootsie would get into a snit if I tried to change on him now. I'd really like to keep my job"

"You seem very content these days. I'm glad."

"I am content. While I admit driving a tour bus isn't the best-paying job around, it does pay my bills. I like doing it. The hours are flexible, the people are usually nice, and when they aren't, I soon get rid of them and never have to see them again. Look in your crystal ball again. Are you sure that warning isn't meant for someone else? I'd hate to bail on Tootsie now."

"Whatever you think best, Harley."

Harley hated it when her mother said things like that. It always felt like she'd made a bad decision when Diva tranquilly agreed with her.

"Okay. I have to ask. *Why* do you think I shouldn't go?" By now Diva was headed to the kitchen and Harley followed along behind her, something she could have done even in the dark since her mother liked wearing tiny bells sewn into her loose, flowing skirts. Diva still dressed much as she had in the late sixties and early seventies, with her pale blond hair long and down her back, tunic tops and skirts to her ankles, sandals and bracelets and necklaces that she made herself out of crystals and beads and leather. Diva and Yogi lived in their own era, and it didn't much matter to them that time had moved on.

Diva's reply drifted back over her shoulder. "It's your choice, Harley."

"Yes, I know it's my choice. That doesn't mean I'll make the right choice. Come on. Give me a clue here. You know something I don't, apparently."

"Rama and Ovid are concerned."

Harley couldn't help it. She rolled her eyes. "What do Rama and Ovid have to do with me? They're your spirit guides, not mine."

"What you do affects me. You're my daughter. But perhaps it's best that you do go. It will help your father feel so much better."

"Oh good Lord. That sounds ominous. I'm not going to have to get up on stage at one of his shows and throw my panties or anything like that, am I?"

Diva laughed. "I'm sure not. Oh, will you let King in? The pet door is broken."

Recognizing she wasn't going to learn anything else until her mother chose to tell her, Harley went to the back door and opened it. King, her father's black and white Border Collie named for Elvis, trotted inside. His paws were muddy, and seeing as how there'd been no rain lately, that no doubt meant he'd been up to mischief again.

"I thought the higher fence Yogi put up kept King from getting out," she said as she gave the dog a pat on the head that promptly elicited an ecstatic wiggle of his entire body.

"It does. Why?"

"His feet are wet. I'll bet he's been fishing in Mrs. Erland's pond again."

"Perhaps he's just been in the garden. Yogi hooked up a watering system. King likes to go back there and sample tomatoes on occasion."

That explained the glazed look in King's eyes. Yogi's illegal tobacco grew right next to the tomato plants, and the crop of both had a relaxing effect on those who indulged. Since King couldn't roll his own and smoke, he'd obviously found eating the tomatoes a nice substitution. Well, whatever kept him from being the neighborhood scourge had to be an improvement.

"He seems much better behaved now," she remarked. "Maybe he's settling down."

"The obedience classes helped, I think. How kind of the Border Collie Rescue to help out."

"They just didn't want to get stuck with him. But I'm grateful for anything that keeps me from having to go looking for him at three in the morning."

"You have an affinity for animals, Harley. I don't know why you resist it. That's a lovely talent to have."

"Right. If you don't mind pet hair over all your clothes, on the floor, on the furniture, in your food—"

"So how is Sam?"

Harley sighed. "He's fine. I can't believe I let Cami talk me into keeping that cat. I had to pay Mr. Lancaster a pet deposit. A hundred dollars, just so I can clean out a litter box and pay good money for a scratching post and toys that I use more than he does. He looks at me like I'm crazy when I try to get him to play with them. I think I've been had."

"We don't often choose animals. They choose us. They're on a higher spiritual plane than we are and can sense people with good hearts."

"Which explains why Sam is so picky about who pets him,

I suppose. It's rather nice having a cat that's smarter than people."

"He's not necessarily smarter, just isn't burdened with preconceived ideas about how things are supposed to be. He sees with all his senses. Just like King."

While Diva smiled at the dog, who seemed to know good things were being said about him and wagged his tail so hard it should have flown across the room, Harley reflected on the simple truth that animals had some kind of pipeline to objectivity. They never let anything like concern about their next meal interfere with behavior patterns that bordered on criminal. If it wasn't for the cuteness factor, dogs would never have been allowed into that first cave. And she wasn't at all sure they were domesticated. Cats were definitely still undomesticated, despite the popular belief that they were house pets. They weren't. They just had good PR agents.

"Listen to this," Yogi said from the kitchen doorway, and

Harley turned, wincing a little at the sight of him still in his Elvis getup. At least his pot belly had shrunk, and with his long sideburns, once he got his annual haircut he'd resemble Elvis pretty closely—if *closely* included cherubic cheeks and a nose that was a bit short, lips that were a little too thin, and height a couple of inches below six feet. The Elvis contest was the only time he ever cut his hair; the rest of the time he kept it in a ponytail.

"We're listening," Harley said as her father hit a few chords on his guitar.

Yogi launched into a pretty good imitation of Elvis singing *Suspicious Minds*. He really wasn't bad. Even his guitar playing had improved.

"I've been taking guitar lessons from Eric," he said when she complimented him on how good he sounded. "This is the year I'll win. I just know it."

Harley couldn't help a big smile. Yogi was always so certain he'd win, and when he lost, always so determined to win the next time. "I'll just bet you do win this year."

He did another Elvis stance. "Thank you. Thank you verra much."

Time to go. Harley left after the usual farewell rituals and stood on the front porch a minute before heading to her car parked at the curb. Huge oaks hung over the street on both sides, shading it save for a few patches of sunlight.

Her parents' house was only a few blocks from the University of Memphis—formerly known as Memphis State, and before that, Normal State, the latter no doubt changed when it became obvious it was a more hopeful than realistic name. The Normal neighborhood had gone through many transitions over the years. In the thirties up to the fifties it'd been full of young families, then older families. In the sixties, college kids and hippies painted flowers everywhere, grew pot in closets with sophisticated lighting, then melded like chameleons into yuppies and left it all in a shabby air of neglect.

In the past decade or so, the transition had started all over again. Some of the older families like hers had stuck it out, but some of the houses were divided into rented rooms for university students. Now younger families had started buying and renovating the older homes in the area. Most of the families at this end of Douglass Street were older. On the other end, swing sets and kids' toys littered yards like some kind of plastic nuclear blast.

A wide front porch ran the length of her parents' bungalow- style house. In summer it held chairs, in winter it held hardy plants. Now it held Harley's younger brother. Eric was just coming up the steps onto the porch. Tall, thin, and nearly always dressed in black, he smiled when he saw her. "Hey, cool chick."

"Hey, dude." Standard greetings over, she asked him about his art classes the coming year at the University of Memphis, the heavy metal rock band he was in, and if he'd be going to the big Elvis finals competition with their parents. Provided Yogi made it that far.

He shook his head, and afternoon light glittered off the earring in one ear. "Not this time. We've got a gig that night.

Thank God."

Harley completely understood. "Yeah, I have to work. I hope. What color do you call that on your head? It looks pink."

He brushed a hand over the gelled hair standing four inches high on his scalp. "Fuschia. It didn't turn out quite like I wanted." "That's a relief. I'd hate to think you were going for that look."

"I'm thinking of shaving my head and tattooing the hair on."

"Now *there's* a look guaranteed to break a mother's heart.

I'll be glad when you grow out of this difficult stage. Think it'll be any time soon?"

Eric just grinned. "Maybe. Maybe not."

That was the thing about her family. They just drifted along at their own speed, heedless of convention or opinions, happy to just exist. Why couldn't she be like that? No, she had to be in this phase where she questioned everything about her life: her job, her direction, why she was still unmarried at nearly thirty, and even if she ever wanted to get married.

Not that she did without male companionship. While she refused to think of it as a bona fide relationship, she certainly enjoyed all the perks of keeping company with Mike Morgan, the hottest undercover cop in Memphis. Three months, and things just got hotter. She liked to tell acquaintances that they'd met over murder. It was certainly a conversational icebreaker. And very nearly true.

So what if the beginning of their relationship had been a little rocky? It'd smoothed out. Perseverance and tolerance helped. Given his line of work, the sharp edges were understandable, if not always desirable. While most of the time, she saw only a killer bod, electric blue eyes, dark hair that was usually a little shaggy around the edges, and a grin that made her stomach do funny flips, he had another side that she wouldn't want to confront in a dark alley. Or even at high noon shivers of the *uh-oh* kind. She'd only caught a glimpse of it a few times, and wasn't especially eager to see it again. She liked him much better when he was agreeable, even if a little intolerant about her stumbling over corpses.

Later that evening, Morgan reminded her about his intolerance of her new direction in life. "Over two months without you finding a body or two lying around." He blew into her ear and she shivered. "I'm glad to see you've reformed." "I like to think of it as keeping better company, thank you."

"No jewelry thieves, no smugglers—what do you do with all your spare time?"

She slanted her eyes at him. "When I'm not being asked annoying questions by a naked man in my bed, I knit scarves for the homeless and hang out on street corners. It's not like I *tried* to find bodies, you know."

"So you say. Baroni must be delirious with relief."

"Bobby," she said, "is a jerk."

"That's not a nice thing to say about an old friend. How would he feel if he heard you?"

"He's already heard it and didn't seem too bothered. We're not speaking at the moment. Sometimes we do that."

Mike laughed softly. "Do I want to know what happened?"

"Probably, but I'm not going to tell you."

He rolled over on top of her and pinned her arms back to the pillows. "I have ways of making you talk, y'know."

She looked up with a smile and whispered, "Do your worst, copper."

"How about," he whispered back as he moved over her in a most intriguing way, "I do my best instead?"

"I'm up for it."

He smiled. "So am I."

Oh yeah.

Tootsie looked a bit frayed when Harley showed up for work a little earlier than usual the next morning. The phone was ringing, and paperwork had piled up on his desk.

"You look like you had a bad night," she said, plopping the leather backpack she used as a purse down atop his desk.

"Want me to help out?"

"Grab the phone. Take a name and number and tell them we'll call back." He looked up at her, frustration in his eyes.

"This time of year is always a bitch." when it finally stopped ringing, blew out a breath of relief. "I don't know how you do it. Some of these people are downright rude if they don't hear what they want to hear."

Tootsie batted his eyelashes. "I use my Southern charm. Works every time."

She grinned. "Must be why I'm not very good at it. I failed that class."

"You just spent too much time in California. It was all that commune living as a child. Southern charm is usually a requirement here."

"Not for everyone. You do recall my Aunt Darcy and cousins?"

"Ah yes. There are those who don't show up for class. What's up?"

She got up from the chair and perched on the edge of his desk while he got back to the computer. "I don't suppose you'd schedule me for airport runs during the candlelight vigil? Or taking tourists to Beale Street? Or Victorian Village? Or AutoZone, or—"

"I'd be happy to, but Charlsie already put in for the airport, and Jake got Beale Street, and Sharon took Victorian Village.

Since your time off, they have seniority. I did have a Dixon Art Gallery run, but you're still banned from there so I sent Lydia. Sorry, baby."

Harley sighed. "I understand. I don't like it, but I understand. Of course, if any of them get sick, I get first chance at their run. Deal?"

"Deal." Tootsie laughed. "Just don't get any ideas."

"You know me so well." She smiled. Thomas "Tootsie"

Rowell was really one of her best friends. He'd hired her immediately when she'd answered the ad in the paper, and they'd gotten along famously ever since. She even attended his shows at times, where he dressed up like Cher or Madonna or Liza Minnelli, or whoever caught his fancy. Hard to admit, but Tootsie was more gorgeous as a woman than most women. He wasn't much taller than she, only about five seven to her five six, and borrowed her dresses from her corporate days of wining and dining. She hated to admit he looked better in them than she ever had. But then, she was much more comfortable in jeans and a tee shirt anyway. Evening dresses had never been her style, and it probably showed every time she wore one. most of the time liked her job as a tour driver and occasional taxi service. That depended on where she was needed most, since the company had recently branched out into offering short runs as well as the regular tours. It'd taken a while to get the licensing and regulations straight, and required more training for the drivers so everyone could get their piece of the financial pie.

But more vehicles were added to the fleet and all the drivers qualified. It wasn't like her former job in corporate banking. If she disliked the clients, she got rid of them at the end of the day, where before she'd had to deal with them on a regular basis. Not to mention several tiers of former bosses, some of whom were nice but most of whom were stereotypical jerks. Maybe she should have finished college, but at the time it hadn't seemed nearly as important as it did now. Ah, her shallow youth was behind her. She was now entering the halls of maturity. Things could be worse.

Tootsie snapped his fingers in front of her face. "Hello? You in there?"

"Sorry. Just thinking how lucky I am to still have a job." "Baby, you just don't know."

"Sure I do. You went to bat for me. I'm convinced you've got something on the ogre. If you didn't, I'd have been out the door back in May."

"Don't get too comfortable. And for pity's sake, don't go around finding any more dead bodies."

"Which makes me wonder—is there such a thing as finding live bodies?"

Tootsie rolled his eyes. "Sometimes you act so blonde."

"I *am* a blonde."

"I know. But you're usually a smart blonde. There's a run you can take this afternoon. I know it's one you'll like. Elvis impersonators."

"A taxi run? I thought I was scheduled for Tupelo." "They cancelled at the last minute. Fortunately for you, we have this one."

She sighed. "I'm in hell."

"Not until two o'clock, baby."

By two-thirty, Harley was rethinking the entire tour guide thing. Just getting around town was a feat of luck and persistence. But now her ears hurt as well. All the Elvises sang at the same time—*is the plural of Elvis called Elvi?* she wondered, then winced.

Normally—and separately—she liked those songs. All at the same time, however, they made her want to ram the van into the nearest telephone pole. As soon as she dropped these guys off at the hotel for their contest, she intended to go to the nearest drug store and buy ear plugs.

When she pulled into the covered parking area to unload her passengers, she managed a smile as she told them she'd be back for them at eight, and reminded them that if their schedule changed they were to call her cell phone or the offices at Memphis Tour Tyme.

A rather portly Elvis paused in the door and said, "Thank you, thank you verra much" as he got out. If she had a nickel for every time she'd heard that or would hear that in the coming month, she could retire.

However, she just said, "You're welcome, Elvis. Good luck."

As always, she glanced back to make sure everyone was out before she left, and only one guy remained in the van. He was in the very back on the last seat.

"Hey," she called, "last stop for all Elvi. This is it, sir. Sir?"

He didn't respond, just remained in his seat staring out the window. Maybe he'd gotten cold feet. She didn't blame him.

Grown men dressed up like Elvis and sweating on a stage had to be daunting. She should know. After all, Yogi went every year. It was his only brand of religion, other than his government conspiracy theories. The last she understood, but the first she found inexplicable. "Sir? Hey, Elvis?"

He still sat there staring out the window, and with a sigh, Harley got out of the van and went around. She'd get him out with a can opener if she had to, but dammit, he was getting out. She deserved someplace quiet for a while before she had to deal with the ride back to their hotels.

"Hey, buddy," she said when she reached his seat, "we're here. Time to go on stage and sing your heart out. Knock 'em dead."

When he still didn't respond, Harley put a hand on his shoulder to give him a slight shake out of his trance. He slumped forward, his head hit the back of the seat in front of him, and she jumped into the aisle.

The hilt of a knife protruded from his back. She froze. This couldn't be happening. Not to him, not to *her*.

Maybe it was a mistake. A bizarre, cruel joke. She leaned closer, and the rusty smell of blood made her stomach lurch. Backing slowly away, she fumbled at her waist for the cell phone that she now kept tethered to her with a chain, and hit speed dial. They answered quickly. "Nine-one-one?" she said in a voice that sounded a lot calmer than she felt. "We have another dead Elvis."

Acknowledgment

I want to thank my good friend Lisa Turner for advice on an interior design shop, and assure my readers that in no way is she or anyone in her family the models for Darcy Fontaine and her daughters. I did, however, shamelessly conceive the plot idea after visiting Lisa's very successful and beautiful interior design shop in Memphis.

About Virginia Brown

As a long-time resident of Mississippi, award-winning author Virginia Brown has lived in several different areas of the state, and finds the history, romance, and intrigue of the Deep South irresistible. Although having spent her childhood as a "military brat" living all over the U.S. and overseas, this award-winning author of nearly fifty novels is now happily settled in and drawing her favorite fictional characters from the wonderful, whimsical Southerners she has known and loved.

Visit her at virginiabrownauthor.com

CPSIA information can be obtained at www.ICGtesting.com
Printed in the USA
LVOW110813070412

276605LV00004B/2/P